PRIMORDIA II

RETURN TO THE LOST WORLD

GREIG BECK

SEVERED PRESS
HOBART TASMANIA

PRIMORDIA II

Copyright © 2018 GREIG BECK

WWW.SEVEREDPRESS.COM

ISBN: 978-1-925711-89-9

"One must wait till it comes."
— Arthur Conan Doyle, The Lost World

FROM THE RESEARCH NOTES OF EMMALINE JANE WILSON

It's only a tiny comet.

It's called P/2018-YG874, designate name: Primordia, and probably came out of the Oort cloud a hundred million years ago, give or take a few million.

Since then, this astral speck of mostly iron had been traveling in an elliptical orbit around our solar system. It would approach our Earth, pass by it, and then head back to the inner star where it was grabbed again and then flung outward for yet another cycle around us. It was a decade-long yo-yo game that has been going on for millions of years and would go on for millions more.

The Primordia apparition, meaning when it was visible to the naked eye, was unremarkable, except for one thing—scientists say the comet's nuclei has a significant concentration of iron and other rare minerals. But what they don't know is that this composition creates a unique magnetic distortion on the surrounding solar geography.

In its slow pass by Earth, the comet came closest to South America, directly over a vast tabletop mountain in Venezuela. It was only observable for a few days, but in that time, strange distortions occurred on the mountaintop—things became rearranged, reordered; pathways were created and doorways opened.

It also caused localized monsoonal weather patterns that had been known by the indigenous tribes for millennia as the wettest season. It was also known that for this brief period, the area became home to gods and monsters, and should be avoided. Those who ventured there never came back.

I know this to be true. Except for one thing: sometimes people *can* come back.

A comet impact on the Earth would be devastating depending on its mass and composition. However, even if it didn't make landfall, the full astral effects of a comet simply passing close to our planet are not yet known or fully understood.

October 2014 – Approaching comet, C/2013-A1 (designate name: Siding Spring), has plunged the magnetic field around Mars into chaos.
NASA's Goddard Space Flight Centre, Greenbelt, Maryland

PROLOGUE

He froze, listening to the stealthy sounds outside the cave. He sat for many minutes in the near darkness with just the dying embers of his fire giving the walls a hellish red glow.

After five more minutes of silence, he exhaled long and slow and went back to sharpening a stick by slowly grinding it against a rough stone. His knife, now rusty, was lashed to the end of a long, straight branch, making a spear—his only weapon, and his only protection.

He paused to look again at the cave entrance. Was that the soft sound of claws raking against the rock—seeking, testing, investigating? The entrance had been sealed over, as it was every night. But the creatures that hunted in the dark were more than powerful enough to force their way in.

Hiding, becoming invisible, and avoiding some parts of the jungle was the only way to survive. Nearly every night, the sounds of death and killing went on out there—but he knew, as long as they stayed *out there*, he was safe *in here*.

He looked through long strands of greasy hair up at the walls. He had spent days, weeks, covering the inside with mud, sealing over every crack, fissure, and pockmark, to make sure there were no ways into his refuge, no matter how small. He knew things came creeping at night, not just big things, but tiny, hungry things, and sleep was when he was the most vulnerable.

He shifted a little, feeling the mud flake on his body. He had also coated himself in the silky clay to create a barrier against biting insects and also to mask his scent from the beasts that had senses of smell hundreds of times more sensitive than his own.

His eyes ran along the walls. On one were hundreds upon hundreds of marks—four strokes, crossed diagonally by a single stroke, over and over, as he counted down the days. So far, they totaled to 2,920—nearly 3,000 long, lonely, and terrifying days he had been here. But there were still many more to go until his chance of escape would arrive.

His eyes shifted to the other wall—there, he had drawn an image of a memory now eight years gone by—it was his motivation and his waking dream; Ricky's, a rib joint, complete with sign overhead, large windows, and people inside sitting at a horseshoe booth. One of the people he had carefully drawn in detail, a girl, looking out at him.

Benjamin Cartwright's eyes began to water as he remembered. His dry lips moved. "Don't forget me, Emma," he whispered. "Don't forg—"

His words caught in his throat as the sniffing came from right outside. Then the cave entrance exploded inward and the monstrous thing reached in for him.

PART 1 – FOOTSTEPS FROM THE PAST

"Life is infinitely stranger than anything the mind could invent" –
Arthur Conan Doyle, The Lost World

CHAPTER 01

Venezuela, the Deep Amazon, Unmapped Tabletop Mountain

Emma crouched and picked up a handful of scree. She looked at the weather-blasted fragments, rolling them in her palm for a few seconds before letting them drop.

She rested her forearms on her haunches and slowly turned her head, blowing air through her pressed lips. This place, this tabletop mountain, or tepui, in the middle of nowhere, wasn't on any map and wasn't explored.

And why would it be? she thought. It was like the surface of another planet—riven with crevices, a few small pools of water, stunted trees, and some hardy grasses.

She continued to scan it, looking for something, anything, some sign that indicated there was something here now, or there *had* been something here in the past. As she watched, a small striped skink clambered out from under a flat stone in pursuit of some sort of gnat. She watched it dart forward, ruby-red gimlet eyes and jerking movements as the tiny reptile hunted down its prey with ruthless efficiency.

After another moment, she turned away. There was nothing here now, no secrets revealed. When the wettest season came, and it would as it had been doing perhaps for thousands or millions of years, then anything that was here was buried, hidden, or maybe even destroyed. And what existed 100 million years in the past became reality, just in this one place in the world.

What was lost would be found again. She placed a hand against the sun-warmed stone. "Are you there, Ben?"

She waited, letting her fingers trail over the ancient rock's surface. But she knew there would be no answer, and maybe not for another two years until the time was right.

There was just an eerie silence on the plateau. Perhaps there were ghosts here, but they wouldn't speak to her. Not yet.

Behind her, a huge helicopter waited. The pilot watched on, but was paid handsomely for stripping down his long-distance helicopter, loading in spare fuel tanks, and also for his discretion.

She bet she knew what he was thinking. Probably the same as everyone else that had heard her tale—*jungle fever, hallucinations, post-traumatic stress disorder, fakery*—and dozens of other accusations that had been thrown at her.

But she knew different, and she looked up into the azure sky. One day soon, the eyebrow-like streak would appear, heralding the return of Comet P/2018-YG874, designate name, Primordia. It would first bring an aurora borealis effect in the upper atmosphere, and then its powerful magnetic field would distort time and space on the planet's surface. A doorway would be opened, right here, and she'd be waiting for it.

Emma Wilson stood and turned, circling her finger in the air. The pilot immediately started engines and the huge rotor blades began to turn.

She was finished here, for now. But before going home, she had one more thing to do.

CHAPTER 02

Venezuela, Caracas, Museum of Sciences

Emma alighted from the taxicab and stood out in front of the striking building and admired the magnificent sculptures and ornate stonework of the great artist and sculptor, Francisco Narvaez.

She looked along the magnificent edifice of the museum, one of the country's oldest. It was dubbed the Museum of Natural Sciences when it first opened, but the name was eventually shortened to *Museo de Ciencias*—the Museum of the Sciences—to reflect the broadening of its scope over the years. It didn't matter what they now called it; like most places of public learning, they were dying, yet more victims of the fast-paced age of Internet learning.

Emma had come to this museum for one reason. Though it housed some of the country's best collections in archaeology, anthropology, paleontology, and herpetology, there was only one thing she wanted to see.

Emma walked up the front steps toward the huge doors, seeing the ghostly apparition of her reflection doing the same in the glass panels. The polished glass was like a mirror, and she saw her familiar features staring back—the luminous green eyes, brown hair that shone with red highlights in the sunlight, and she knew there were still a few freckles smattering her upturned nose and cheeks.

But as she got closer, the ghost became clearer, and so did reality. She paused, staring for a moment. There was a streak of silver hair at her forehead that she didn't bother masking, and at the corner of each of her green eyes, fine lines came about from squinting into the sun, plus a line between them, creating a permanent vertical frown, perhaps from worry. The face was older, wiser, and as some even said, haunted.

So be it, she thought as she blinked it away and pushed in through the huge doors, feeling immediate relief from the Venezuelan heat. She inhaled the odors of old wood and paper, floor wax, and something that might have been preserving fluid.

The rapid clip of shoes on marble turned her head, and she smiled and waved to a small, middle-aged man with perfectly groomed swept-back silver hair, wearing an immaculate three-piece suit. She took his outstretched hand, pressing firmly. She needed to win him over, and quickly.

"Greetings, Ms. Wilson, greetings." The man beamed up at her. "Your travels were comfortable?"

She nodded. "Yes, thank you, Señor Alvarez. You look just like your pictures: *handsome.*"

The man beamed and also blushed a little. He continued to shake her hand for several more seconds as he smiled like a schoolboy. He finally shrugged.

"*Ah*, but I need new profile pictures." He pointed at his head. "My hair is now fully grey."

"Suits you." Emma looked around. "Beautiful museum. Thank you for taking the time to see me."

He turned, grasping her elbow and raising one arm to point to a corridor leading into the depths of the building. "Fact is, we are very quiet these times." His lips turned down. "The young people of today, impatient, get their information, and perhaps their view of history, from the Internet." He sighed.

"I know; their loss," Emma replied.

The pair walked on in silence for a few more minutes with just the sound of their heels on the polished floor, and the occasional squeak of heavy wooden doors as they pushed through them.

Alvarez wasn't kidding, Emma noticed, that they seemed to have the place to themselves. The man walked with his hands in his pockets and half-turned.

"You have been to our country before? The Amazon?"

"Yes, eight years ago." She grunted softly. "Eight years, three weeks, and two days ago."

Alverez's brows shot up. "You seem to remember it very well?"

Emma's eyes darkened. "It left...an impression."

The man watched her face for a moment and then made a small noise in his chest. "Sometimes it is not a good experience for some people."

He walked on for a few moments more, and obviously decided to fill the quietude with a little more small talk.

"Did you know the Amazon is still the world's largest tropical rainforest?"

She smiled and nodded. "I did know that."

He returned the smile. "Well then, did you know that the previous estimate of our magnificent jungle being 55 million years old has now been pushed back even further than anyone first thought? There are large tracts in the deepest parts of the jungle that may have existed for up to 100 million years."

Her grin widened. "I even knew that too."

"You have done your homework, Ms. Wilson; I salute you." Alverez bowed his head slightly. "And now I can see why you are one of the few people in the world to even know about our artifact." He stopped before a locked door, and then reached into a pocket to rummage for a moment before producing a large set of keys. "But exactly, *how* did you learn of it?"

Emma felt a tingle of excitement as she waited. "I heard about it from Professor Michael Gibson of Ohio University. He wasn't sure if it was even real. He thought it might have been just a story."

"Excellent archeology professor; I know of him." He put the key in the lock, but paused to study her. "A long way to come for something that is certainly real, but is as confusing as it is confounding."

"Curiosity." She kept her eyes on the door.

"Killed the cat, yes?" He grinned up at her.

"It's killed more than that," she responded flatly.

His brows drew together momentarily. "Quite so." Alverez then turned back to the door, unlocking it and pushing it open. He flicked on lights in a large room filled with exhibits that had most likely been stored or were yet to be classified.

Emma's eyes were immediately drawn to a large cabinet against a far wall, and he flicked on a small spotlight that shone down on a bank of solid-looking drawers with brass handles.

She had to stop herself from racing ahead of the man and calmly walked at his side as they crossed the room. Alverez reached for one of the largest drawers and slid it open. Emma felt her heart begin to pound.

"*La huella de Dios*," Alvarez said, almost reverently.

Emma whispered the translation, "The footprint of God."

She stared at the object; it was a shard of stone, roughly two feet long and one foot wide, and at one edge, there was what looked like a portion of a human footprint with the toes pushed in hard. At the other end of the stone shard was a three-toed print of some sort of dinosaur. From the way the prints were pressed in, it looked like the human was running, the other creature in pursuit. Emma closed her eyes for a moment and felt moisture at the corner of each.

"The matrix rock is dated at around 100 million years old, the late Cretaceous Period. The last one of the Mesozoic Era." He turned to her. "The great age of the dinosaurs."

Emma continued to stare, her eyes blurring. "Do you think...?" She sniffed and quickly wiped a sleeve across her eyes.

Alverez nodded. "Impossible, I know. But the rock has been scientifically carbon dated. But there were no humans then. Many experts believe it is the distorted print of some sort of as yet unidentified animal. And others that it is proof that God walked our land to admire his creation." He shrugged and grinned again. "This is why we call it the Surama mystery, named after a place that is a tiny dot on the map in the center of the Amazon." He chuckled. "Who would believe it anyway?"

"Do you think... I can touch it?" She turned to him, hoping her flirting would now pay off.

"What?" He seemed confused, perhaps by the audacity of her request.

"It's important." She stared into his eyes.

His frown deepened. "But why? What would you...?"

"Please," she urged. "It's important to me."

Alverez's jaws worked, as he seemed to mull the request over. "Señorita Wilson, you must be very careful, and do not lift the stone free." He glanced over his shoulder. "Quickly then." He watched her closely.

Emma raised her hand, fingers outstretched, and edged them toward the dark stone. She touched its coolness, and ran them into the slight depressions, feeling the pads of the foot, the toes.

"It was found over a hundred years ago in the mouth of a river after heavy rain. It was washed out of the dark lands of the deepest Amazon." Alverez watched her as she ran her fingers over the footprint, almost lovingly. "Who, or what, made those prints has been long gone for 100 million years."

"Not for me they're not," she whispered. She snatched her hand back and turned on her heel.

"*Huh*? You are finished?" Alverez straightened as he watched her leave. "*Ah*, perhaps we could talk, have coffee, or..."

Emma turned briefly as she got to the door. "Thank you very much, Señor Alverez, but I have much to do and very little time left."

She walked out front and skipped down the steps, her mind working overtime as she thought through what she needed to do. Rather than grab a taxi immediately, Emma walked down the street, turning down avenues with her mind somewhere else, some time and place long, long ago.

She imagined Ben in that dark primordial jungle, running for his life as he was pursued. For all she knew, that race for survival had happened right here, where she stood now.

The last time, they were just a group of dumb kids who had no idea what they were up against. And they had all paid dearly, most with their lives. But this time, she'd be ready; she'd gather a team with appropriate expertise, and she'd need firepower. She had a lot to do, and she'd left everything to the last minute. But her determination to be there when the wettest season returned burned within her as brightly as the day she had scaled down from that hellish place and then watched as it vanished.

Personnel, logistics, timeframes, and finances all ran through her mind, and she paid little attention to anything else. Without thinking, she found herself in a less-salubrious area of the city. The veneer of respect was extremely thin in Venezuela, and when tough times hit, some people hit back. In this place, she wasn't just a woman or even a human being anymore; instead, she was a target.

As she passed an alleyway, she was grabbed around the throat and a small-caliber handgun jammed into her cheek. Emma would have cursed her stupidity, but her throat was already constricted.

She let herself be dragged into the darker depths of the alley. Another man appeared in front of her. He had the brutish appearance of a thug—fleshy broken nose, jaundiced eyes, and a stained gap-toothed grin.

The pressure on her throat eased.

"Take it." She kept her eyes on him as she held out her bag.

Broken Nose snatched it from her. "Let's see if today is a good day," he said in ruined English. He looked up at her. "But I think, not good for you."

The bigger man holding her guffawed into her ear.

"Take the money and let me go. I won't report you," she said evenly.

"Oh, I know this," Broken Nose said, turning one squinted eye on her again. "But I think we not finish with such a pretty lady yet." He went to empty her bag. "Americano?"

She ignored him, knowing how this was going to go, and the theft was the last of her worries. They'd rob her, beat and rape her, and if they wanted to cover their tracks, they'd cut her throat. Every city in the world had scum just like them.

Her anger welled up. The big guy holding her shifted his grip so he could see over her shoulder as Broken Nose emptied her bag.

"Last chance," she said.

He began to shake her bag onto the ground and frowned. "Shut her up."

The gun shifted from her cheek, and the beefy arm around her throat moved even more as the big guy went to either clamp a hand over her mouth, or something worse.

For a split second, he wasn't fully in control of her; it was the opportunity she was waiting for. She let herself drop, sliding down in Beefy's arms, and he bent forward to grab at her. But when her knees were bent, she jammed her heels into the ground, launching herself back up at him like a spear, the top of her head aimed directly at his chin.

It was a direct hit—his head snapped up and she grabbed his gun hand, her finger going over his on the trigger. She jerked his hand around, the muzzle now pointed at the surprised face of Broken Nose. She didn't hesitate for a blink and fired.

The man's ear disappeared in a spray of blood and cartilage, and he howled as his eyes went wide with shock and pain. He dropped her bag and she wrenched the gun free from the still-groggy Beefy's paw, and then used it to club his temple. He fell like an oak tree.

That was enough for Broken Nose, and he turned and ran. Behind her, Beefy groaned with a purple welt on his chin and matching lump growing on the side of his head.

Emma expertly ejected the magazine, and the round in the chamber, and tossed the pieces into an open trashcan. She gathered her things, straightened her clothes and hair, and headed out of the alley.

She'd been busy since she clawed her way out of the Amazon jungle. She'd trained hard, toughened herself. She might be nearly ten years older, but now she was made of iron.

When Primordia returned, she'd be ready.

*****

Emma Wilson walked calmly from the alleyway and waved down a taxicab. Across the road, another car sat pulled in by the sidewalk, windows down. Inside, a long camera lens pointed at the woman, and the whir of an auto-drive captured her every movement.

When Emma's taxi pulled away, the camera was lowered, the car started, and it followed.

CHAPTER 03

Ohio, Greenberry – 3 Months until Comet Apparition

Emma knelt beside the bed of Cynthia Cartwright after bringing her a cup of luke-warm tea. She couldn't help notice that the older woman looked frailer than usual. The toll of losing her son, Ben, to a damn mystery in the Amazon had aged her considerably.

Cynthia had listened to Emma's story and had believed every word. After all, in 1908, the Amazon in similar circumstances had consumed one of Ben's ancestors, and it was his notes that had led Ben to that god-forsaken place.

Cynthia had begged, and then demanded, Emma find her son and bring him home no matter what the timeframe, cost, or the dangers. She had made her wealth available to Emma to bring it about, and Emma had pledged to do so.

Bottom line was, Emma would have done it anyway, but having the Cartwright money at her disposal meant she could do the job right. She loved Ben, and he had been trapped only because he sacrificed his freedom so she could escape—if he was alive, she'd find him and bring him home, even if she died trying.

Emma stood and tiptoed from the room, and then headed up to her office. Cynthia had invited Emma to move in and she accepted, quickly becoming an unofficial daughter to the old woman.

She eased the door of her office shut and turned. Inside, there were several large computer screens, charts, and newspaper clippings dating back over a hundred years. Each told of weird phenomena, unexplained events, and sightings of strange creatures down in the Amazonian jungle. She'd been busy.

She sat down and pulled her chair closer to one of her screens and opened the astral chart on comet mapping.

There was just one she was interested in: Comet P/2018-YG874, designate name, Primordia. It had finished its elliptical curve around the sun and was well on its way back toward Earth. In a few months, it would be at its apparition point—the closest point to Earth where it becomes visible to the naked eye. At that time, its astral effects would be felt, but only in one place on the globe—a tabletop mountain, or tepui, in the Venezuelan jungles of the Amazon.

It was a place she knew that was near inaccessible. And even more so during the height of the comet's effect, as everything electronic was knocked out—nothing worked—and if you could find it, you couldn't fly over it; even a compass went haywire.

Emma sat back, staring at the screen for a few more moments. She knew what would happen then—on that mountaintop, the world was turned on its head, as perhaps a snapshot of the first time the comet ever passed close to Earth was replayed over and over again, every 10 years. But it wasn't just a vision of a long-dead history, but the worlds' *actual* primordial past became a reality—then became now; there became here.

That window remained open for just over 24 hours, and when it closed, everything on that plateau vanished back to where it came from, and any visitors still inside that portal went with it. The way she understood it, the primordial jungle was still there, but only there in prehistory, 100 million years ago.

And that's where Ben Cartwright was now. There was only one way to find out if he was safe, or even still alive, and that was to be there when the window opened again.

She sucked in a deep breath, filling her lungs as she reviewed her list. Last time, they had been dumb kids on an adventure, high on excitement and self-confidence. That had proved fatal.

This time, she'd be ready. This time, she'd have her eyes wide open, and she'd make damn sure that with the firepower and people she took with her, she'd give herself a fighting chance. She looked down at her list again—first things first: firepower.

CHAPTER 04

Lincoln's Roadhouse, Denver, Colorado

Emma pushed in through the door and stood just inside for a few moments, allowing her eyes to adjust to the semi-darkness. It was two in the afternoon and the bar was near empty—except for one table near the rear wall.

Four hulking men sat there, shots and chasers in front of them—boilermakers. *Little early for the hard stuff*, she thought, *but maybe not if your goal is chasing away demons.*

They were dressed in denim and leather, and some might have mistaken them for bikers, except there was stubble but no beard, and their hair was crew-cut short.

The door opened and closed behind her and she ignored it, continuing to focus on the men. To her, they looked exactly how she expected them to look—ex-military on leave, temporarily or for good. She saw that one had a sleeve half-rolled up, and on the brawny forearm, there was a tattoo of a skull wearing a beret with a sword through it—Special Forces.

This is them, she thought, and walked straight up to the table. Four sets of eyes turned to her, appraising, enquiring, amused, but not defensive or alarmed.

"My name is Emma Wilson. I'm a friend of Ben Cartwright."

The men's eyes narrowed. "He sent you, did he?" The one with the tattoo carefully put his beer down.

"In a way, yes, he did," she replied.

"You mean you *used* to be a friend." His eyes slid back to her, and this time, his jaw was set.

Emma stood her ground. "No, I mean, *I am*. I think he's still alive, and I also think, no, I *know*, he needs your help."

One of the other men with a ginger crew-cut tilted his head to her. "Yeah, yeah, I know who you are now. You're the chick that went down to the Amazon with Big Ben…and was the only survivor of the expedition." His eyes drilled into her. "Eight walk in, and only one walks out—*you*. That's some luck."

Tattoo guy lifted his chin. "And how is it that a Special Forces guy of the caliber of Captain Cartwright doesn't make it out, but a little girl like you does?"

"First up, I'm no little girl." She glared at them. "And second, I'm alive because he saved my ass. I wouldn't be alive today if it wasn't for him. Bottom line, he got trapped there because he allowed me to escape." Emma leaned her knuckles on their table. "I swore I'd rescue him, and I damn well will." She straightened. "But I need some help."

The men grinned and tattoo man chortled, lifting his beer to sip again. He drained a good third before lowering it. "We all need help with something, darling."

Emma had been in Ben's condo over the years and looked through his correspondence, his records, and old photos. And she knew the guys from his old mission team were the closest thing he had to friends.

She folded her arms. "If it was one of you in a jam, he'd be there like a shot to help. He was like that; always had his buddies' backs."

Tattoo snorted, but he looked less comfortable now. "Look, Ben was my brother in the field. Woulda died for the guy. But he's been gone over nine years. I don't know what happened in there to him, to you, and to all your friends. But you don't go missing in the Amazon for nearly a decade and then come walking out. Know what I'm saying?"

Emma folded her arms and smirked. "What if I told you that in a few months, there'd be an opportunity to rescue him? That he'll be there, waiting for us. I *know* it."

The men sat and stared for a moment. Tattoo's face dropped a little. "Give it up, miss, he's gone." He sighed. "If there was a chance he was alive…" He shrugged. "We ain't got the time for wild goose chases into the heart of darkness." He looked up. "The Amazon eats people. But you already know that now, don't you?"

"Yeah, I know it. And that's why I need you. I expect it'll be a few weeks' work, plus some prep time." She began to grin. "And I know that a thousand bucks a day expenses, for each of you, isn't bad pocket money for just chasing geese."

The men looked at each other for a moment, but then she added the knockout blow, "Plus a $100,000 bonus, for *every* one of you…*when* we return."

The redheaded man spluttered and sat forward. Tattoo lifted his beer and drained it, and then slid it back on the tabletop. "Okay, you've got our attention." He stuck a large hand out. "Drake Masterson." He pointed to the redhead on his left, Fergus O'Reilly, and then to the next man, who was the color of dark coffee and had a lobe missing from one ear, Brocke Anderson, and then to the last, the youngest, but possibly the biggest. The man looked sullen and his eyes burned into Emma with something she thought might have been distrust or maybe animosity.

Drake thumbed toward him. "And last but not least, Ajax Benson."

The big man smiled, but it was without a shred of humor of friendship, and all he did was momentarily display a silver tooth at the front of his mouth.

She nodded to each man. "Emma, Emma Wilson."

Fergus reached behind himself and grabbed a chair from the next table. He skidded it up to their table. "We're not saying yes. But like Drake said, you've got our attention. So sit down and tell us more."

"Of course." *Got 'em*, she thought. She turned to the bar. "Another round here, and I'll have the same as they're having."

*****

Camilla Ortega slid into the bar behind Emma Wilson. She ordered a single scotch and then sidled into a booth at the other end of the bar from the table of men that Wilson was talking to.

She'd been an investigative journalist for over 20 years with *Nacional De Venezuela*, one of the most prestigious newspapers in all of South America. Nearly half of those two decades had been dedicated to finding out what happened to the Cartwright expedition of 2018.

She sipped her drink as she watched from the shadows. Her personal theory was that the American woman had killed them all and had then wormed her way into the aging Cartwright widow's affection with the intention to inherit the now-childless estate fortune.

The story had been going nowhere, but then one of her friends in immigration told her that Ms. Wilson was suddenly making trips down to South America again, and Camilla's journalistic antenna had quivered. Wilson was up to something, she just knew it, and she also knew this might be her last chance to find out what happened.

She sipped and watched. Camilla had no proof of anything, but the one thing she did know was that sooner or later, killers always returned to the scene of their crime—just like Emma Wilson had started doing.

Camilla carefully withdrew a notebook and pen from her bag,

placing them out of sight on the seat beside her. She pretended to be staring off into space as she faced the group. But her hand moved rapidly as she took notes. There was something else she'd picked up along the way in her journalistic travels—lip reading—and as Emma and the men discussed their plans, she took it all down.

After 10 years, it looked like a criminal mystery was about to be solved. And this time though, Camilla would be right there to scoop it.

CHAPTER 05

1948, over the deep Amazon, Venezuela – Time of Comet Apparition

Airman John Carter grinned as he sped over the treetops in his Corsair Fighter. The USS *Bennington*, the huge Essex-class aircraft carrier, was heading back to Bermuda, and he and a few other pilots had been ordered to patrol the eastern seaboard of the South American continent.

Basically, it was a belt-and-braces job. The war had been over for three years, and no more resistant stragglers had even been encountered. After the conflict ended, most of the serving men and women went back to their lives. But not Carter; he loved the Navy, loved flying, and had decided that this was going to be his life. So he stayed.

And this was why—he banked, looping even lower over the dense green jungle below him. He pushed the stick forward, feeling the huge Pratt & Whitney engine call on its 2000 horsepower, and accelerated with ease. Up here, he was free as a bird, and with the world war over, he could enjoy his flying time free of the fear and fury of war.

Carter was a couple of hundred miles in from the east coast of Venezuela, over what was uncharted jungle. He snorted—*like just about all of it down here,* he thought. But he wasn't worried, as his Corsair had a range of over 1,000 miles and was as reliable and tough as John Wayne with a six-shooter. Sure, the birds were a bit tricky to land on a carrier's deck, hence why they were called *bent wing widowmakers*, but he and his airplane knew each other like an old married couple.

Carter's Corsair and five others were spread in a line over 250 miles and would continue to zigzag on for another 200 before heading back to the *Bennington*. So far, the sky had been a clear blue, except for a growing smudge on his horizon.

He squinted; it was strange, and even though it looked a little like a storm, it was only over a small part of the jungle. He'd never seen a weather pattern like that before. He radioed it in and got the okay to give it a little look-see.

Carter rose to 2,000 feet and saw the thick, purple clouds slowly hanging over just one area of the jungle, and as he got closer, he saw that the effect had a type of ceiling, and even more oddly, it rotated, getting thicker and darker at the middle. He closed in on it and decided to rise above it to look down into its eye.

That's when the shit hit the you-know-what. As soon as he was over the top of the boiling clouds, warning lights flashed and then to his horror, the Corsair's powerful engine sputtered.

"Don't you do it to me, baby."

But she did—the massive Pratt & Whitney engine shut down.

"*Mayday, mayday, going down…*" He quickly glanced at his instruments panel to give his bearings, but the dials were frozen, all of them.

Jesus Christ, he whispered. He knew that the radio was also probably dead, but his training took over; it was all he had left.

"This is Lieutenant John Carter, last known position 5.9701° North, 62.5362° West, approximately 240 miles in from the Venezuelan coast. Engine has failed, I am going down, I repeat, *I am going down…*"

Carter looked out of the cockpit window as his plane dropped into the boiling cloud. His visibility vanished.

The Corsair was a magnificent and efficient fighter plane, but she was no glider, and very quickly, she started to turn nose down and gather speed.

"What the…?" Outside his cockpit window, he thought he could make out, in amongst the fog-like cloud, other airplanes glide past, but bigger than his Corsair.

Still well over a thousand feet above ground, Carter had no option but to bail out, and just as he reached up to slide his canopy back, he broke through the cloud and saw the jungle below him.

But it wasn't like the jungle he had just been flying over. In fact, it was a jungle like he had never seen before in his life—strange towering trunks with grass-like fronds instead of leaves, pulpy ferns, spiny-looking cycads dozens of feet around, and in the distance, a glittering lake that caught rays of light from a growing hole in the cloud ceiling above him.

Carter was relieved to see those other airplanes he spotted still soaring over the treetops. But wait, *no*, they weren't aircraft at all, but freaking birds, *giant freaking bat-like birds* with claws on their wings.

I'm losing it, he thought.

"*Mayday, mayday*," he yelled again into the mic. Carter gritted his teeth and wrestled with the controls. He was thankful to be low enough to bring it in, but he needed somewhere to put it down. He pushed all flaps up, trying to compensate for the heavy nose of the machine.

There—in the distance, he saw the clearing, close to a cliff edge, and he prayed as he headed toward it. At the last instant, something lifted from the treetops—a head on a neck that must have raised five stories into the air. It turned to glance at him with large liquid eyes, and he yelled his fear and jerked the stick, trying to bank away.

But time was up, and speed and gravity won. Carter came down hard and fast, shearing the tops of trees and then coming down on the gravel-covered clearing. The corsair's nose was too low, and instead of sliding, it dug in, stopping way too fast for a soft human body to take. The initial jerk slammed him, his face, and his forehead, into the instrument panel.

Hope they find me, was his last thought before darkness took him.

CHAPTER 06

University of California, Digital Collection Library

Emma sat at a desk and scrolled through the historical newspapers. The files the university had available were from its own stocks and from obtained collections that stretched back hundreds of years. Now, thankfully, all digitized, so no more squinting into huge microfiche machines and slowly inching along at a single page at a time.

The digital files meant she could set clear search parameters, and to begin with, she confined her search to anything after the 1700s, in both North and South America, and in any year ending in 8.

That was her magic number, as the comet, Primordia, was on its elliptical orbit in a periodic recurrence of every 10 years, and it arrived every decade in a year ending in 8. Even though it only lasted a few days, to the locals, this had always been known as the wettest season.

During the last one, Emma was in the Amazon, and she had personally seen the coma streak in the sky looking like a silver eyebrow. But then, when it was at the closest point to Earth, in what was called its perihelion or maximum observable focus, this particular comet did something unprecedented, something unbelievable; it distorted the time and space directly over a vast tabletop mountain in Venezuela. No one would believe her, but she knew it was true. She'd seen it herself.

It was then that strange distortions occurred on the mountaintop—time and space became rearranged, reordered; pathways were created and doorways opened. It was only observable for a few days, but in that time, a gateway to a little piece of Hell opened upon the Earth.

Emma sat as if in a trance as her mind took her back to the tepui and their expedition of December 2018. She and her friends had been transported back 100 million years, or perhaps that primordial timeline had been transported here.

In the past, she had tried to obtain answers from physicists, theorists, and even science-fiction authors; and trying to get her head around quantum realities, spatial time distortions, and past-life theories, had only left her more confused than ever. But whichever it was, that hellish place had killed all her friends in little over a day, and she'd been the only one to escape.

She'd given up trying to convince people that she was telling the truth, or that she wasn't mad. Only Ben's mother, Cynthia had stuck by her, but Emma soon realized it was up to her and her alone to rescue Ben who gave up his freedom so she could have hers. When the doorway closed, Ben had been trapped behind it with all those primordial horrors, and she prayed daily that he somehow survived.

She shook her head to clear it and looked at the results that had been returned from her historical search of news events. She wasn't exactly sure what she was looking for, but she now had over 200 entries, going back to the late 1700s. She organized them by story headline and began to sort through them, discarding anything mundane about trade, armed conflicts, or politics, and after 30 minutes had narrowed it down to several dozen that spoke of strange weather, disappearances, or sightings of inexplicable things in the jungle.

She even found an article about the naming of a new comet in the late 1700s. *Primordia.* She whispered the name, now even hating the sound if it.

She opened an article from the NY Times from 1908, titled: 'President Roosevelt Offers Reward for Giant Snake.'

She read on: Theodore 'Teddy' Roosevelt was the 26th President of the United States, and also an explorer, soldier, and naturalist. He'd heard tales of a monstrous snake in the Amazon, and offered a $1,000 reward to anyone who could catch it. Amazingly, the reward was only withdrawn in 2002 and had stood at $50,000 when it ended.

She remembered she and Ben had talked about the possibility of one of the prehistoric animals from the plateau somehow escaping into today's jungle. It would be an oddity, but also it would become a thing of legend—and all jungles had them.

Next, there was a 1928 column about an expedition to find missing explorer, Percy Fawcett, who vanished in the Amazon. It caught her attention as Fawcett claimed to have shot a giant anaconda over 60 feet in length. He also claimed to have found giant footprints that he believed came from a creature from the dawn of time.

The dawn of time. Emma felt a tingle of excitement. She believed him, but she bet no one else did.

Her mouth quirked up at one corner at the next story from 1948— Airman John Carter from the USS *Bennington* went missing in a Corsair Fighter. She sighed, remembering. *You're not missing to me; I know where you are*, she thought as she smiled sadly. *Thank you for the loan of your plane, Airman Carter. We tried.*

Emma leaned her head back on her neck, shutting her eyes. She reached up to rub at them. "What am I looking for?" she said to the ceiling.

Something, anything, she knew, that indicated a way up or down the tepui, or that where she had been transported to could be accessed sooner than the decade-long wait. Or even some sort of concrete proof anywhere, anytime.

But there was nothing.

She guessed something that was there for a little over a single day once every 10 years was a blink-and-you'll-miss-it event; especially when that event took place in one of the most remote, inaccessible, and inhospitable places on Earth.

She opened another window on her computer and searched for South America, 100 million years ago. One of the results was an app that ran a tectonic plate movement simulation. She ran it.

It showed the formation of the last great supercontinent called Pangaea. It started to break apart about 175 million years ago, and 100 million years ago, South America was still the basic shape it was today, except it was ringed by a shallow coastal sea, and interestingly, was only separated from the west coast of Africa by a few hundred miles.

She leaned in closer to look at the 100-million-year-ago tropical green mass of a primordial jungle that was still the impenetrable Amazon of today. *That's where you are, Ben, in there somewhere*, she thought.

She was a rock climber, and those skills are what gave her the edge getting on and off the plateau. But she needed a way in and out for a team that didn't necessarily require those skills this time. She steepled her fingers at her chin, thinking.

"We can't risk climbing again." She rubbed her chin and stared into space, letting her mind work. *And no one will fly over it, or even could, as instruments don't work. There's got to be another way*, she mused.

Emma drummed her fingers on the tabletop for a few moments, and then quickly grabbed her things, pushed her chair back, and headed for the doorway. She suddenly had a whole bunch of new things to investigate and now only a few months to get it all together. Time mattered; and the comet was already on its way again.

CHAPTER 07

Ben slowly lifted his head from the mud and opened one eye. Predators homed in on identifiable shapes, and two eyes, especially ones with white sclera, were like neon lights in the dark.

To survive, he used all his Special Forces training of concealment and stealth, but he knew that the adversaries he faced here had senses hundreds or even thousands of times greater than any human foe he had ever faced.

He opened his other eye and scanned the ground, then looked back along the tree trunks and bracken stems, then once more overhead, looking up into a strange tangled canopy in this area that was heavy with giant cycad branches, palm fronds, and massive ferns like cascading waterfalls of green.

Finally, he allowed his eyes to drop back down to three turkey-sized creatures that picked at fallen berries. They were beaked, like a bird, but squat and pebble-skinned, and their four stubby legs ended in blunt, three-toed clawed feet. Their dull eyes constantly swiveled, like some sort of chameleon, always moving and keeping a lookout for predators.

Ben ran through his plan: get a little closer, spear one of them, then snatch it up, and get back to his shelter, pronto. His stomach grumbled; he needed food, and though he'd found some berries and tubers he could digest, he needed protein for energy and also to preserve his muscle mass. In this place, it was only the strong that survived.

He began to squirm forward—*slide, stop, slide, stop*—until he was as close as he could get. He drew his spear forward, and then began to ease to one knee. He brought one foot forward to plant it in the mud, the ooze squelching up between his toes. He braced the muscles in his arm, his gaze unwavering as he exhaled, then…

Something burst through the ferns and screeched so loudly that Ben literally felt himself blanch from shock. He threw himself down into the mud.

The thing stood about seven feet in height and seemed all box-like head, serrated teeth, and a green and brown camouflage tiger stripe that would have rendered it invisible in the twilight jungle.

It was some sort of theropod and its jaws clamped down on one of the turkey things with a wet, bone-breaking crunch. It then shook it quickly from side to side, much like a dog that had caught a rabbit.

The other plant-eaters fled, one straight at Ben, and he only had to flick an arm out to grab its neck and twist sharply.

With the hunter occupied and the sounds of ripping flesh loud enough to mask him, Ben began to back into the brush. He made sure to drag his dead prize through the mud, coating the creature to also conceal its scent. One of the many things he had learned in his long years here: to stay alive, you needed to be able to vanish—no scent, no sound, and no movement.

He began to squirm into one of the tunnels he had carved out through the roots, stems, and branches of the ground bracken, straining his body to fit inside.

He couldn't help farting, and he froze, grimacing. He waited to hear if there was any sound of pursuit. After a few minutes, he exhaled.

Idiot; can't take you anywhere, Cartwright, he thought, and pushed on. In another few minutes, Ben was well away.

*****

The largest theropod, the leader, was joined by several others of its pack, and after it had its share of the small animal, he allowed them to tear at the remains to finish off even the skin and bones. The small creature was barely enough to take the edge off the pack's appetite—they needed more, always more.

The leader sniffed the air, catching the scent of the methane. Its sensitive snout was able to analyze the tiny airborne particles in the gas and understand everything about the animal it came from; the food it had eaten, that it was warm-blooded, its health, its sex, and finally, the direction it went.

It grunted once, calling the pack in, and they began to follow the scent.

CHAPTER 08

Smithsonian National Museum of Natural History, Washington DC

Emma was on a mission, and she headed for the Smithsonian's special exhibits gallery. She was rapidly ticking off her list of things she'd need. Her plans were coming together, and she tried to think of everything that caused their downfall last time—sure, there was the gross underestimation of everything they'd all walked into. But there were resources they could have made use of to improve their chances.

Her jaws clenched when she thought of how naïve they all were when they sat around in Ricky's Rib Bar and high-fived at the launch of a grand adventure—they were all dumb kids who thought that money, enthusiasm, youth, and a spirit of adventure was enough. It wasn't, and it killed nearly all of them.

Her teeth were grinding so hard they ached as she entered the special exhibits hall and slowed as she came to the display she was looking for.

At the sight of it, her brain yelled a warning and her heart began racing in her chest. But her legs kept moving her closer.

The *Titanoboa* exhibit showed a reconstruction of the massive snake. It was as wide as a car and muddy brown. It was frozen in the act of devouring some sort of antelope. The back end of the animal was disappearing down the huge fang-toothed maw—it made Emma feel a sudden wave of nausea.

In the exhibit with the model were two people, a young man and woman, who crawled over the snake's body, touched-up paintwork, and cleaned the display site as they chatted to each other. Emma just stared, and eventually, the young man noticed her, smiled, and wandered closer.

"Pretty awesome, *huh*?" He turned back to the snake and stuck his hands in his pockets. "It was around at the time of the dinosaurs and probably ate them for dinner." He turned to her and grinned. "Wanna know why we think that?"

Emma shrugged. "Sure."

"Regurgitation debris." His eyebrows went up.

"Vomit?" She tilted her head.

"Exactly. We found crushed dino bones that were pulverized *before* they were fossilized. The fragmentation size led us to believe that a snake crushed them, ate them, and then regurgitated them." He chuckled. "The big guys do that sometimes."

"Don't we all?" Emma returned the smile.

"Yep." Andy laughed. "Weird thing is though, the *Titanoboa* outlived the dinosaurs by millions of years. We still don't know how."

Emma's eyes slid to the model. "It's too small," she said, her gaze trance-like.

"What is?" he asked, frowning.

"It's too small, and the body was striped, like a tiger, except *green* and brown." She licked lips suddenly gone dry. "And it was far more muscular, sinuous, and powerful-looking." She shrugged and nodded. "But it's close, given I understand you only had a few vertebrae to work with."

He turned to stare and his female colleague had stopped what she was doing to listen. Her eyes narrowed. She wiped her hands on a rag and wandered over.

"You're Emma Wilson, aren't you?"

Emma nodded and blinked, her name snapping her out of her trance. "Yes, I am."

The woman shook her head and turned to her colleague. "This is the woman who said her friends were attacked by a giant snake in the Amazon ten years ago." Her lip curled a little.

Emma folded her arms. "And you two must be Andy and Helen Martin, brother and sister paleontologists who are also specialists in herpetology." She smiled at the young man. "You did good work on the *Borealopelta markmitchelli* fossil find."

Andy grinned. "Thank you. It was a relative of the *Ankylosaurus*, and undoubtedly the best-preserved specimen in the world. You can actually see all the plating. Fantastic to—"

Helen nudged him and turned back to Emma. "What can we do for you, Ms. Wilson? We're a little busy right now."

"I understand," Emma replied. She tilted her head. "But I see your eyes light up when you talk about your fieldwork and making such magnificent discoveries. And I know funding is hard to come by. After all, it's not every day you get to find something truly magnificent."

Helen's jaw tightened, but Andy nodded.

"I don't know what you've read about me, but I can guess." Emma looked from one to the other. "The fact is, my friends and I mounted an expedition to the Amazon, and we discovered something there that was as magnificent as it was deadly. We failed because we underestimated everything about the place, the animals there, and the jungle."

Emma looked from one scientist's eyes to the other. "We're going back, and this expedition, I'll be taking everything I need. This time, we won't be underestimating *anything*."

The pair looked at Emma for a moment before their eyes slid to each other. Helen lifted her chin. "I'm guessing you want us to go, as part of that *taking everything you need* speech."

Emma hiked her shoulders. "You're the first specialists I've asked. This is a great opportunity. And consider this: I'll fully fund your research for a year, and any discoveries we make there are yours."

Andy's eyebrows rose, and the corners of his mouth couldn't help twitching up. Helen's face remained implacable.

"And what's in it for you?"

Emma met her gaze. "Fulfilling a promise I made to someone a long time ago. I left someone behind, and I intend to find them."

"After ten years? I think you mean what's left of them." Helen tilted her head. "So, a waste of time."

Andy sighed, and then looked up at his sister. "It's probably a hoax, or all a big mistake. But if there's even the sliver of a chance…" He lowered his voice. "Sis, come on, we gotta think about this."

"And if there is a sliver of a chance its true, it'll be beyond dangerous." Helen's brows were still drawn together.

Emma's jaw set. "I won't sweet-talk you; it *will* be damned dangerous, and deadly. That, *hidden place*, killed all my friends in a little over a day. But we weren't ready then."

"And you are now?" Helen's eyes were half-lidded. "Who else is going?"

"I'm bringing some firepower this time. Four ex-Special Forces soldiers with jungle experience, all kitted up. Then there's you two, and me. And that's it."

"*All kitted up*? You can't be shooting up a foreign country. You'd get everyone locked up," Andy scoffed.

"The guns are coming. And if you decide to come, and I hope you do, then you'll be glad they're there." Emma smiled flatly. "In or out?"

Andy didn't even wait. "In."

"I know I'll regret this." Helen sighed. "...*probably*, in."

Emma nodded. "In one week's time, we meet for introductions and our first expedition briefing. I'll send through the details." She stuck out her hand. "Welcome aboard."

CHAPTER 09

Ben had found a new home. He hated to have to leave his old one behind, and he thought it had been well hidden and fortified. But, he found that the longer you stayed in one place, the greater the odds that he'd eventually be found.

And he'd been right. He was lucky that he had an escape hatch, or he would have been dug out like a grub from a rotting log. One to two years, and then he was usually on the move again.

His new cave descended into the ground as opposed to into the side of a rock face. All around it was thick growth—good for concealment, but unfortunately, the twin fact of that was that it meant it gave good concealment for any approaching hunters. Every time he went out or came back, his neck prickled at the thought of something waiting patiently to ambush him.

He always prayed that if it did happen, it would be quick. Ben still remembered after all these years, watching in horror as their guide, Nino, was torn limb from limb and then eaten while still alive. He shuddered at the red-raw memories.

Close to the mouth of his cave, there was also a massive tree trunk, rising easily 80 feet into the air. It had fur-like bark, and its massive canopy was more like long ribbons of grass or reeds than leaves. Over the months, Ben had used his knife to chop out wedges into the bark, creating a type of ladder, and every so often, or just when the mood took him, he climbed to the top of it. Then, hiding in amongst the grassy canopy, he looked out over his primordial land.

Ben sucked in a deep breath of the humid air, catching the familiar fishy scent of animal dung that he now knew to be dinosaurian. There was also the sweet smell of rotting vegetation, the sharp tang of plant saps, and also strange-scented flowers. Huge insects zoomed by, and higher up, he could see leathery-winged pterodons riding on thermals. Some of them were no bigger than ravens and flitted from treetop to treetop. But others were enormous, like airplanes.

In the distance, huge heads on long necks rose and fell as the land leviathans fed on grasses, trees, and pretty much any plant matter they could get into their gargantuan mouths. They trumpeted a little like elephants, and the mournful cries traveled along the valley floors for miles to be answered by another of their kind lost in the hazy distance.

Ben sat forward; he had learned to keep moving, and the land he was currently in stretched to a wet, green valley with raw, towering cliffs. Even the geology of this primitive place was huge, as continental drift was still pulling, pushing, and uplifting the earth, and then eroding it back down.

He had created a small perch within his branch nest, and momentarily, he looked down toward the ground. He knew that hunters were probably down there somewhere. But up here, he felt safe. Beside him was a woven sack of fist-sized rocks—he'd collected them and carried a few aloft every time he scaled up to his nest, and if anything got too interested in his trail, he'd rain the rocks down. Nothing liked having a baseball-sized rock hit their heads, no matter how thick those boxy, tooth-laden skulls were.

Ben grinned mercilessly; he had other safeguards as well. This was his patch, and any intruders would soon find he was not going to make for an easy meal.

He sighed and leaned back, placing his arms behind his head. Hazy sunlight shone down on him, and he turned to stare toward the plateau—*his plateau*—right now; it wasn't like it would be in the future. The iron-hard granite walls were sloping on some sides and only rose a few hundred feet where the cliffs fell away, unlike the thousands of feet the sheer walls would rise in his home time. Today, his tepui was young and still growing up.

But just looking at it filled him with hope and horror. He knew he'd need to make his way back up there one day. He hoped that his theory that the wettest season would once again grab that junior tabletop mountain and allow anything and anyone on there to be thrown forward into the future. When it did happen, he'd damn well make sure he was there.

Ben almost wept with joy, impatience, and frustration, and he couldn't help thinking back over his long time spent here. It was like a jail sentence where all the other inmates wanted to tear you limb from limb, *literally*.

In his travels, he'd seen vast volcanic plains that looked like the surface of alien planets. He'd crossed jungle valleys that contained monstrosities no one had ever seen or recorded. There were stinking swamps with soft-bodied things with hook-like teeth that drained blood or had segmented bodies and dozens of sharp-tipped legs and pincers.

His eyes slid back to the juvenile flat-topped mountain and felt his stomach knot. Everywhere in this damn place was dangerous, but up there on that huge risen landmass like an island in the sky, lived an alpha-apex predator that was worse than anything that hunted in these lowlands, and it was the reason he had been made to flee all those years ago.

He sucked in a deep breath and continued to stare, like he did most days. The gargantuan snake, the *Titanoboa*, wasn't just another monster. This thing was like a force of nature. He couldn't help replaying that last handful of minutes where he had led the monstrous snake away from Emma.

Then the chaos of swirling wind and boiling clouds had vanished and he found himself alone. Alone, except for something that was from his worst nightmare pursuing him. It had pushed him to the cliff edge, and when he stood on the precipice, he didn't see the Venezuelan Amazon he recognized anymore; instead, it was this place.

It was then he knew why no one could find the place unless it was during the wettest season, once every 10 years. Because it just wasn't there anymore. The doorway had closed, and he had been trapped on the wrong damn side.

Ben had no choice but to leap then into the vast unknown of this brutal, primordial world. He began to chuckle sourly.

"And I'm the only guy here, and will be for the next 100 million years. Just me and the monsters."

Ben looked back to the plateau. There was something that bothered him; in his travels, he found few incidences of the *Titanoboa* in the jungles. The massive snakes seemed to prefer it up on the plateau. Or something kept them up there.

Ben knew he'd have to move on soon. He'd already stayed here longer than he should have. It was like a sixth sense that told him he wasn't safe anymore.

He wished he could go back to the ocean. Sure, it had its own vast menagerie of wonders and horrors, but he'd liked it there...until he was evicted. His mouth pulled up on one side as he remembered: the endless blue water, the fresh fish, and his only friend, *Ralph*.

"Still miss you, buddy." He sighed and prepared to scale down, but paused, listening.

*****

The hunters tracked the scent of the strange animal for miles. Its warm blood smell, its salty tang of sweat, and its exhalations were irresistible to them.

The lead theropod, a seven-foot-tall biped with toes that ended in scythe-like claws, paused, turning its head bird-like to listen to the sounds of the jungle. The thing they hunted was close, they could smell it strongly now, but strangely, it was still out of sight.

The hunter crept forward, about to edge between two large tree trunks, when its three-toed foot snagged on some twine strung between them. Immediately, a horizontal branch whipped out, and along its length were sharpened spikes that came at it faster than the creature could react.

The theropod was frozen to the spot as the three-foot-long sharpened spikes were embedded deep into its gut, holding it in place.

High above it came a sound. It was the first time the hunters had ever heard it, and never would again—it was the sound of a human laughing.

CHAPTER 10

The Cartwright Estate, Greenberry, Ohio

Cynthia Cartwright had let Emma use the family home to bring everyone together. It was the largest house in Greenberry, and the most discreet place she knew.

Emma saw the old woman talking softly and earnestly with the huge and formidable Drake Masterson. The big man held her tiny hand in one of his large paws and patted it, nodding as he listened. She could imagine her extracting promises from him to bring her son home. And Emma could also envisage him in return saying, and honestly, that he'd die trying.

Emma trusted and liked the big guy, and she was thankful he had agreed to lead them in. He gave her…confidence.

She guessed that now that the four ex-Special Forces guys knew there was even the slightest chance of Ben being alive, they probably would have gone in to get him for free, such was the bond within their fighting unit. But she knew that risking their lives needed compensation—she just hoped they all lived to enjoy it.

The soldiers were like a different species to the others in the room. All were huge, wide, and loud. The redheaded Fergus O'Reilly joked with his buddy Brocke Anderson, whose blinding white grin lit up the room. She wondered how he lost his earlobe—was it shot off or bitten off? Time would tell.

Brocke noticed her looking at him, lurched forward to pick up the coffee pot, and theatrically held it out to her; she smiled and shook her head. As he went to put it down, Fergus nudged him and held out his own cup.

Emma let her eyes slide to the biggest and youngest of their group—the still-sullen looking Ajax Benson. She made a mental note to speak to him, try and understand him. There was something he was keeping bottled up, and given where they were going, she didn't want any underlying issues bubbling to the surface. As Ben told her once, small imps of the mind can grow to become monstrous demons once in a field of combat.

Combat? She snorted softly at the thought. It was ridiculous of her to think like that, but after surviving the plateau once, she had a right to feel a little battle hardened.

Andy and his sister Helen, Emma's paleontological firepower, stood together by the fireplace and the pair chatted as Helen looked over the photograph collection on the hearth—she paid extra attention to the smiling face of Ben, as though trying to memorize his features.

Emma had a moment of doubt about her selection—the pair of scientists seemed too young and naive. She was about to throw them into a grinder they had no way of fully appreciating.

Over the years, Emma had grown armor plating, as well as a little single-minded ruthlessness in pursuit of her objective—rescuing Ben—nothing else mattered. The Special Forces guys looked like they ate barbed wire for breakfast, but these two…they looked more like they'd prefer to be eating smashed avocado on wheat toast and sipping soy latte at their favorite Bohemian café.

She girded herself; they were picked because they could help her bring Ben home—end of story. She'd lay out the risks and then they could choose to go or stay. She still had time to replace them.

She swallowed; it was time to bring things to order. Emma cleared her throat. "Morning, everyone." She smiled and looked at their faces as the group turned toward her.

She first crossed to Cynthia and took her by the arm, leaning closer. "I'm going to talk to the team now. You don't have to stay if you don't want to."

The small woman suddenly seemed to steel herself. "You're going to talk about rescuing my Ben, *our* Ben. I want to hear." She looked behind her and pointed to her favorite chair. Fergus sat in it. "I'll just sit quietly and listen."

Emma raised an eyebrow at the redheaded man and he immediately stood, made a show of wiping the chair seat down, and then turned to bow. Emma led Cynthia to it and helped her sit, poured her another tea, and put a small slice of her favorite orange sponge cake on a tiny blue and white plate.

Emma then moved to one of the large walls beside the fireplace and took down a few of the pictures, leaving it blank. On the table, she turned on the projector sitting there and plugged it into a laptop computer. Behind her, the wall lit up.

The first image appeared, and she stood with handheld remote and folded her arms. It was a picture of South America showing a red dot on the edge of the Canaima National Park.

"Where I, *we*, began our expedition." She breathed deeply. "Almost ten years ago to the day."

"Begging your pardon, Emma." Drake Masterson turned in his chair. "But how did you know to start *there*?"

She expected the question. "We had maps, a notebook, and a legend to follow. And I know what you're going to ask next; no, we don't have all of those resources anymore. They were all lost."

"But I guess the legend remains," Andy added.

"Yeah, that's a good start," Fergus said. "And given the Amazon is over three million square miles in size, it shouldn't take us any time at all to find what we're looking for." He winked at Brocke.

Ajax snorted and shifted his huge bulk. "Who cares? We bumble around in the jungle for a week; maybe some schmuck gets sick, or injured, maybe even killed. Then we all come home with money in the bank." He looked at her. "By the way, if the schmuck that happens to get killed is you, I want to make sure we'll still get paid."

Drake Masterson glared at him, but Emma stared the young man down. "You'll be paid. And you all have something else that we didn't have the first time." She looked at each of their faces.

"You have someone who was there, who survived, and who can tell you what to look for, and even better, what to look out for." She eyeballed Ajax. "Happy?"

"Yes, ma'am." He grinned and saluted with two fingers.

"Good. And over the years, I've drawn maps and made notes from my memory...several maps." She progressed the images to another view of the jungle that was taken from a lower level, this one starting on the Rio Caroní River.

Everyone sat forward as they followed the dotted line, branching off the main river, with notations, such as: *Covered River, Shallows, Sunken Idol, River Of Paradise, Swamp, And Forest Of Tree Ferns.*

Drake nodded slowly. "Not bad."

Fergus grunted. "Scale is probably up the shit; but yeah, it's a good start. We can work with that."

"We've worked with worse," Brocke added.

Emma moved them on to some hand-drawn images collected together; there was the tepui from a distance, the massive edifice like a giant wave of rock rising from the jungle. The next was a temple with gargoylish sentinels on each side of the massive doorway.

Andy squinted and then stood, coming closer to the illuminated wall. He pointed and then turned to Helen. "The Snake God—the *Yacumama.*"

"Mother of the river," Emma replied. "That's what Jenny..." Emma grimaced. "...called it."

"How high is that tabletop?" Ajax asked.

"Probably about 1500 feet, give or take a hundred. Not the highest in the jungle, but it was sheer on all sides." She walked closer, her arms folded. "There was a hidden passage in the temple, a chimney that we could climb all the way to the top. Took us several hours."

"Okay, good," Ajax said.

"No, not good, as it's not there anymore. It...collapsed."

"So we do it the hard way," Drake responded. "Going to take a lot more time to scale. I know you have climbing experience, so does my team." He turned to Andy and Helen. "Anyone else?"

"Well..." Andy bobbed his head, his eyes looking up and to the left into his head, as though rummaging for the necessary experience.

"No," Helen said firmly. "Neither of us."

Andy looked to her and then sighed. "Nah, not really. Some gym stuff on the climbing wall, but nothing...outdoors."

Ajax guffawed, momentarily showing his silver tooth. "Don't sweat it; it's exactly the same." His grin widened. "Except you're not gonna have some sap holding your line on the ground, and there won't be little colored bits of plaster to hang onto, plus no cushioned mat to land on if you fall. Oh, and then there's the bit about being higher than the tip of the Empire State Building. Otherwise, yeah, exactly the same."

Emma couldn't help smiling at the shade of pale Andy went. "There are other caves, or rather *one* other I know of. It was the one I came down in. But it was no easy climb and took two days. I don't want us to waste the time and take the risk."

"Take a chopper. I know some guys down there who'll loan us a Hewie—armor-plated, and we can refit the gun, .50 cal. We're in and out fast, and we got decisive firepower." Drake opened his arms wide. "You're welcome."

"Own the sky, own the war." Brocke clapped his hands together once.

"Too easy." Fergus leaned across and bumped knuckles with the man.

"Won't work," Emma said. "In fact, nothing electronic will work. Whatever magnetic distortion the comet, Primordia, makes, it renders all electronic devices useless. The locals think it's just some weird weather effects, maybe ball lightning, but they avoid the place for a week."

Ajax lifted his chin. "Then we go early and wait. You said the effect of this distortion thing only occurred for a little over a day. So we get there the day before, and wait for it. When it's over, and the effect's gone, we fly out."

"I thought of that," Emma said. "And I've spent ten years researching the phenomena. In 1978, they dropped some survey beacons on the tabletop mountain we're interested in. Afterward, when they went to recover them, they found they had vanished. Not just destroyed, but gone-gone, like they'd been canceled out of existence."

Emma folded her arms. "My theory is that if you happen to be there when this effect begins, the distortion is so powerful as the doorway is opening that anything underneath is obliterated."

"Well, that's fucked up." Ajax sat back.

Emma waggled a finger in the air. "I believe there's another, faster, and safer way."

CHAPTER 11

Ben settled down in his cave with one mud-crusted arm behind his head. The theropod meat he'd dined on was tough and needed to be chewed until his jaws ached. But it was tasty, and nourishing.

Loneliness was the mind killer now, and as he drifted off to sleep, he let his memory take him back to the only friend he ever had in this hellish place. He closed his eyes and dreamed.

Ben traveled mostly during the night, heading east. He had crossed the Venezuelan Coastal Range, a line of huge jagged mountains that ran along the northern coast. There were no roads, and the only paths were animal tracks, and following those was a high-risk option, as it invited ambush from wily predators on the lookout for unwary animals.

It had taken him over a month, but finally, at one of the peaks, he had stared down at the vast, blue ocean. It sparkled, calm, inviting, and azure as the sun rose over it. It took him the rest of the day, but by dusk, he had stood at a slope looking down onto long sandy beaches to his left, and to his right, steep cliffs to the water's edge, with the dark and mysterious mouths of caves, some huge, some small.

Caves meant danger. But then again, empty caves meant safety, and even better if they were ones that were hard to get to. Ben could see that some of these caves were 50 feet up from the ground and were very promising indeed. It was there he headed first.

Ben stood peering down from the cliff that dropped 80 feet to a horseshoe-shaped, sandy beach. It had a fair-sized lagoon that was barricaded off from the ocean by a breakwater ring of jagged rocks.

He then got down on his belly to inch forward and looked down over the edge. One of the largest caves was about eight feet down and with a nice ledge he could navigate—big enough for him, but way too small for serious predators.

Ben rested on his arms. "Well, looks like I just found home for the night."

He strapped his spear and woven bag to his back and started down. With the fading light, he peered around the edge—he sniffed—fishy shit odor, but that was it.

He clambered in, pulled his spear out, and crouched there for a moment, letting his eyes adjust to the gloom. There were a few screaming pterodons, but tiny ones no bigger than gulls.

Ben smiled. "Hello, breakfast. Mind if I join you?"

He took off his pack and sat with his back to the rear of the cave, watching the sun set on a shimmering ocean. After a full day trekking, in another moment, his eyes became so heavy he didn't even remember when he had fallen asleep.

CHAPTER 12

"I got it. HALO drop." Brocke clapped his hands together. "High Altitude Low Opening. If the tabletop mountain, or tepui thing, is as big as you say, then we can drop from high up, and only open our chutes over the top. Plus, if we're really high, maybe the magnetic disruption won't be an issue."

"Brilliant." Fergus sat forward. "And if it *is* an issue, we jump out a couple of miles from our target site and glide to where we need to be."

"Jesus, and I thought the cliff climbing was going to be tough." Andy's mouth dropped open. "I can't do that."

"That's me out too." Helen just looked wearied.

"None of us can," Emma said. "Besides, how do we get off, if we were *all* ever to make it down in one piece?" Emma asked.

"Re-gather and repack our chutes. Base jump off when we're done." Ajax sat back, smirking.

"We encountered a massive updraft as the doorway or portal began to close. You jump into that, you'll end up being blown a hundred feet back into the jungle." Emma smiled. "But you're not far off."

"Come on, darling, the suspense is killing me," Fergus said, chuckling.

"We use our first ever mode of air travel. And one that doesn't care about magnetic interference." Emma smiled. "A hot air balloon."

There was silence for a few seconds before Ajax slapped his huge thigh and guffawed with his head thrown back. "Seriously?" He rocked forward. "A freaking balloon? We're all dead, just kill me now," he said, braying again.

Fergus rubbed his face, and Brocke also wouldn't meet her eyes. Emma's jaw jutted out, and she saw Drake Masterson watching her closely, assessing her.

Ajax sat forward, grinning from ear to ear. "Hey, maybe she's Mary Popp—"

"Excuse me."

Ajax stopped talking and looked around.

"*Excuse me.*" Everyone turned to where Cynthia was sitting forward, with the perfect lines of her eyebrows arched. She pointed one thin finger at Emma.

"This woman not only survived but walked out of the Amazon jungle all by herself. She is one of the bravest, toughest, and smartest people I know." She turned to Drake Masterson. "My son, Ben, will be there waiting for you. Help her get him and bring him home."

Drake's eyes were unwavering. "Yes, ma'am. That's the plan."

Ajax cleared his throat. "But seriously, just how long do you think we have? Riding in a balloon will take weeks, and we have to rely on the right winds and weather. Plus, fuel tanks are heavy."

"Not unless we get real close first," Drake said. "Good-sized balloon, that will take up to a dozen people, can be broken down quite small—bag, basket, burner, and fuel tanks. I know the commercial bags of about the size we'd need weigh in at 155 pounds." He thumbed at Ajax. "The big guy here could carry that on his back and not break a sweat."

"Easy." The young soldier grinned with confidence.

"He's right." Emma paced. "Baskets are wicker or aluminum. We don't expect to be in the air for that long, so we won't need many propane tanks—average of fifteen gallons in a high-pressure tank will buy us eight to ten hours air time. More than enough."

Drake nodded slowly. "Doable."

"But what happens if the wind is blowing in the wrong direction?" Andy asked. "Emma's notes said there was near cyclonic winds and low clouds. We could be blown off course."

"Yeah, balloons are a little like sailing ships," Drake agreed. "It doesn't help if the wind is in your face. *But*, also like sailing ships, you can tack across wind, using flaps and vents in the canopy, and also lower or raise the balloon to chase the best thermals." He bobbed his head, as he seemed to be thinking out loud.

"I do some sailing; up and down the west coast." Andy had his hand up. "Catamarans to dinghies, and even acted as a deckhand on a seventy-foot racing sailboat during the last America's Cup." He grinned and looked around, but no one seemed to care. "*Um*, and yeah, you have to chase the wind. But you follow it by watching the water, seeing where the breeze is going, and you have white caps or ripples to indicate its direction and strength. But tip over in a boat, you just swim or hang on. Tip over in a balloon…" He shrugged.

"Without a doubt, it's going to be a challenge, and the cloud might be an issue," Drake agreed. "We can bring it in to come down real gentle in a balloon, but if you snag the bag and rip it, it'll take time to repair. Not great if we're under time pressure."

"Very true." Emma was delighted someone had read her small report, and also seemed to be in her corner. "The cloud was damned thick, but it lifts as the day progresses. Also, I remember it opens at the center, directly over the plateau. A little like the eye of a cyclone. I remember seeing the sky—I *know* I did—it was calm and clear."

"Good. Every second we can preserve is one more second we can spend looking for Ben." Drake picked up his coffee mug. He toasted Cynthia, who nodded her approval.

"You took days to get there," Fergus said. "I understand you were following the clues, searching for the right pathways and tracks. But now you know the basic ways there, can we not shortcut some of the legs? I don't see why we need to travel by boat." He shrugged. "Why can't we use a seaplane?"

"Works for me." She paced a little closer. "Some of the hidden streams were very narrow and might present a problem if we have a lot of equipment."

Emma remembered the coffee-dark hidden streams, and then finding the sunken idol that led the way to the beautiful *Rivers of Paradise*. She also remembered how that brief hiatus had then led on to the miasmic swamps. It had all taken them days to traverse.

"So I agree it'd be advantageous if we could leapfrog over some of the thicker jungle. But where we finally emerged from the swamps, we had no GPS, satellite, or even compass, as the magnetic effects of Primordia were kicking in. Plus, when you added in the thick, low-cloud cover, we had line-of-sight navigation only."

She moved the images along to the tabletop mountain, but it was a picture taken when not in the wettest season. The plateau rose up monolithic, impressive, and imposing from the jungle floor.

"This is what we'll be looking for. And in the wettest season, its top is hidden by the cloud cover." She left the image up and turned to the group.

"You said there was a small clearing on the bank of the Rio Caroní River, before you turned inland, correct?" Drake asked.

"Yes, it was where I was found...*after*." Emma looked up.

"And you still had electronic capability there?" Drake lifted his chin.

Emma nodded.

Ajax sat forward. "Then we don't need to tell you, but in the dense jungle, you can spend a day going just a couple of miles. Much better to be above it, if only to lower the risk of running into snakes, spiders, poisonous plants, and all manner of creepy crawlies that a big jungle hides in its belly."

"Then that coastal clearing will be our base camp and launch point. Should be enough water for the flying boat to land and get us to the bank. Plus enough clearing for us to prepare our balloon and electronically mark our position." Drake held his hands wide. "Save us a helluva lot of time."

Helen leaned around her brother. "Mr. Masterson, just how fast *can* a balloon travel?"

"Call me Drake." He saluted her with a couple of fingers.

"Helen," she replied.

"Nice to meet you." His eyes gave her a quick appraising look as if he just noticed her, and he smiled as he spoke. "Balloons don't quite travel as fast as the wind, but on a good day can scud along at between five and eight miles per hour. Sure beats hacking or paddling all day for a few miles."

"Are they safe?" she asked.

"Mostly. Accidents happen when they're overloaded, or the fuel mix isn't right, or the heat blaster is set too high." He kept smiling. "Or if you go up when the winds are too strong."

Helen frowned and he waved her down.

"But these days, the package is pretty tight. We play by the rules, and the balloon will probably be the least of our worries."

"I suppose we can wear parachutes," Andy added hopefully.

Drake nodded. "Sure, you can wear one. But as we won't be going up that high, by the time you yell *rip-cord*, you'll be eating jungle." He chuckled.

"But Emma's notes say that the plateau is around 1500 feet high. That's *high*," Andy responded.

"Relatively," Drake replied. "Skydivers jump from over 10,000 feet. A parachute needs a good 100 to 200 feet to fully deploy, and then takes more time and distance before your velocity is slowed enough for you to land without breaking every bone in your body. Like I said, you can wear one if it makes you feel better."

Andy sighed theatrically, and Drake held his hands wide.

"Bottom line, Andy, is that more people die from parachuting accidents than they do ballooning. Like I said, we follow the rules, we'll all walk away smiling."

Andy didn't look comforted. He turned to Emma. "And what about protection?" he asked. "You said you'd be better prepared this time. We have Mr. Masterson and his colleagues; is that it?"

Emma smiled and held out an arm. "Drake, the floor is yours."

The Special Forces soldier got to his feet and stood in front of the group. "Thank you, Emma." He put large hands on his hips, and he seemed to fill the room. "Everything we bring is designed for self-defense purposes, and I hope we never have to use any of it. *But*, if we *are* threatened, then we must respond fast and decisively."

He nodded to Fergus who lifted a black carry-all bag onto the coffee table and unzipped it. He handed Drake one of the objects—it was a metallic gun that looked like it was made from black plastic. It had what looked like another gun strapped underneath it.

"Cool." Andy sat straighter, and Helen groaned.

"What I have here is a—"

"M16," Andy shot out.

Brocke snorted. "Looks like we have an enthusiast."

"Close," Drake said. "I'm holding an M4 carbine tactical assault rifle. A shorter and lighter variant of the M16, and now the primary infantry weapon of the United States Marine Corps combat units." He paused to glance at Andy. "And we will all be getting one."

The soldier held it forward. "The M4 is a 5.56×45mm, air-cooled, direct impingement gas-operated, magazine-fed carbine. It has a 14.5-inch barrel and a telescoping stock." He balanced it in one hand. "It weighs 6.5 pounds empty and 7.49 with a 30-round magazine inserted. The M4 is capable of firing in semi-automatic and three-round burst modes and is also capable of mounting a Heckler & Koch M320 grenade launcher." He indicated the smaller, stubbier-looking gun attached underneath.

"Oh wow." Andy's eyes blazed like a school kid.

"Oh Jesus Christ, this is overkill." Helen bared her teeth. "And I, for one, will not be going to war down there."

"*Begging your pardon.*" Drake's gaze was direct, and though he hadn't raised his voice, the authority in the tone was like a fist slamming down on a desk. "If only one-tenth of what Ms. Wilson's report says is there, happens to *really* be there, then you'll be glad you have something more than a university degree to defend yourself."

Helen's eyes narrowed and she folded her arms and sat back. "Nope. I won't be taking one, end of story. That's your job, if I'm not mistaken."

Drake remained calm. "Yes, we are to be your shield and the sword, ma'am. But survival is everyone's job."

Emma held up her hand. "We'll all need to do training, regardless of whether we decide to take a weapon. Last time, we had a few guns, but many of us had no real idea how to use them. I won't make that mistake again. That's why I've personally undertaken extensive weapon training, taken a first-aid course, and some basic zoology, paleontology, and biology studies. But I'll still go to Mr. Masterson's training sessions, because he's a survival expert, and I have this peculiar desire to survive." She turned. "Go on, Drake, please continue."

"Thank you." He held up the rifle. "The M320 grenade launchers will only be attached to ex-military personal M4 rifles; however, as the unit can be detached and used independently, we will be practicing with these as well." He stared hard at Helen until she looked away, still looking like she smelled something bad.

Drake pointed at the bag and Fergus removed what looked like some weird striped clothing, shoes, plus other smaller items.

Drake held up a shirt that had numerous pockets and flaps. "There'll be knives and other items for survival and defense, but this will be your best buddy night and day. The digital tiger stripe jungle uniform—lightweight, cool, odor free, and damn tough as all hell. There'll also be tactical all-terrain and water boots, with built-in snakebite protection and rapid drying. But no padding, as it absorbs water, so take these home today and start wearing them in."

He held up some goggles. "Last but not least, old, but reliable— the Generation-3 Auto Military Spec U.S. Night Vision Goggles. They're a little dated now, but they work, are easy to use, and they're low-tech, meaning a lot less can go wrong. They'll do for us."

"May I?" Andy held out his hands.

Drake tossed the goggles to him and Andy put them on, flicked a switch, and his mouth broke into a grin underneath the plastic and rubber seals.

"Weapons training begins tomorrow morning, 9am, at the Bristolville, Grand River target range."

"Can you make it?" Emma asked the pair of paleontologists.

Andy nodded and Helen shrugged.

"There'll be other sessions before we depart. There's a lot to learn and not a lot of time—call it cramming for the most important test of your life." Drake smiled grimly.

The rest of the afternoon was spent on a few questions, getting to know each other a little more, and some trip and logistics planning. Drake headed out onto the back porch for a smoke, and Emma joined Cynthia on the couch. She looked a little wearied.

"Do you think you're ready?" Cynthia asked.

"No." Emma turned to her and half-smiled. "But just as ready as we can be."

"It will have to do. Ben is waiting for you, I know it." She reached across to take Emma's hand and squeezed it. "I know you'll find him."

Emma held her small, thin hand, but kept her lips tight. She hoped Ben was there, and if he were, she would do everything in this world to bring him home. But one thing she wouldn't do is make promises she might not be able to keep.

She patted the old woman's hand and then stood. "And now, I've got to order a hot air balloon."

*****

Drake sat on the back step, slowly rubbing the hunting knife against the whetstone. The slow, circular rotation, over and over, made a soft hissing noise as he filed the large blade's edge to razor sharpness.

Special Forces soldiers knew to keep their weapons in top condition, but there was something about the repetitive nature of the task that allowed Drake to think, and sometimes that wasn't a good thing. Memories came back, not all of them welcome.

Drake hadn't thought about big Ben Cartwright in years. The captain was a tough guy, and one of the best that he'd ever served with. If it wasn't for Cartwright, Drake knew he'd be a pile of bleached bones somewhere out in the Syrian Desert right now.

The mission came rushing back—it was a night incursion into no-man's land to get in behind enemy lines and find and destroy an ammunition store. There were eight of them, eight of the best of the best Special Forces, the Gravedigger Unit. Two of them were out at point, Gino Zimmer and Ron Jackson; both good soldiers, but that night not good enough.

On that night, there was no moon, and they had their quad night vision goggles in place, the eerie four lenses and their body armor making the Special Forces operatives look like armor-plated robots.

They walked into a patch of desert that immediately had the hair on Drake's neck rising. But it wasn't until Cartwright raised a clenched fist that the unit halted. The captain reached up to his quad lenses and must have flicked them from night vision to thermal.

In the next few slices of a second, the captain had yelled a single word that turned their world upside down: *"Contact!"* And then all hell broke loose.

They'd walked right into the center of a terrorist's nest—spider holes all around them, and only slits showing their positions. With thermal imaging, Drake could make out the thin slice of red-warmth, telling of the bodies hidden inside under those camouflaged trapdoors.

They'd engaged—loud, bloody, and brutal. And they didn't stop until the air was filled with a red mist, smelling of cordite and the tang of coppery blood.

They'd wiped out every single terrorist that night but lost four good men. Zimmer and Jackson were the first to buy it—the price of letting your guard down.

Yeah, without Cartwright's sixth sense, he'd be dead. All eight of them would be dead.

Drake continued to circle the blade on the stone. He owed the big guy, and it was time to pay his dues.

*****

In a car concealed under the shade of trees and as close to the Cartwright house as she could get, Camilla Ortega held up the sound gun, with the earphones over her head. She had her eyes closed and she concentrated on the voices. In her other hand was a pen, and she made notes as she picked the valuable details from the group's plans. Beside her, a dark-eyed man sat leaning back in his seat, looking bored.

"The meeting is breaking up," Camilla said.

"Good; they been in there all morning, and I'm hungry." Juan Marquina exhaled loudly and shifted, making the seat complain under his weight. He let the telescopic lens camera rest in his lap so he could wipe sweaty hands on his shirt.

Camilla glared at him. "This might be the biggest story in our newspaper's history. In fact, I'm betting it'll make headlines in both

North and South America. So I think you can hold off on your donuts for a little while longer, yes?"

He picked up the camera again. "Yeah, because the picture guy always gets the awards." He snorted derisively.

"Get ready. I want photographs of the mercenaries. I can use them." She licked her lips as she lowered the sound gun and dragged the earphones off her head.

"I don't get how we're ever going to track these guys in the Amazon. They got mercenaries, guns, money, and all you got is a skinny expense account, and a lovable, but ever so slightly overweight, camera guy." He grinned.

"Slightly?" She chuckled. "And you got me. But we won't be tracking them." She turned in her seat. "Because we'll be invited along." She pushed open the door.

*****

The doorbell rang, and Emma swung to Cynthia and frowned. The old woman shook her head. Everyone else simply looked back at her. Emma pointed to the weapons, and Drake and Fergus quickly gathered everything up and started to store them away.

She went to the door and pulled it open to see a 30-something, black-haired woman with eyes just as dark staring back at her with the hint of a smile on her lips. She stuck out a small brown hand.

"Ms. Emma Wilson; I'm delighted to meet you in person at last."

Emma reached forward automatically, still confused, and the woman grabbed her hand and pumped it.

"And you are?" Emma forced the hand to stop pumping.

"Camilla Ortega, journalist for *Nacional De Venezuela*."

Emma released her hand, and her gaze became flat. Immediately, she sensed danger.

"Yes?"

"Call me Camilla, please." The woman's smile remained fixed in place.

Emma folded her arms, waiting.

"Nice place you have here." Camilla looked over Emma's shoulder into the house for a few moments, and then her gaze returned, and she seemed to force a smile. "You know, Ms. Wilson, I feel I've known you forever. I was just doing mundane local stories at the newspaper when they brought you, just you, out of the jungle all those years ago." Her eyes were intense as she scrutinized Emma. "But you fired up my journalistic passion. And now, after all this time, you are finally going back." Her eyebrows just lifted a hint.

Emma shook her head slowly. "Nope."

She became coy. "I think, we may finally solve the mystery of the missing Cartwright expedition, yes?"

Emma felt alarms going off in her head. *How the hell did this woman know this?* she wondered. Her jaw set, and she leaned forward.

"Listen, Ms. Ortega, I don't know what you want or expect. But you have your facts wrong. I have nothing to offer you, and don't intend to be talking to the media, local or otherwise."

Camilla's red lips remained lifted at the corners. "But you've given me so much already, Ms. Wilson."

Emma's frown deepened.

Camilla went on. "I know you've hired mercenaries, have a few scientists working with you." She tapped her chin for a moment. "And now I believe you will be preparing for a little trip down to our magnificent jungle once again."

"Piss off." Emma went to shut the door, but Camilla's arm shot out.

"Wait." The woman's eyes were gun steady. "I can be your best friend or your worst enemy, Ms. Wilson. One call from me, and you'll never get a visa to our country, ever again."

Emma felt her heart sink, and she shut her eyes for a moment. She had spent years trying to plan for everything, every conceivable risk, but had overlooked the most basic one—people. She steeled herself and glared back at the woman, but now Camilla looked more empathetic than triumphant.

"Hear me out. Please." Camilla's hand went to Emma's arm. "I can help you. But this mystery has been part of my life almost as long as it has yours. I only wish to help you solve it. Because it will give you closure, I think." She shrugged. "And I can help you in Venezuela; I *know* people."

Emma felt torn—their plane was to fly to Caracas, but then she and her team would immediately board a private charter seaplane to transport them and their cargo to a destination she would reveal to the pilot only when she was onboard. It was costing her a fortune in under-the-table fees.

The last thing she wanted was to be hauled in by Venezuelan immigration officials and questioned. A horrifying thought of being detained, even for a few days, might mean she'd miss her slim window of opportunity—Primordia would come and go—for another goddamn ten years.

Emma felt the knot in her gut tighten. She couldn't even afford to gamble on having her shipment confiscated or scrutinized. Her mind whirled as she tried to think.

"I can help; I promise." Camilla's hand was still on her arm, and it moved to her hand where she then squeezed her fingers. "I *promise*."

Emma looked at the journalist—small, but robust-looking, well-dressed, but not dainty, and with an ornate silver crucifix around her neck. Did she really care if this woman wanted to risk her own life, or worse, lose it?

"You don't know what you're asking."

"No, I know *exactly* what I'm asking," Camilla responded confidently. "You're going into the Amazon jungle. I've been into its interior several times on news stories. I'm fit, and I can climb, hike, swim, and shoot with the best of them. So can my cameraman."

"Cameraman?" Emma scoffed. "Deal breaker."

"No, he won't film anyone that doesn't want to be filmed. In fact, each day and at the end of the expedition, we can review the footage and edit out anything you don't like." She stepped back and crossed her heart, briefly touching the silver crucifix at her throat.

Emma noticed. "Do you believe in the devil, Ms. Ortega?" she said evenly.

Camilla frowned, but her lips curled up slightly. "I believe in good and evil."

"*Hmm*, I never used to believe in him. But I do now." Emma continued to look deep into the woman's eyes, trying to decide.

"You won't frighten me off." Camilla tilted her head. "So…"

Emma knew she didn't have the time to wrestle with this now. Besides, there was something she needed the woman to do. And something that only a local with knowledge of the Amazon and its workings could do. If she wanted to come so badly, she needed to earn her way in.

Emma decided. "I need you to do something for me. Consider it a test. Or an entry fee."

"Sure, what is it?" Camilla smiled benignly.

"To find and contact someone in the Amazon, the jungle, that I haven't been able to. Can you do that?" Emma lifted her chin.

"Sure can; try me." Camilla looked serious.

"I'll give you the details—it's important. Do it, and you're in."

Camilla nodded. "Consider it done."

"Good; we leave for Caracas in ten days. Be ready."

Camilla continued to look serious. "We will be, and thank you."

They swapped phone numbers, and Camilla then turned and made a call. In a few moments, a car pulled up with a larger man sitting in the driving seat that had obviously been parked close by.

Emma sighed and closed the door. Now she had to break it to the team that they'd suddenly picked up a couple of extra members…who were press. She groaned.

"They're gonna kill me."

*****

Camilla jumped into the car and slammed the door. She turned and grinned. "We're in."

Juan's mouth dropped open. "You're good; you're *real* good. So what's the plan?"

"We leave in ten days, so we need to prepare. We join their team. We'll be with them the entire way. Filming the entire way."

'They'll let us film…*everything*?" Juan's eyebrows shot up.

"I told them that they could review the footage. But I never said we'd delete anything. Just make sure you back everything up to the secondary camera drive." She turned back to the front of the car. "We'll be there, right there, when we all find out what happened to Mr. Ben Cartwright and his friends. And if Ms. Wilson had anything to do with their disappearance, then she may find her stay in Venezuela is a lot longer than she expected."

CHAPTER 13

Ben woke to sunshine on his face, and he blinked a few times before even remembering where he was. The warmth of the rays had also warmed the guano in the cave, and a miasmic steam began to rise off the fishy-smelling paste.

He sat up as the small reptilian birds flew past him, in and out, gathering the morning's fish from the ocean surface. Ben turned about and immediately spotted a few nests close by with grey, leathery-looking eggs nestled within.

He scrambled over and lifted three, tearing the oblong cases open and drinking their protein-rich contents. He wrinkled his nose at the bitter sardine taste of the first two, and then the third from a different nest turned out to be a bit further along, containing soft bones and a hint of salty blood. It didn't matter what they tasted like; he needed the protein for his energy. Nothing was wasted anymore.

Ben wiped his mouth, and several times across his beard, and sat staring at the view while ignoring the stench of the small pterodons. It was entrancing and he moved closer to the cave mouth and then inhaled the odor of the sea—the fresh saltiness, drying weed, and warming sand. He hadn't realized how much he missed it.

It all felt familiar, and he could have been back at home, looking out over the expanse of never-ending blue water from a pier down at a California bay. That is, except for the sight of long necks lifting, swan-like, from the water, and diving back down to be gracefully raised once again with flapping fish in their toothy mouths.

He watched them for a while longer, mesmerized by their grace and beauty. *Like a pod of whales*, he thought, as the group of plesiosaurs moved together, some huge, their slender, shining necks rising 20 feet from the end of large cetacean-like bodies, and others small, no more than six feet in length, obviously their calves.

Ben closed his eyes and sat for a while, letting the sun warm his upturned face. He relaxed, something he was rarely able to do in this time of tooth and claw, and let his mind drift to not if, but when, he would be back home.

What would he be doing now? he wondered. Would he be fixing up a motorbike in his garage? Would he be drinking with his buddies at one of the local bars? He inhaled, smelling stale beer, ancient cigarettes, and the press of bodies.

Or would he be out somewhere with Emma, sitting under a tree, talking, or perhaps just holding hands and staring into each other's eyes. He groaned, feeling a wave of homesickness wash over him.

While there is life, there is hope, he reminded himself. His eyes flicked open to the sound of squawks and clicks from down along the beach. Two theropods, both only about four feet tall, walked like a pair of ostriches along the sand at the high tide line. Now and then, their necks would drop to pick something from amongst the weed to be gulped down. Probably dead fish, he guessed.

Even though they were both fairly small, he knew from experience that those triangular heads contained teeth sharper than those of a wolf. And they cut like shears. Best to avoid ones even that size.

In another few minutes, they were well out of sight. The tide was drawing out, and Ben looked down into the large, natural pool below him. It was roughly circular, hundreds of feet across, and a perfect lagoon. And by the look of it, the breakwater rocks had trapped a good deal of sea creatures in its depths.

The water was extremely clear, especially in the shallows that ran for several hundred feet, but then there seemed to be a ledge where it gradually dropped deeper and then toward the far edges closest to the ocean, it must have been over a dozen feet deep, and a type of kelp weed stopped him from seeing the bottom. Still, even in those shallows, he saw fish darting back and forth.

He grinned; they had no idea what a human was like, or whether they were even dangerous. He bet he could spear one with ease.

His mouth watered; he hadn't eaten fish in years. Even raw fish with the ocean's natural saltiness would make a change from berries, tubers, and even a dinosaur's tough and gamey meat.

Ben turned to look over his shoulder, which immediately elicited some loud and serious warnings from the small pterodons sitting on their nests.

"Hey, guys, looks like I might not be able to join you for dinner tonight."

He chuckled, lifted his spear, and looked down over the edge of the cliff. "We can do this," he said. He noticed he spoke to himself quite a bit now. Hearing his own voice was better than not hearing any voice at all. It somehow made him remember he was a human being.

There was a ledge that would take him all the way to the horseshoe-shaped beach. He was kinda looking forward to it; even as a kid, he loved peering into rock pools and turning over stones to see what weird sea thingies lived underneath—crabs, octopus, starfish, urchins, and tiny fish with huge mouths like a mudskipper.

He pulled off the tattered remains of his boots, now held together with vines and animal hide, and began to thread his way down the cliff ledge. It only took a few minutes and in no time, he was able to leap the last few feet, feeling the sand scrunch beneath his feet as he landed. Ben made fists with his toes, smiling as he remembered the sensation from his childhood.

He turned to the water, feeling good. In fact, better than he had in years. *A change of scenery is as good as a holiday*, he remembered his dad used to say. He continued to stare, thinking of the paradox he was trapped within—his father or mother wouldn't be born for another 100 million years. Somewhere in some corner of this prehistoric world, there was a special sort of creature that would evolve into one of his progenitors.

"Better not step on it," he said with a grin.

Ben paused at the notion—and what if I do? Will I simply cease to exist? Vanish? Will it change the entire course of human evolution and then some other species will rise to be the new rulers of the planet? It made his head hurt just thinking about the paradox.

Ben glanced quickly up and down the coast, not seeing any threats for miles heading north along the sand, and looking down south, it ended in cliffs that rose hundreds of feet. He felt pretty safe with empty beaches, cliffs at his back, and a pod of plesiosaurs more interested in fish than a weird upright, hairy creature on the shore.

He began to walk along the tide line, looking at the strange in amongst the familiar. There were bivalve and coiled shells, crab bodies, and jellyfish. But also, the front end of a creature that might have been a dolphin but had a plated boney head, large disk-like eyes, and backward-curving teeth like those of a barracuda. There were ribbed shark egg casings, starfish as big as hubcaps, and after a while, something else he noticed. It wasn't something that was *there*, but something that *wasn't*—there wasn't a speck of plastic—no modern flotsam and jetsam.

He scoffed softly; *the ocean was better off before we arrived*, he thought. He waded into the shallows of the lagoon and saw sprats darting about over a rippling sandy bottom. He lifted his gaze to the deeper water near the rock barrier and raised a hand to shield his eyes from the still-rising sun.

The lagoon was bigger than he expected now that he was down at water level, running for hundreds of yards to the left, right, and out to the breakwater. Where the water began to deepen, he could just make out colorful weed growing like underwater trees and spiny starfish with long spiky arms hung in amongst them. Shrimp, crabs, and colored fish also moved about, and as he hoped, none paid him the slightest bit of attention—in fact, many of the fish came closer to him to investigate.

"I bet if I fed you, you'd be eating out of my hand in a week."

Ben looked along the breakwater and mentally mapped out a route along the jagged rocks that separated the lagoon from the sea. It could be navigated, and he planned to try and circle the entire lagoon one day. But for now, even the lagoon depths were an unknown place, and out beyond it, the deep, dark ocean was far too forbidding to even contemplate.

Save that for later, he thought.

The sun had risen a little more and lit the shallows. Golden sand, beneath only about two feet of water—he waded in. It was warm, and he smiled, enjoying it. Fish darted by him. They were only about eight inches long and like silver streaks of mercury.

A little further out, something bobbed mid-water, and he moved toward it. He reached in and lifted it. It was a coiled seashell—striped in brown and ivory, and also occupied. Tentacles emerged and one large eye regarded him with disdain.

"Nautilus, nautiloid, or something like that, right?" He held it up, turning it one way then the other. His stomach rumbled, and he'd eaten worse things, but he had other fare on his mind. He let it plonk back into the water, where it hovered for a moment, and then motored away backward.

He shuffled further out, coming to where the natural edge of sand fell away into deepening water. It was still extremely clear, but it was about three feet there, and then must have dropped to three or four times that further out.

Ben got down on his knees first, and then ducked under the surface and opened his eyes. The water felt glorious on the skin of his face and was so clear he almost didn't need goggles. Holding his breath, he was always amazed at the sounds of the ocean. He could just make out the clicks, pops, and grainy movements of sand as the sea life went about its business.

He surfaced, flicked his long hair back, and rubbed his face. His heart told him to swim further out. But his brain urged caution and listening to his logical self was what kept him alive so far. He decided that until he knew the waters a little better, he'd take his investigations slowly.

Ben got to his feet and continued his exploration along the edge of the sandbank.

He spun; spear up.

His sixth sense told him he was being watched. He let his eyes move over the water, and peering below the surface, he could see for hundreds of feet below as well. But there wasn't any dark shape lurking there. There were only lumps of rock or patches of weed gently billowing on the bottom.

After many minutes, he managed to tear his eyes away and walked back into the shallows where he spotted a large conch shell on the bottom. He reached in and lifted it.

"Nice; I would have loved you on my desk back home." He turned it in his hand for a moment more and then stuck it in his pack.

Ben had almost finished his search by moving back and forth in the shallows. And then, *movement*, plate-sized, and along the bottom. He raced after it and jabbed down with his spear, receiving a satisfying *crunch*.

"*Yes*." Ben lifted his spear. The large crab came up and he strained to hold it. It was a big one with blue tips on its legs and large claws. It must have weighed in at about five pounds. "You'll do."

He walked up the sand and jabbed the spear hilt into the sand. Then he removed the large conch and placed it atop a large rock, like a cap.

"The first of my collection." He looked at it, and then turned to the splayed crab. "Man's gotta have a hobby, right?"

Ben feasted that night. But raw crab was a little harder to remove from the shell than cooked crab so a lot was left behind. Still, the claws each held a fistful of meat.

Ben kept the shells with shreds of meat to use as bait for the next day's hunt. He slept soundly, safely, and his mind relaxed and took him back to a little rib joint in Ohio.

He smiled in his sleep as a dark-haired girl with luminous green eyes and a spray of freckles across her cheeks and nose put a hand over his.

I love you, she mouthed.

I love you too, he said and lifted her hand to kiss the knuckles.

Her expression became sad. *I came, but you weren't there.*

What? Ben asked, frowning.

You weren't there, Ben.

No, no, I was, he beseeched.

You weren't there, you weren't there, you weren't there—her voice became shrill, loud, and squabbling.

Ben opened his eyes and blinked. The pterodons were fighting over the remains of meat in his crab shells.

"Hey! Piss off." He shooed them away, and then rubbed his face. He picked up a shard of shell and tossed it at a few that were still bickering. "And thanks for fucking up my dream." He scowled. "It's gonna cost you a few eggs for breakfast."

He turned back to the sunrise over the perfect ocean. He sighed as the sight immediately calmed him. He'd stay here for as long as he could. It was safer than the jungle and a hundred times safer than the plateau. Ben headed down to the water to start his new day.

First job was placing the broken crab shells in the lagoon water, and then that day, he decided to walk down along the beach, scouring the tide line, but remaining wary. The open beach had no cliffs at its back, so any hungry or fleet-footed theropods might have run him down if he wasn't careful.

He found some driftwood he could use, and also another shell for his collection. In the late afternoon, he also speared another crab in his lagoon, albeit a smaller one that had come to sample the contents of its kin's broken shells. It was another good day.

But the next day, he had no luck at all for food. The only thing he found was another large shell in the water. It was huge conch, spiny and a foot long.

Standing knee-deep in the water, he admired its beauty. But it was odd as the shell hadn't been there before, and as it was empty, it certainly hadn't crawled there. Also, the night had been calm and no waves entered his lagoon to wash it there. Must have been the tide...*somehow*, he thought.

"Another beauty." He added it to his collection.

The next day was the same, no crabs, and only a few fish in his shallows, but once again, another magnificent specimen of a shell, although this one even further out and closer to the edge of the sandbank.

Ben reached in to lift it. Again, it was a fantastic shell, but instead of looking at it, his eyes never left the water. The drop-off still was fairly shallow here, and crystal clear, so he didn't see anything other than the clumps of weed and patches of corals and sponges. But today, his sixth sense alarms were going off.

He squinted. At the bottom of the sandbank slope, there were two more shells; big, unique ones. He wanted them, and he stared for a moment. There was nothing close by, and the water was clear and warm.

But he just couldn't bring himself to wade in or dive into the deeper water.

"*Nah*, not today." He turned and shuffled back to the shoreline.

The next day, Ben woke extremely hungry. He'd dined again on pterodon eggs, but his large frame craved protein. The sky was just turning an azure blue and was cloudless to the horizon. The air was still and the morning sea mist was rapidly burning off. He could see from his cave perch the large torpedo shapes of fish out at the breakwater in his lagoon. He wanted them. His hunger *demanded* them.

Today's the day, he thought.

Ben climbed down, looked once again up and down the sand, and then hefted his spear and crossed to the rocks and then headed out along the breakwater. It took him 15 minutes to make it toward one of the deeper ends of his ocean pool. The rocks formed a barrier but were more like broken teeth in that they let the tide run through between them, and on high tides obviously also let in good-sized fish, without anything larger gaining access.

On the inner side was the lagoon, and on the other, the vast ocean. He leaned forward on one of the rocks to stare out at the magnificent sea. Where he was, it looked deep. So deep, he couldn't see the bottom, and it was dark indigo that might have been 20 feet deep or 100.

Ben leaned further forward and looked northward. He could see another jutting promontory several miles up the coast. He wondered what it would be like if he went there, keeping along the coastline until he came to America. Would it feel like home? He doubted it.

He pulled in a deep drought of warm sea air, flooding his lungs, and scanned the horizon. Oddly, there were no plesiosaurs anymore—

gone home or chasing schools of fish somewhere else. Or for all he knew, they were there, just diving deep.

Ben continued to watch for a few more moments; it made him feel uneasy. One thing he knew was that the ocean was just as dangerous as any jungle and staring into the deep-dark blue might mean that something was staring right back at him and he'd never even know.

Ben turned back to the calm of his lagoon. On this side, the water was like a massive swimming pool. But even though the water looked inviting and the sun already warm on his shoulders, he couldn't quite bring himself to dive in—*yet*.

He liked the idea of having his own personal swimming pool and aquarium. But he needed to be cautious—it was what kept him alive so far, and looking down, the water was deeper here and the weed could hide a multitude of things he had no idea even existed. He read somewhere once that it was a one in a million chance that an animal became fossilized. That meant there could be thousands of creatures that evolution tried out that we didn't even know about.

As Ben stared into the lagoon's depths, silver fish longer than his arm skimmed back and forth along the surface. There were oysters on the water's edge, and he used the butt of his spear to break a few free and extract their meat. He was tempted to eat the pulpy, grey meat then and there, but today, he had other plans. He mashed them in his hand and tossed the remains onto the surface before him. He hoisted his spear and eased down a little closer to the water.

In seconds, silver torpedoes rocketed through the cloud of debris, picking off the larger portions, and then literally swarming to then look like knots of boiling mercury.

Ben only had to jab into the center of the cauldron of feeding fish to feel his spear strike flesh. He then hoisted a good eight-pounder from the water.

"*Yeah*, that's what I'm talking about."

He brought it to him, and then lowered it to the rocks beside him where he carefully pushed it off the blade of his spear and used the sharp edge to sever its neck to kill it.

By the size, Ben thought two fish would make a nice meal, and probably breakfast. He rinsed the blood from his hands and left his first catch on the rock close by, bleeding out, and turned back to the water. The oyster debris had gone, save for a milky cloud that a few fish glided through sensing the food, but not finding any.

Ben eased a little bit closer to the water but saw that the fish were thinning out rapidly as they lost interest now that the food was gone. He kept his spear ready, but in a flash, the fish vanished. He could smash another few oysters open or maybe use the head of the fish he'd just caught as bait. He turned to look at it.

"*What the fuck?*"

It was gone.

The rock was still smeared with blood, and he was certainly high enough not to have had any waves wash it off, but there was no sign. He had left it on a flat rock, just between two boulders that created the barrier between the lagoon and the ocean. Blood had leaked down the side of the rock that washed between the two bodies of water.

He looked up, checking for any pterodons, but though there were a few, even the small ones' wings flapping sounded like you were shaking out a wet towel, so no way they could creep up on him.

Ben stared hard back into the water of the lagoon. The fish was as dead as they come, and there was no silver body floating on the surface. He stepped lower, peering deeper into the water—it was impossible to see the bottom because of the weed, but he was sure there was no silver shape down there.

Ben was furious and for a few seconds, contemplated diving down to feel around at the base of the weed—somehow, the fish must have slipped off the rock and glided down in amongst that forest of weed. All his work was wasted—*crap*, he fumed, as he had been proud of his success.

"Fuck it," he muttered. The sun was getting hotter, but for some reason, he felt a chill run up his spine and he looked one way then the other. He didn't see any threats, but he was spooked now, and his Special Forces intuition was setting off a warning.

"Okay, maybe just *one* fish today, and then I head home," he whispered, squinting out over the lagoon. He began to step down closer to the water, planning on cracking open another few oysters when what felt like a wet glove latched onto his ankle...and then stuck there.

"Wha...?"

He spun and looked down.

"*Shit!*"

A jolt of fear rocketed through him—there was a tentacle, thick as his wrist, coming up out of the water beside the rock, and in the few seconds, he was frozen watching it as it inched a little more up his calf to grip on.

Ben leaped to the side, but the thing held on tight, and looking down into the water, he finally realized where his fish had gone, and horrifyingly, what was lurking there.

Its camouflage was so effective that even so close, Ben had to concentrate to make it out. The massive creature was spread out like an enormous rug beneath the water, and the bulbous bag of a head had two plate-sized eyes staring dispassionately up at him. It was easily 30 feet across and as he watched, it changed color, flaring red and becoming brilliantly visible from its camouflage in amongst the weed beds.

As part of his Special Forces training, Ben had dived in deep water where the giant Pacific octopus dwelled and knew they could get to 150 pounds with an arm span of 12 feet. They were smart, curious, and strong as hell. But this thing was three times that size and might have been one of its ancestors.

Maybe it was just curious, and maybe it was hungry. But Ben had no intention of letting the thing drag him into the water, as he knew underneath the massive cephalopod's body would be a horned beak, probably a foot across on this monster, that would sever limbs and crack his skull open like an egg.

Ben also realized that this must have been the thing that had been gifting him the shells. It scared the shit out of him knowing that it had been watching him probably since he arrived. And it was baiting him, trying to lure him to deeper and deeper water. And when that failed, it had decided to come get him itself.

"*Fuck you.*"

Ben brought his spear around and jabbed at it, and then began to hack with all his might as the head began to breach the surface. It ignored him and started to bring more arms to bear on its task.

"Shit, shit, shit."

Ben continued to stab, but it was like trying to put holes in a soft and super tough rubber blanket, as the limbs or boneless bag refused to be penetrated. There were tentacles around both his legs now, and his feet began to skid on the rocks…toward the water.

"No. Fucking. Way." Ben lunged with the spear, this time catching the edge of one eye, and blue blood spurted from its side. The tentacles curled back up for a few moments, a little like a boxer protecting its head in the ring.

Ben backed away. *Would it stay in the lagoon?* he wondered, or rather, he hoped. He remembered seeing a nature program once that showed an octopus leaving a rock pool to chase down a crab. It was fast and ruthless, and once it had caught its prey, it hauled it back into the water to dine at its leisure. Ben didn't want to find out if the bigger variety could do the same.

Ben used the moment to clamber higher on the rock and scale down onto the ocean side. He peered back between the boulders, spear held ready, and saw the bulbous thing start to heave itself from the water. The large disc-like eyes caught sight of him, and the body flared a fire engine red—*if ever there was the color of anger, this was it,* he thought.

Perhaps the lagoon belonged to it, and the monstrous octopus was about to show the soft two-legged creature that it was boss around here. He bet he knew who'd win that fight.

Ben looked up and down the breakwater. The rocks on the ocean side looked slippery and also covered in oysters closer to the deep, dark water—he didn't like his chances of moving quickly. At worst, he'd slip and hurt himself, but at least he'd end up in the ocean. Though he desperately wanted to avoid those bottomless-looking depths, if need be, he'd damn well swim for it.

He considered his options; he could go south and try and swim around the octopus, and all the way back to the beach. Or swim to his north, where the breakwater met the cliff face? Though he doubted he'd be able to scale the sheer edifice, he might have been able to at least get up and out of the water, and perhaps higher than the heavy creature could climb.

He grimaced with indecision. How long would he have? How long would it take him to climb with that big bastard in the water, throwing sticky tentacles at him while he slipped and slid on the rock face?

Ben glanced between the rocks again and saw the huge muscular body launching more tentacles from below to latch onto the rocks and haul itself out. Its body now undulated in stripes of red, green, and brown, and he knew it wasn't going to give up and just go away. His time was up—the beach or the cliff? He chose—the beach it was—and he ran for it.

Skipping across jagged rocks in bare feet meant he'd be crippled for days, but he had no choice. Back between the huge stones, he saw the octopus now fully out of the water and pulling itself up to the top of the border rocks. Thick tentacles were thrown like climbing ropes over the jagged stones and the bag-like head began to appear.

Ben knew he'd never get past now, and worse, the thing had the high ground. He had one chance left. He gripped his spear and dove into the ocean.

He swam hard and fast, knowing he had seconds to get around the huge beast before it was fully over. If it decided to launch itself into the water, it'd have him in seconds. Ben knew his one chance was to get around it, clamber back onto the rocks and then, damn his feet, just freaking run like a mountain goat over the rocks and back to the beach.

Ben swam, almost right beside the huge cephalopod and past it, and then flicked over onto his back for a quick glance back. It was moving fast, but maybe it had decided to stay out of the ocean. The huge body was all writhing tentacles like a coiling bag of snakes and flaring redness as it perched high on the rocks.

He was almost past it, and a glimmer of hope started to flicker in his chest. But the huge eyes continued to stare at his flailing arms and must have found them irresistible, as a warm rippling effect ran over its skin color—satisfaction, delight, or hunger? Ben might never live to find out.

To Ben's horror, it started to descend, and he was going to be trapped in its element. He wasn't far enough along, and he glanced at the rocks and knew it'd be hard to pull himself out of the water quickly here. So, instead, he wedged himself in amongst the boulders, feeling oysters and barnacles slice into his back. He ignored them, gritted his teeth, and pointed his spear outwards.

"*Come on!*" he yelled in defiance.

The massive octopus began to clamber down and at the water line, stopped, and spread itself out like a parachute on the rocks. Colors flashed and rippled on its body, and the lead tentacles touched the ocean water, coiling back as though being scalded.

To Ben, it looked like it couldn't decide what to do. Then, instead of coming in, it lifted itself and began to slide across the rocks at the water line. Horrifyingly, the boneless creature flowed like some sort of glutinous liquid—straight toward him.

Jesus Christ, it's going to drop down right on top of me. Ben eased out of his shelter and was about to start swimming again when the ocean exploded around him.

Something like a submarine launched itself from the depths beside him. Ben's eyes were so wide with panic, they nearly bulged out of his head, and his sudden, sharp intake of breath was mostly seawater.

He spluttered and thrashed as the biggest thing he'd ever seen in his life surged up on the rocks to grab at the bulbous head of the octopus. It was shining gray-black with a triangular head as big as a truck that split open to be nearly all mouth and full of tusk-like teeth.

Ben thought it might have been some sort of colossal whale ancestor but discarded that thought as he remembered mammals didn't even exist yet. Then he saw flippers and a long reptilian flattened tail thrashing behind it as it brought itself up higher onto the rocks so its jaws could snap the more than thousand pounds of octopus from the breakwater.

With a muscular flip, the colossal body was gone with a massive surge wave that threw him against the rocks. He clung there, feeling stars pop in his head from shock.

Now he knew why the octopus wouldn't go in the water, and also why the plesiosaurs had vanished. This thing must have been patrolling the shoreline. He looked back up to where the octopus had been, and he coughed water. Nothing remained. He turned back to the ocean.

Thanks, he whispered, and scrambled up onto the rocks, and then quickly over the breakwater to the lagoon side in case the great beast came back feeling like some human dessert.

He sunk down to sit, resting his back against the stone. He sucked in deep breaths, willing his heart rate to slow.

"How was your day at the office, dear?"

He started to laugh, but then a wave of nausea wracked him, and he began to shiver. Shock, he knew, and he screwed his eyes shut.

"Hold it together, buddy." The sound of his own voice reassured him. "We're still here," he said softly. "Just you and me."

He slowly opened his eyes and stared at the calm lagoon. It seemed like an oasis compared to the ocean now. And even better, the previous owner had just been violently evicted, so it was finally all his.

Ben contemplated spearing a fish now that the pool belonged to him, and he hefted his spear, but his hand shook so violently, he knew he'd never hit a thing.

He blew out a long breath and looked up toward his cave on the cliffs. The small flying pterosaurs darted in and out as if nothing had happened. His mouth pulled into a lopsided grin.

"Sorry, guys, looks like eggs are back on the menu after all."

*****

Ben watched from his cave mouth perch for many days, still shaken by the octopus attack. He saw the huge sea creature cruising up and down along the coast, its dark shape just visible when the sun was low, as the massive paddle-finned leviathan stayed just below the surface.

After a few days, it had vanished, and then in the next, the plesiosaurs were back.

"That's a good sign," he said, eyes still on the water.

Ben sucked in a deep breath and once again headed back down to his lagoon. He'd spent his time fashioning a long length of twine from a strong fibrous and elastic vine. At one end, he had carved a hook from a large seashell, and finding half a fish carcass on the tide line, had used it to bait his hook.

Ben swung it back and forth a few times, before tossing it out as far as the line let him. His goal wasn't to catch fish, but to draw out any more lurking octopus. He trawled his bait for days but attracted nothing but fish bites.

It was as he hoped—from his diving days, he knew the big cephalopods were territorial and rarely tolerated their own kind; even mating was over in a matter of moments and then the males had to make a break for it to avoid being eaten by their paramour.

Ben lifted his chin and took in the sea air, swelling his chest and then letting it out slowly. He sucked in another one and this time, let it explode out as words.

"*This lagoon is mine*," he shouted, and the cliff walls echoed it back at him in a chorus of agreement.

He felt the sun already hot on his chest and face, and he waded into the clear cool water, took one last look around, and dived.

He opened his eyes below the surface and was once again surprised how well he could see in the glass-clear water. Large fish came to check him out, and he picked at shells on the bottom, examining them, before surfacing and flicking back long hair. He wiped his face, blinking a few times, and couldn't help the smile breaking out on his face. It was, *invigorating*.

He moved quickly back to the shallows and turned, feeling his neck tingle, and then he spun—nothing followed him. No large shadows crept forward to try and ambush him. No massive leviathans that were all teeth, or bulbous bags that flared red with plate-sized eyes and eight crushing arms, watched from the depths.

But schools of fish did. He waded up onto the sand and retrieved his spear, and the next time a silver torpedo closed in on the shallow water, he stabbed down, skewering it.

Ben wasted no time gutting and cleaning the fish, and then tossing the bloody remains into the shallows, where they were immediately gorged upon by the fish's kin. He wanted them to get used to seeing him close by, and also used to thinking when they did see him, it meant feeding time rather than death.

Days passed. Ben felt his strength and good spirits returning with each moment of this idyllic life. Sunrises were clear, clean, and magnificent, and his personal lagoon was usually always replenished after the high tide let water gush through the breakwater that acted like teeth, allowing in the fish, but keeping out the larger predators.

After one particularly high full-moon king-tide, Ben awoke to see the recognizable fin of a shark cruising in his lagoon. The age-old creatures had been around for 400 million years, so he kind of expected he'd see one sooner or later.

From his lookout cave, he could see down into the lagoon, and judged the predator to be only about eight or nine feet in length. But it was squatter and more barrel-shaped than the streamlined modern sharks he knew and would have probably weighed in at about 500 pounds.

Though it was a big fish, Ben didn't think it would be much of a problem. "I can share." He nodded to the creature. "You stay in your side of the lagoon, and me in mine, and we'll a-*aaall* be friends, okay?"

The sudden surge in the lagoon and a few seconds of thrashing that ended in bloody spray meant the shark had already begun its hunting.

Ben waggled his finger at it. "But listen up, buddy. You eat all my fish, and you're toast, got it?" He grinned, quite liking the company.

Over the coming days and weeks, Ben would spend his evenings down on the lagoon's water line, talking to his shark. When he had caught his own fish, and cleaned them, he'd always throw the remains to 'Ralph,' named after a beloved dog from his youth.

It didn't take long for Ben to start speaking to the shark. First, just saying *hello*, in the mornings, but soon, he was having long conversations with the shark about his fears and his hopes, and basically anything that came to mind.

Oddly, it felt good to talk to someone, even if it wasn't another person. Ben fiddled with a shell as he watched the shark.

"I bet you're surprised to see me," Ben said, watching Ralph glide close to the sand. "I know, I know, I shouldn't even be here. In fact, you shouldn't be seeing me, my kind that is, for another 100 million years, give or take a million."

He dug his toes into the sand. "How did I get here? Long story, Ralph." He chuckled. "Oh, you've got nothing *but* time, you say."

So Ben told Ralph about finding the letters between Sir Arthur Conan Doyle and his great, great grandfather, the original Benjamin Cartwright. He told him of his friends who came with him; all funny, happy, enthusiastic, idealistic, and fatally naïve.

"I killed them," he said, staring trance-like at the fin as it slowly cut the water in front of him, always moving, but staying close to the shoreline. Ben was sure he could see it roll slightly every now and then, so it could keep one black bead-like eye on him.

"No, not really, but, if I had used an ounce of sense, I may have made sure we were all better prepared...or better still, didn't come at all."

He gave Ralph a crooked smile, and then sighed. "Anyway, this gateway sort of thing opened on the plateau, between your world, I mean, time, and mine. Happens once every ten years." He looked up. "My girlfriend, Emma Wilson, got away." He grinned broadly. "But she's coming back for me. And when that damned gateway, or portal or freaking door, or whatever the hell it is, opens up again, I'll be there, front and center."

The shark came up real close, its snout seeming to lift from the water. Ben shook his head. "No, Ralph, I'm sorry, but I can't take you with me." He laughed and tossed the shell out into the center of the lagoon. The shark spun away to investigate the splash.

Days came and went like that, and to begin with, Ben regarded their relationship as something akin to that of coaxing a wild wolf into your camp—there was wariness, but also a mutual respect. When Ralph was hunting, Ben stayed out of the water. And in turn, when Ben was in the shallows trying to spear a fish, Ralph usually stayed away, cruising along the deep end of the lagoon.

Once he had cruised in a little too close and got pushed away with the butt of the spear. After a while, the stout shark seemed to get it and remained out in the deeper parts of the enclosed rock pool. In fact, as if in payback for the scraps Ben tossed him, there were times when Ralph seemed to herd the fish toward Ben's waiting spear.

Some days, Ben spent his time out at the breakwater, on the rocks, leaning on his arms and looking out at the huge sea beasts, or up and down the coastline. Northward, he could see the jutting landmasses that might have been headlands or perhaps islands in the far distance. He knew his home was up there somewhere, and often wondered what it would be like now—perhaps miles of shallow coastal estuaries, foreboding swamps, or vast plains of grasses, and forests of weird trees that looked like 50-foot-high Q-tips.

Ben was about to turn away, when he noticed something else. It was in the far distance and in near to the jutting shoreline. But oddly, it looked square against the horizon.

He frowned; other than geologically, nature didn't really do squares or geometric shapes. If he had been back in his own time, he wouldn't have given it a second glance, as he would have immediately known what he thought it was—*a sail*.

"Insanity, or a solitude-induced hallucination?" He laughed softly as he watched the thing. It seemed to tack away and finally vanished from sight. He continued to stare for many more minutes, but there was nothing bar some humidity mist rising from the ocean's surface.

"Wasn't a sail," he said softly.

But Ben kept looking for the square, while in his stomach he felt the leaden heaviness of longing and homesickness. When he had finished for his day and turned, Ralph was always cruising back and forth behind him. "I thought I saw...*nah*, nothing." Ben saluted. "Night, big guy." And headed for his cave.

Like clockwork every evening, Ben marked off more notches on the cave wall, always carefully keeping track of his calendar. He knew it would take him many weeks, and maybe even months depending on what he faced, to return to his plateau. But he had years to go just yet.

There was time to enjoy his paradise, and over his many years, he had found so few safe havens such as this that he shouldn't rush to leave it.

There were still dangers here, and from time to time, he spotted two-legged hunters patrolling the tide line. They rarely hung around for long and avoided the water, seeming to know that in those depths things waited that were even more fearsome than they were.

As the sun was going down one evening, Ben felt the change in the air pressure, and noticed the horizon was filled with a wall of clouds, like a dark tsunami bearing down on him.

Storm coming, he thought, and made a mental note to secure his items in the cave, and sleep well back in its depths that night. It meant sucking in more of the pterodon shit, but at least he'd stay dry.

"Hello?" Ben squinted. "What's that?"

There was something else in the distance. Coming down along the coast and in close to the shoreline, he spotted what looked like a huge fallen tree, just floating. It was hard to make out clearly, and as the sun set, he began to lose sight of it.

"Damn," he breathed. At first, he thought it might have been the sail again. But, even now, he thought that was his mind playing tricks on a fatigued and lonely mind. He squinted, concentrating. It had to be a tree stump, and he kinda hoped it would float all the way down to him and wash up during the storm—he could certainly work with the wood.

He rubbed his red eyes. "I'd give my left testicle for a good pair of field glasses right now."

Then it was gone. Ben sighed and moved further back into his cave as the angry clouds swallowed the light.

The storm hit a few hours after dark in an explosion of furious wind and rain. At first, sleep was impossible as the thump of huge waves against the cliffs was like the beat of a titan's drum. Outside, lightning forked, thunder cracked, and he could only turn his back and pull some of the large leaf fronds he had gathered up over himself to stop the wet wind rushing in at him.

Ben's body made a small barrier to the storm's fury and a few of the small pterodons came and nestled in close to him. He almost regretted eating so many of the little guys' eggs. Almost. And they still stank terribly.

Regardless of the thunderstorm, Ben managed to catch a few hours sleep, and when he woke, it was to the sound of his flying roommates greeting the dawn with their usual squawks and chirrups as they headed out to skim the surface of the ocean with their toothed beaks to catch sprats from the surface, or to go and pick at the lines of debris washed up after the storm.

Ben sat up and rubbed his face, and then pulled his beard flat. He let his hand run down its foot-long length, and then glanced at his knife-tipped spear. He had promised himself he'd scrape the beard away when he set off back to the plateau, and *would*, even though he didn't relish the idea of scraping his face with the now chipped and rusting blade of his former hunting knife.

Ben eased forward, keen to see what damage the storm had inflicted on his lagoon, and the first thing he noticed were the tracks on the sand—massive and strange—like someone had beached a boat in the night. The drag marks had to be at least 20 feet wide, and on each side, there were footprints, or rather, claw prints, and each as large as a manhole cover. He'd never seen anything like them.

He crawled further forward until he was at the lip of the cave mouth and rested on his hands and knees following them. They came from the ocean well down the beach, and then whatever it was, was dragged all the way along the sand toward his line of cliffs. The deep gauges finished at his lagoon, where they vanished.

The sun wasn't fully up, and it was still too dark to make out anything in the water, but he swallowed, feeling a knot begin to form in his stomach.

"Hey, Ralph, did you have any company last night?" Ben asked softly. It looked like some sort of large dinosaur had patrolled the beach in the dark. But as the sand was so churned up, and also many of the tracks obliterated by the downpour, it was hard to determine where the thing eventually went. Or even, if the tracks were leading to or from his lagoon.

Further down along the beach, there was no sign of anything larger than a few pterodons squabbling over something in amongst the weed.

He stared out at the horizon for a few moments, and as the sun rose, he watched the light slowly go from a blush in the distance to creating a golden highway along the vast blue ocean. His lagoon was still in the shadows and remained an inky black. But it looked calm and mostly untroubled by the storm, save for some debris floating within it.

Might be something he could salvage, he thought. Ben strapped his spear to his back, grabbed up his fishing line, and began to scale down. He walked along the sand, feeling a slight chill against his chest from the morning breeze.

"Ralph, you there, old buddy?"

The water of his lagoon was calm, but not pond still. There were swirls and bubbles popping, and some sixth sense kept Ben from going to the water's edge this morning. He let his eyes run along the entire surface and was confused that the fin of the shark wasn't there somewhere.

"You went home?" Could Ralph have been washed out in the storm? Ben wondered. "Most likely," he answered.

Ben leaned against the only rock on the beach, perhaps a massive piece of sandstone that had broken off the cliffs a thousand years before. He laid his line on top of it and turned back to the water. Still no fin, and his friend not being there depressed him.

"*Ralph*!" Ben yelled, and the name echoed against the cliffs, but it still didn't bring the shark to the surface. Ben pushed off the rock as the sun began to peek over the top of the breakwater, and he took a few steps toward the lagoon's edge.

And then froze.

The devil was in there, watching him.

And when he saw it, it knew he saw it.

And it attacked.

The giant sea crocodile exploded from the water, and a mouth larger than Ben was opened wide.

Ben threw his arms up and stumbled back, but only took two steps before falling beside the only rock on the beach.

The massive creature's jaws struck the rock, and that split second gave Ben the chance to sprint away for his life. Ben didn't stop until he was up the cliff face and into his cave. Only then did he turn and look back with his heart beating fast and hard in his chest.

"Oh shit." His spirit sank.

The massive fallen tree he thought he had seen last evening hadn't been a tree at all. In his lagoon was a crocodile that must have been 40 feet long if it was an inch. It was close to the shore, and just its eyes and snout were at the waterline—it had reset its ambush, perhaps hoping Ben would try for the water again.

"Ah shit, Ralph." Ben sat back. He knew his friend was gone for good. He also knew he'd never get close to the water again.

Ben sat watching for another few hours as the sun rose higher and higher. The crocodile pulled itself up onto the sand to sun itself. It was a monster.

The crocodile's jagged skin rose like spikes all along its body and down to a flattened tail-like a paddle. The claws were massive and broad, and the body was wide as a bus. But it was the mouth that was its most fearsome attribute—the jaws gaped open as it rested, and Ben could see shreds of flesh between its tusk-like teeth—he knew it was his friend. Ralph wouldn't have stood a chance being trapped in the lagoon. His speed was useless when he was within a confined space.

Ben remembered from his time in Florida that modern crocodiles nested at certain times of the year, and also stayed close to their nests if they found a good spot—like this one.

Ben looked up at his cave wall with all the calendar marks. "Well, looks like I've been evicted." He gathered up all his things into his woven mesh bag, strapped his spear to his back, and packed a few pterodon eggs in for his travels.

He turned to the rear of the cave. "Goodbye, kids; it's been fun."

The small pterodons just squawked their response. Ben then went to the cave mouth and looked down one last time.

"Hope Ralph gives you indigestion, you big bastard."

Then he started up along the ledge to the top of the cliff.

PART 2 – THE GODS CAN'T PROTECT EVERYONE

"*One must wait till it comes*" – Arthur Conan Doyle, The Lost World

CHAPTER 14

**Eagle Eye Observatory, Burnet, Texas – 5 Days to Comet
Apparition**

"Here we go." Jim Henson stared into the viewing piece of the
12.5-inch Newtonian reflector. The massive steel tube of highly
polished glass lenses and mirrors, plus large view aperture, gave the
man crisp images of the solar system.

"Just like clockwork." He squinted and used one hand to gently
turn the imaging dial with the precision of a safe-cracker.

"*Huh*?" Andy Gallagher leaned away from his computer screen.
"P/2014-YG332?"

"No-*ooo*. Not even close." Henson pulled back from the telescope.
"P/2018-YG874, *Primordia*—look at the date."

Gallagher checked his calendar. "Oh right—the magical number
8." His eyebrows rose. "Hey, did you know that '8' is a lucky number
in China? It means—"

"Yeah, yeah, money, luck, good fortune, or something." Henson
waved it away and then squinted back into the eyepiece. "I love this
little guy. He isn't big, and probably originated in the Oort cloud over a
hundred million years ago. But he's perfectly formed—good coma, tail,
and nice glow, which undoubtedly means there's some sort of iron base,
rather than just being a lump of super-compressed ice."

"Venezuela," Gallagher said. "That's where it'll be closest, i-
iiin…" He typed on the screen. "…five days, forty-seven hours, forty
minutes, and counting down."

"Of the nearly 6,000 known comets visiting us in the inner solar
system, we only get to see around one per year with the naked eye. But
Primordia is a real beauty." Henson pulled back, snapped his fingers,
and pointed to Gallagher's screen. "Get some pictures, will ya?"

"Right." Gallagher started typing furiously at his keyboard. Beside
them, the enormous computerized 25-inch aperture Truss-Dobsonian
reflector came to life. The powerful computerized telescope looked like
a barrel on a robotic arm, and it whined as it lifted and swiveled to gaze
into space.

The Truss-Dobsonian sent its images directly to Gallagher's

computer. "Here we go." He focused on the small streak in the sky. "Our baby is just passing by Venus now."

Gallagher folded his arms as he watched, but from the distance of 162 million miles, it seemed stationary even though it was probably traveling at around 50 miles per second in space.

"I'd love to be there," he said dreamily. "To the closest planetary point where its apparition becomes observable, I mean."

"*Meh.*" Henson wrinkled his nose. "There might be some sort of aurora borealis effect, and you'd see the coma for sure, but would that be worth trekking into the center of the Amazon jungle?"

Henson and Gallagher looked at each for a few seconds.

"*Hell yeah*!" they both shouted.

They chuckled for a few moments, and then Henson sat back.

"Maybe one day." He spotted something on the desk beside Gallagher. "Hey, Pete, toss me those Doritos, will ya?"

Gallagher picked up the bag, twisted it shut, and then tossed it into the air. "Look out; it's Primordia—*incomi-iiing*!"

CHAPTER 15

2018 – South Eastern Venezuela – 2 Days Until Comet Apparition

Emma shifted in her seat and then reached for a bottle of water. She was parched dry from all the airline travel, and her back hurt; both her legs were going crazy from inactivity, plus her nose, lips, and eyes were so dry she felt like she had just crawled out of Death Valley.

She shifted to try and straighten a kink in her back, but gave up and slumped again. She felt fatigued already…and scared, and resentful, and anxious as all hell.

It wasn't like this was the first time she had flown into Venezuela. She remembered the youthful exuberance, the excitement, the curiosity…the damned stupidity. Now, ten years older, and with full knowledge of what she was getting herself into, she couldn't help feeling just as stupid.

She looked around and sighed. *She* knew what awaited them, but the others didn't. Even though she had made them read her report, cover to cover, she knew there was no way they could fully comprehend what they were walking into. Her expression dropped as her mind took her back there for a moment.

Who could possibly believe that there was a place where creatures from Earth's primordial past lived and breathed? That it was a land of brutality, miasmic swamps, and horrors waiting to tear them limb from limb?

She drew in a breath and let it out slowly. Maybe it was for the best that they didn't really believe the truth. Would she have been able to get them to come with her if they did? She doubted it.

She let her eyes touch on her team. Including her, she now had a party of nine: her soldiers, Drake, Fergus, Brocke, and the foreboding Ajax. There were her paleontological experts, Andy and Helen Martin. Plus two extra gatecrashers: Camilla and her cameraman, the large and jovial Juan Marquina, who to her amazement, had even won over Drake and his team with his good humor and his serious knowledge of the Amazon.

Emma knew she might be leading them all to their deaths. She felt a wave of guilt wash over her and screwed her eyes shut for a moment.

Then they slowly opened, and the steely resolve had returned. *This was a rescue mission*, she reminded herself. *That's what really mattered.*

Following the many hours and 2,300 miles of flying, they had a smooth landing into Caracas. Their cargo was unloaded, and Camilla had earned her keep by negotiating a low level of scrutiny over what they contained, for a handsome amount of extra fees.

Along with their cargo crates, they were hustled to a large truck, and then headed directly to the Rio Caroní to wait for their flying boat to arrive.

"Looks good." Drake nodded to the sky as a twin-float seaplane circled and then came down to glide smoothly along the surface. "DHC3 Otter; that'll do nicely."

"Good STOL," Fergus observed.

"STOL?" Andy asked.

The redheaded soldier grinned. "Short take-off and landing; *STOL* for short. In these parts, if you're gonna navigate narrow rivers with all sorts of bends and twists, you might not have a lot of clear water to come down on. A shorter landing and take-off craft is better for getting you closer to your target insertion or extraction point."

"Got it." Andy nodded, and then walked a few paces over to his sister. He pointed to the plane. "DHC3 Otter; got good STOL."

She frowned at him, and Fergus chuckled.

Emma watched as the single-propeller craft eased into their wharf. There was a single pilot, middle-aged and grey-bearded, who touched his cap and masterfully maneuvered the floats and rudders to guide his plane in against the wood. Ajax and Brocke grabbed it, pulled it in close, and then tied it off, the propeller slowing and then jerking to a stop.

It only took them 15 minutes to load up and board, and after she met the pilot, Jake, a retired Canadian commercial pilot, she supplied him with their destination coordinates.

He nodded and whistled as he looked at her map.

"You know it?" she asked.

"No one really *knows* it. But been over there," he said, pushing his red cap up on his forehead. "Not much down there. Just miles and miles of nothing."

"That's what I'm expecting. How long?" Emma asked.

"Good weather, so, two hours, give or take." He straightened his cap. "Say the word."

She grabbed his shoulder and squeezed. "Word."

Emma headed back into the cabin. Just two more hours, she thought. It had taken them nearly an entire day to come down via boat the last time.

She found her vacant seat and dropped into it. The DHC3 only took 10 passengers, and with the bulk of Drake and his oversized buddies, it felt crowded as hell inside. And hot. But right now, and for the next couple of hours, it was all up to Jake's flying and navigation skills.

Emma settled back as the propeller started up, and the craft vibrated all around her. She leaned her head on the backrest and stared out the window. They were here, and now they were closing in. When Jake dropped them in the middle of nowhere, it would all be down to her memory and a truckload of luck.

The DHC3 began to ease forward, and Emma let herself relax and settled deeper into the seat. She closed her eyes.

*****

Emma perched on the precipice, one hand on the cliff edge and the other gripping onto the wrist-thick vines. Around her, the wind howled like the scream of banshees, and debris was whipped around so hard and fast it stung her exposed skin and forced her eyes into slits.

Over the roar of the tornado, she yelled for Ben to run toward her. But instead, he backed away, not from her, but from the monster that reared up before him.

She went to climb back, but he turned to her and held a hand up to stop her, and then shook his head.

As she watched, the giant snake, the *Titanoboa*, lifted the front of its 70-foot body nearly 20 feet into the air. Its soulless glass-like eyes were fixed on the man, and its huge muscular body emanated the raw power of an alpha-apex predator.

Ben turned back, seeming transfixed by the thing or maybe just resigned to his fate. He just stood there, a mouse before a cobra. He finally held up a gun, pointing it at the creature, but it was rusted and old, and eventually, his arm dropped to let the ancient revolver fall to the ground.

The snake gathered itself in behind it, coiling its huge muscled body. Emma saw Ben half-turn to her, and her eyes met his. He mouthed something to her. Was it: *Hear me? Help me?* She couldn't hear it clearly, but knew it was the most important thing he wanted to tell her.

Emma became frantic and began to clamber back up over the cliff. Ben turned to the snake, distracting it, and then he took a step toward it.

"*Don't!*" she screamed.

The snake struck, its massive diamond-shaped head moving faster than her eyes could follow—or for Ben to react. One second, the man she loved had been standing there, and the next, he was in the thing's mouth. The snake lifted its head, and gulped, letting Ben slide deeper into its gullet.

"*No-ooo!*" She clambered up onto the cliff. "*No-ooo!*"

The snake spotted her, and then faster than anything its size should be able to move, came at her like a heavily scaled river of terror. She backed up and felt her foot right on the cliff edge. A hurricane-like blast of wind pushed her sideways, and she overbalanced and fell. Her legs dangled, and she scrambled for the vines as her body began to slide into the abyss.

Emma looked down, barely making out the jungle thousands of feet below her, as everything seemed oily and distorted. She had one arm on the cliff edge and she began to slide.

The snake must be close now, she thought, and she tried to find the cave to leap into—it was there—she could make it. Emma went to swing into it but was jerked to a stop—it had her arm.

She screamed.

Emma's eyes shot open as she furiously slapped at the thing on her arm that held on, shaking her. Her teeth were bared.

"*Whoa*, easy there." Helen backed up, holding her hands up and away. "Nightmare much?"

"*Huh*?" Emma blinked away the images that still floated in her mind. "No, yes, I'm okay. What is it?"

"The pilot," Helen said over the sound of the propeller. "He's calling for you."

"Oh, okay." Emma unstrapped and launched herself toward the cockpit doorway. Inside, Jake turned to nod. He lifted some earphones, held them out to her, and she slipped them on so they could talk to each other without being drowned out by the engine.

"Look outside," he said.

She did, seeing nothing but the endless green of an impenetrable tree canopy, with the dark highway of the river splitting it in half.

"This is where your instructions and map has put us." Jake glanced from Emma to the cockpit windscreen. "Are you sure about this?"

The river continued into the distance, narrowing here and there, the occasional small clearings at the water's edge. But for the main part, it was unbroken, and there was no evidence at all of any side rivers.

"Yes, I am."

But she knew they were down there. Plus, she had a secret weapon. That was if Camilla proved to truly be of value.

"Bingo." She pointed.

Camilla had succeeded—about a mile or so in the distance, there was a ribbon of smoke rising lazily into the humid air.

"*There*; that smoke, put us down there," Emma said.

"Yes, ma'am." Jake accelerated in the air, and in no time, they were over the top of a tiny clearing, and looking down, she could see a single canoe pulled up and a fire burning.

"Yeah, that's it." Emma felt her confidence soaring.

The pilot half turned. "Taking her down. Make sure everyone is strapped in."

Emma got to her feet and scurried to the cabin where she yelled instructions, getting everyone to sit down, redo seatbelts, and prepare for a fast disembark. Once done, all heads turned to the small porthole windows.

The DHC3 banked, lining the river up, and then they came in fast as though Jake was in a hurry to get them down. In another few seconds, there was the thump and bounce of the flying boat's floats meeting the flowing waters. Even though it seemed smooth, the plane rattled and jerked over even the smallest of ripples until they slowed and settled.

The pilot brought the craft around and then eased it in toward the shoreline. Emma saw from the window a single nut-brown man with a bowl-cut hairdo and round belly watching solemnly—she knew who it was, recognizing him even after all the years—*Ataca*, their original guide and her eventual savior.

Jake guided them into the shoreline, and the nose of the plane bumped up onto the bank. Drake was already up with his men and they threw open the door to leap out, immediately setting to secure the plane with ropes, hammering in spikes to lock it in place.

Jake cut the engine, and after another moment, the sound of the jungle came alive around them, and with it the rush of humid heat, and the smells of decaying vegetation, acidic sap, strange blooms, and brackish water.

Emma leaped down and staggered for a moment on the soft earth. She quickly straightened and waved to the solemn-looking Pemon Indian. As she approached, she saw that he had aged—so had she, but obviously years in the jungle were a lot harsher. The once fierce-looking young man with a smooth face, black bowl-cut hair and daubs of vivid paint on his cheeks, now looked shrunken and less colorful.

She smiled broadly. It was Ataca that had helped her a decade ago when she had staggered from the jungle, more dead than alive, babbling and fevered. Emma went to him and held out her hand, knowing that hugging was not something that the Pemon understood or even wanted.

"Ataca, my friend, thank you for coming."

He took her hand and held it rather than shook it. His felt like bone and leather, and to him, she was sure hers was silk, and not designed for a life lived here.

"You come back," he said in soft, halting Spanish.

She smiled. "And you learned Spanish."

"A little." He hiked sharp, brown shoulders. His face became serious. "The wettest season comes. And you are here for your friend."

It wasn't a question. "Yes." Emma looked out over the jungle for a moment. "Yes; if he's alive, I'll bring him home."

Ataca looked saddened. "All my life, *ah*, one person only ever comes back from the bad place." He looked up into her eyes. "That was you."

She half-smiled. "And I will again."

Ataca's dark eyes slid to her group. "And will they?"

"Yes, *of course*," she said, more forcefully than she wanted to.

The Pemon Indian grunted and went to turn back to his canoe but paused. "I will ask my gods to protect you, *again*." He looked toward her team once more, who were unpacking the last boxes. "But I don't think the gods can protect everyone."

"Wait." She rushed back to the plane, drew out a plastic bag, and jogged back to the small man who was already sitting in his canoe. She crouched beside him and put the bag in front of him. "This is for you, as a way of thanking you...for everything."

He looked in the bag and his eyes lit up. It was only a bottle of whiskey, a few hundred American dollars, and two shiny new hunting knives. Ataca smiled, nodded, and reclosed the bag.

He picked up his paddle. "I will come back, after the wettest season has ended. I hope you will be here. *With* your friends." He pushed away from the bank.

Emma raised a hand to wave, but the small man never turned. *Thank you*, she thought. *But this time, I hope I don't need you.*

Drake Masterson joined her and stood watching Ataca disappear with his hands on his hips.

"Your guide?"

"He was." She turned to him. "I wish we could get him to come with us. He knows more than he's telling us."

"About the Amazon, sure. But about where we are going; probably not more than you do now," Drake responded. "I know the Pemon; they're very superstitious and see the jungle as a living thing which they're a part of. Your friend might be fine for a while, but also might not be able to hold it together if some of his gods or demons come to life before his eyes."

She scoffed and looked over her shoulder. "And you think they will?"

Drake grinned. "Time will tell." He turned about. "This will be base camp; where we'll launch from and where we all agree to return to—even if we split up." He checked his watch. "According to your timetable, we now have twenty-one hours, seventeen minutes until this phenomenon begins. So let's call 'em all in, so we can begin."

"Yep; first things first." Emma went and checked the plane was fully unloaded, and then confirmed her instructions with Jake—he was to be back in four days. If everything went to plan, they should all be back here waiting for him.

The older man nodded and saluted from the edge of his cap, and then started the propeller. Emma backed up, squinting and hugging herself as she watched the seaplane maneuver out toward the center of the river, accelerate, and then take off.

Jake didn't circle back, salute from the cockpit, or dip his wings like they did in the movies. He just lifted and headed home. Emma felt emptiness in the pit of her stomach as the plane vanished into the distance. It was like watching the modern world leave her behind, and now she belonged to the jungle.

She blew air through her lips, turned, and then clapped her hands once. "Okay, everyone, in here, please."

The group assembled in front of her. Behind them, stacked in the center of the clearing on the riverbank, was their pile of boxes and bundles. Phase one of their journey was complete.

"This is base camp. It will take us a day to reach the plateau—"

"I thought it was going to be less than that?" Andy complained.

"Hopefully, it *will* be less," she replied. "The last time I was here, navigating via the streams, it took us several days. We'll be able to lift up above all that, and if the winds are favorable, then yes, we should arrive in plenty of time. We can be early, but we *cannot* be late. So, you might notice we're building in slack for any unforeseen *eventualities*."

Emma looked up at the sky, and then at her watch. "From now on, we treat this expedition like it's a military mission. Drake will be calling the shots with me acting as advisor." She waited. And though Helen's lips were clamped, and Camilla seemed a little amused, there was no pushback. She held out a hand to the formidable Special Forces captain. "Drake."

"Thank you, Emma." Drake Masterson had both hands on his hips as he eyeballed the group. "This is a rescue mission. And from what we understand, it's going to be a damned dangerous one at that. We will be entering extremely hostile territory. My job, and the job of my men, will be to keep everyone alive."

Andy's hand shot up.

"Go." Drake nodded to him.

"Are we launching the balloon from here?" Andy asked.

"Yes, but not yet. Tasks will be handed out to everyone, and I mean *everyone*. Because everyone here needs to pull their weight, and no one is here just because they have a nice smile."

"Damn," Juan said with a grin.

"To begin with, my guys get the hard stuff." He nodded to his men. "Everyone else, under the supervision of Emma, will be unpacking the gear and laying it all out. We'll need to suit up in our jungle clothing, and also do a weapons check, load up our packs, and then…"

Drake looked at the forbidding wall of jungle. "…*then*, we'll be launching the balloon."

"And what will you be doing?" Andy said with a cocky grin.

Drake turned to him. "To launch the balloon safely, we need about an extra hundred feet of clearing. So for the next few hours, Fergus, Brocke, Ajax, and myself will be hacking out some more space. We'll then lay out the canopy bag and give it a once-over. We'll construct the basket and check the heat blaster." He lowered his brow to Andy. "You are welcome to pitch in, Mr. Martin."

Andy shook his head and held his hands out. "See these? These are academic's hands, and the toughest things they've dealt with lately are paper cuts and maybe a hot coffee spill."

Drake snorted. "I've read your bio, Mr. Martin, and I know you've done plenty of fieldwork in some pretty nasty places. We could use your help."

Andy puffed up a little. "Okay, sure, I'm in."

"Good man," Drake said, and then checked his watch. "It's too late to launch today, as by the time we've done all of this, nightfall will have overtaken us. Launch is first thing in the morning."

He looked along their faces. "Questions?"

There were none, and he nodded to Emma. "Then let's begin."

CHAPTER 16

Venezuelan National Institute of Meteorological Services

"Well, well, well; old Santiago was right after all." Mateo folded his arms as he read the data on the bank of screens before him. He turned to the young man sitting at the desk behind him.

"Hey, Nicolás, you see that storm cell gathering energy over the northeastern jungle?"

Nicolás had an open-mouthed grin, but his brow was furrowed. "Yes, I see it, but I don't believe it." He switched to the satellite images. "It doesn't make sense—it's just over the deep eastern jungle. But nowhere else." He swiveled his seat to Mateo.

"It comes again." Mateo turned back to his screen. Santiago, his former boss, mentor, and friend had retired just last year. And he remembered well seeing the same phenomenon exactly ten years ago. Back then, he was the fresh-faced kid, and just like Nicolás was as confused as he was intrigued by the occurrence.

"Every ten years, almost to the day, and always over just that part of the jungle, there looks to develop a localized hurricane, but coming out of nowhere, and centralized. But strangely, it *stays* centralized." Mateo watched the cell become ever more dense every few moments.

"I've never seen anything like it. Or even ever read about this unique occurrence." Nicolás turned back to his screen, and his fingers raced over the keyboard. "It's impenetrable," he breathed.

Mateo chuckled. "Give up; I tried the same thing when I first saw it. Satellite, thermal, or even geographic readings over the site are near useless."

As they watched, even the satellite image started to blur over the affected area as if there looked like a smudge was starting to obscure his screen. The localized cloudbank swirled and was so dense it looked like an error in the software or hardware.

"Every ten years, we have what the locals down there call the *wettest season*." Mateo watched, feeling like an old friend had come to visit them again.

"What should we do about it?" Nicolás asked.

"Do about it?" Mateo turned. "What should we do about the sun coming up, or going down? Or about the sky being blue, or the trees green? We do nothing but observe, document, and enjoy a unique weather phenomenon."

Mateo reached forward to pull a battered old paper folder from a shelf. He looked at it for a moment, and then thumbed through it, finding the pages he wanted.

"History repeats. This was given to me ten years ago by my former boss; you'll see my notes of the last occurrence." He held it out. "And now I hand it to you to make *your* notes."

Mateo pointed to the open pages as Nicolás read. "Every ten years, like clockwork, there is a unique phenomenon that happens in these parts." He shrugged. "The conditions manifest over a single area, only remain for a few days, and then just as abruptly, dissipate and then vanish. It's been happening for as long as anyone can remember. Maybe forever." He looked up.

Mateo nodded. "Theories are that it is caused by an upswelling of thermal activity in the area that alters ground heat, and then the associated humidity and air density."

Nicolás flipped back through the book. "2018, 2008, 1998…" He let the pages fan. "…there are pages stuck in, handwritten, that go back hundreds of years." He looked up. "What happens down there?"

"No one knows," Mateo said. "Our best technology can't see through it, so for all intents and purposes, whatever is or was there ceases to exist as far as we're concerned." He chuckled. "Maybe everything goes to the Land of Oz."

"We should go there," the young meteorologist said.

"No, we won't. And I don't think anyone would be mad enough to try and visit that strange cauldron at this time. Even if they could get there," Mateo said wearily.

Nicolás nodded, and then began to read from the notebook. "One day, someone will." He paused. "Hey, the weather satellite will be in a complimentary position for the next twenty-four hours. Mind if I continue to monitor the site?"

"Knock yourself out, kid." Mateo had already lost interest.

CHAPTER 17

Ben had been traveling all through the night, like he had for the last few days. Dawn was coming fast and he needed to find shelter soon. Though there were the nocturnal night hunters, there were fewer of them than the ones who hunted by sight.

Ben had found out the hard way that the daylight hunters, even the smaller ones, had eyesight comparable to that of birds of prey, with vision that was mostly triggered by activity.

When he had to move during the day, it meant having to crawl along the ground, avoid rapid movement, and stop for many minutes and just let his eyes scan the foliage.

Many times, he had seen them, the hunters, like weird crocodiles standing up on hind legs, remaining motionless in the dark of the jungle, just waiting for something to amble close enough for them to ambush. And they were fast—the prey animals rarely outran a pack of hunters.

Ben often marveled at the predator's natural camouflage—mottled patches or splotches, tiger stripes, or skin that looked to be able to mirror its surroundings and change color.

He looked up at the outline of the plateau in the distance, just recognizable against the blush of the sunrise. Clouds were beginning to form over its surface and were slowly rotating. Around him, a soft rain fell. It was as warm and slick as oil, giving him good sound cover.

He couldn't help grinning—after 10 years, he was coming home. Ben wanted to run forward, screaming and waving, his impatience drawing him nearly mad with an urge to act, and fast. His long wait might be finally over. But he knew that impatience would kill him as surely as putting a gun to his head.

He'd find shelter now, and then in the next night, he'd begin to work his way up the slope to the tabletop mountain.

"I'm coming, Emma," he breathed. "I'm coming home."

CHAPTER 18

At dawn, Emma woke to the sound of a tiny whine and opening her eyes saw the cloud of gnats, mosquitoes, and larger insects trying to find a way in through her mosquito netting.

She sat up and saw that Drake and the others were already moving about. They had all spread around a campfire at the water's edge, with one of the soldiers taking turns on guard. Though the river here moved too fast for small caimans, there were bigger ones this far in, and sleep was when people made themselves vulnerable, so there was no need to take unnecessary risks.

She watched the dark water for a moment more as she pulled her knees up to her chest. The thought of waking to the feeling of her foot clamped in a caiman's jaws and being dragged into the water sent shudders up her spine. But this green hell was something she'd only have to experience for a number of days, and she tried to imagine what it was like for Ben, who was forced to live in a jungle far more dangerous, day after day for a decade.

If he was *still* living in it.

He's alive, she demanded of herself. She had to believe that for herself and for everyone else she was driving forward.

At her feet were her jungle clothes ready to put on: the tiger-striped Army uniform, belt with knives, ammunition pouches and holster, plus the calf-high boots with in-built snakebite armor.

Emma grabbed her water, sipped, and began to dress, making sure she stayed within the netting until she could reapply her chemical shield.

It took her ten minutes to work everything out, lather on the bug spray, and then throw back her netting. Brocke was grilling some fish he'd caught, and Drake, Fergus, and Ajax had laid out their ordnance, checking it over.

Emma turned from the river to the jungle and chuckled. "Holy wow."

The guys must have worked like machines all afternoon and evening, and now she saw what they'd accomplished. The clearing they had arrived on was now three times as large, and several hills of green debris had been pushed up to one side.

The orange balloon canopy was laid out, and she could see why they needed so much clearing space—it looked huge. Also, the basket had been constructed from the panels—it was about ten feet square, light but formidable, and would fit them all in with room to spare.

Emma inhaled the humid jungle air deep into her lungs. She felt good; she was certainly getting her money's worth from Ben's old comrades and felt vindicated for bringing them along.

She also knew they weren't doing it just for the money—the motto: *no one left behind*, was something that was in their DNA. Ben was more than just a fellow soldier; he was a blood brother to them. They'd bring him home, or she bet they'd die trying. Her years of planning were taking shape, and so far, she regretted nothing.

Emma saw that Andy was lending a hand with the weapons, and even Helen was in amongst the soldiers, chatting and helping out. She then looked across to her outliers—Camilla and Juan. The pair hovered close by, and from time to time, Juan would take a picture or tell a joke, a funny one, by the look of the expression on the team's faces.

Their work was nearly done, and she thought if nothing else, they all certainly looked the part in their camouflage outfits—a private army about to do battle deep in the Amazon jungle's dark and mysterious center.

Emma reached for her holster, slid out, checked, and then replaced her sidearm—it was a new SIG Sauer M17, straight off the line. The 9mm handgun was a dark earth tone, and was lightweight, corrosion-resistant for tropical environments, accurate, and reliable. Against the adversaries she had in mind, it might prove to be more of an irritant. But it made her feel safe, and she had practiced enough over the years to know she could hit a dime from 50 feet.

She'd feel even better when she was packing an M4 rifle. She almost felt...confident.

Emma went to turn away but noticed that Camilla was staring. She nodded to the journalist, and in return, the woman scurried to the fire, poured two coffees, and came toward her, holding them both in front of her.

She held one cup out. "Good morning, Emma. Did you sleep?"

Emma took it and raised it to the woman. "Thank you, and yes, surprisingly well. You?"

Camilla shrugged. "A little."

Emma just nodded. Given they'd be on the plateau soon, she might regret not getting more sleep.

"So." Camilla sipped her brew. "Where do you think Ben will be?"

Emma noticed her eyes twinkled as if they were sharing a secret. "Somewhere on the tepui. I don't know where. Maybe he'll find us."

"Really?" Camilla lowered her cup. "Do you *really* think he's alive? I mean, *really*?"

"That's why I'm here. We're *all* here." Emma turned to face the smaller woman.

"Closure." Camilla nodded. "For you and for Cynthia Cartwright. Can't have been easy on her. You coming back, but her son, not." She looked up into Emma's face and tilted her head. "I hear she's not well these days."

Emma's eyes narrowed. "That generation was from far stronger stock than us. She's fine."

"But if she dies, who inherits the Cartwright estate?"

"Ben does," Emma fired back.

Camilla turned side on. "But if Ben—"

"*Ben does.*" Emma's jaw jutted momentarily. "He *will* be coming back." She leaned in close to the woman's face. "Got something to say, say it."

Emma's raised voice turned every head in the camp. She noticed that Juan was filming her and Camilla.

The journalist stood her ground, and the corners of her lips just turned up a fraction. "Well, you see, it's just that you win either way. You find Ben, and live happily ever after. Or you don't find Ben, inherit the Cartwright estate, and live happily ever after."

Emma saw red and leaned in real close so only the woman could hear. "Watch that mouth, or else."

"Or else?" Camilla straightened. "You'll leave *me* here...*as well*."

Emma had the urge to grab the woman's shirtfront and shake her. "No, but I'll break your fucking jaw."

She stormed toward Drake and his team. Juan filmed her the entire way.

CHAPTER 19

3008 BC – Sacred Tabletop Mountain – Time of Comet Apparition

Kueka was the last high-borne priest remaining. A few others had managed to flee, but he and his warrior escort had waited too long, and now he would pay.

The others of his group had scattered, but the chance of their survival could be counted in the breaths of a bird, rather than in days or even hours.

The priest bounded up the steps of the temple, past the majestic stone idols, and also past the bowls of large, fragrant blooms, fresh fruits, and other offerings to their gods.

He paused, confused—*where were the guards*? They knew not to leave until he had returned. They would pay with their lives.

Kueka cursed; he had always known his gods were angry and demanding ones, and the sacrifices were becoming costly. Too many lower-caste men, women, and children had been offered and accepted, greatly thinning out their tribe. Now it seemed the eyes of the great gods had turned upon the high borne.

It was said to be an honor to be sacrificed to the great snake god. But it was an honor that Kueka wanted to ensure never fell upon him. As head priest, he was said to be able to talk to these monstrous creatures. But today, no god was listening, as were any of his people. It seemed no one was left to listen.

The small man bounded down the steps and leaped through the hole in the wall, accelerating to the pathway that would lead back down to the base of the plateau. The wettest season would be over soon, and everything would vanish back to the underworld. He must escape before that happened. Or he'd be trapped. But first, he must survive.

He sprinted down the cave passageway, closing in on his escape route, when he skidded to a stop. The burning torches along the way threw distorted shadows on the rough-hewn walls, but in the dancing light, there was one shadow looming ahead that he wished was just a trick of the light. The snake god, one of them, was waiting for him, and blocking his way.

Kueka half-turned. From behind, he heard the heavy sliding of another huge body—he was trapped between two of the great beasts. He couldn't really talk to them; that was just to fool the tribe. There would be no entreaties, no mercy, and no hesitation. He'd end up food, just like the rest.

He had one chance, and he darted to the side where there was an alcove for storing building materials. He clambered in and quickly used the cut stones that were stored for construction, lifting them quickly into place, one on top of the other, sealing the entrance to the small hole, and also sealing himself in.

He had no choice; he'd wait until the creatures left. Surely that would be soon.

CHAPTER 20

Drake stood, finished his coffee, and then flicked the dregs into the jungle. After breakfast, two coffees, ablutions, and all jobs done, it was still only 8am. He was satisfied with progress.

"All right people, we're gonna start inflating the bag. It'll take two hours, need everyone involved, and once done, we will immediately board and set off—morning breeze is a good breeze, so we'll use it." He turned to Emma. "Once we're up, it'll be over to you for navigation."

Emma also stood and wiped her hands on her pants. "That's right; we can use GPS and compass for only a while. Then once we arrive over what I'll call the fern forest and are closing in on the plateau, I expect everything to go haywire again. Also, by then, I'm expecting low cloud and fog. That's where we'll be relying on skill, precision, and some luck."

Luck, thought Drake with disquiet. If there was one thing a soldier hated to rely on, it was that. He kept quiet and watched the woman. He couldn't help admiring her. She was single-focused in what she wanted to achieve, and there was a steely resolve and toughness about her that he wouldn't dare bet against. She was confident, and she made him feel confident.

Helen raised her hand. "Remind me again how we are going to find it, if we've got no compass, GPS, and if there is fog, no line of sight?" She stared at Drake from under her brows. "I mean, I've been doing some reading on recreational balloons, like this one, and though they're pretty tough, you don't want to bang into the side of a building or a mountain when you're a thousand feet in the air. The canopy punctures and deflates, and we're all going to drop like a rock."

The soldier grunted. "Modern balloons are tougher than that, and a lot more navigable. But the plan is we rise above the cloud layer. Emma believes we can drop in through a permanent eye effect that is over the center of the plateau." He turned. "That right?"

"It'll be there," Emma said with conviction.

"How high *can* we go up?" Camilla asked, and raised her chin.

"Well, some hot air balloons can go to one-hundred-thousand feet, and that's well into the stratosphere." Drake stuck his thumbs into his belt and tried not to laugh as their faces went a few shades paler. "But this recreational model isn't designed for that. We can certainly get some good height, and if we needed to, we can climb to five thousand feet. Though I expect we'll only need to climb to around two and a half, or maybe three, depending on the cloud mass."

"Will we need breathing equipment?" Andy asked, still looking excited.

"No, not at that height," Drake replied.

"Still no parachutes?" Andy pressed.

"Oh shit, parachutes." Drake slapped his forehead, and Andy's mouth dropped open, but stayed curved up at the corners. Helen looked like she was going to pass out.

Drake couldn't help himself and guffawed. "No, no, like I said before, we won't need them. These modern balloons are pretty tough and can be lowered and raised quickly. We should be fine."

"Should be," Helen repeated.

Drake ignored her. "Anything else?"

Andy's hand shot up again.

"Jesus," Drake said with a groan. "*Yes*, Andy?"

"One more thing; what happens if we *don't* find the plateau?"

Okay, good question, Drake thought. "Well, it's like this; with all our propane cylinders, we have about twenty-four hours flying time—a lot of that is getting there and back. The plan is we find the plateau, rise above it, and then descend down to the top of it, where we will either tie off the balloon or deflate and store it. We find our man, then reinflate and leave. All up, well within our burn boundary."

Drake bared his teeth for a moment as he thought it through. "Unfortunately, we do not have a lot of time for sailing around looking for something. We either find it, or we don't." He turned to Emma. "If we don't find it within the first twelve hours, well, we'll need to head back."

Emma's jaw clenched and she didn't say a word.

Drake stared into her eyes for a few more moments, and bet that as far as she was concerned, there was no way she was returning until she was good and ready. He'd have to cross that bridge when they came to it.

He clapped his big hands together. "Okay, people. We got work to do. In two hours, we are airborne."

And they were.

CHAPTER 21

20 Hours to full Comet Apparition

Comet P/2018-YG874, designate name, Primordia, was on its approach to the third planet from the sun. The magnetic bow wave that preceded it caused collisions between electrically charged particles in the Earth's upper atmosphere, creating an aurora borealis effect over the jungles of South America.

In one of the most inaccessible parts of the eastern Venezuelan jungle, clouds began to darken, and in another minute or two, they started to swirl and boil like in a devil's cauldron, throwing down a torrent of warm rain.

Beneath the clouds, a gigantic tabletop mountain became cloaked in the dense fog, and brutal winds began to smash at its sides and surface. Thunder roared and lightning seemed to come from the sky, air, and even up from the ground itself.

The first of the bestial roars that began to ring out even drowned out the crash of thunder, and before long, the hissing, roars, and screams rose to be like those from the pits of Hell.

It had been ten years since the primordial sounds had been heard in this part of the Amazon, and even the creatures on the jungle floor over 1,000 feet below the plateau scurried away in fear.

It was the wettest season, and Primordia was returning.

CHAPTER 22

The balloon lifting off and soaring above the treetops gave Emma an odd feeling in her stomach. Not so much nausea, but more a sense of unreality as it felt more like she was on a fun park ride instead of a flight into a primordial hell.

Sure, now and then, there was the growling sound of the burners blowing hot air into the canopy, but for the most part, with no engines, there was only the odd creak of rope and squeal of the wicker basket under their feet.

Looking over the side when moving so slowly meant they had time to see and enjoy the jungle below them.

Juan reeled off dozens of photographs as Camilla pointed things out for him to capture. Andy and Helen leaned over together and grinned like school kids as they watched flocks of birds sail over the interwoven branches of the tree canopy. Occasional bands of monkeys stopped to stare up at them and scream, with a few trying to pelt either fruit or dung up at them.

"How'd you like a face full of my dung?" Andy yelled back at them, as Helen gave him the sort of look of distaste that only an older sister could conjure.

After a few hours, Emma stared down almost trance-like, as she tried to make out the winding brackish river they had navigated all those years ago. But she found it impossible to see through the green mesh of the massive trees. The treetops were so thick in this area that it actually looked like solid ground. But she knew it was an illusion as the real ground was another few hundred feet below it.

That permanent twilight world was a green ocean, and below the surface, things swung in branches, hung from tree trunks, and burrowed through leaf litter. There was another entire world hidden down there, and she was thankful they were floating above it, and not having to paddle or trek through it.

Another advantage was even though the balloon moved at around five miles per hour—jogging pace—it was faster than if they were crossing over the ground on foot or canoe. They also were able to travel as the crow flies, thus cutting out miles and miles of meandering river twists and bends.

Camilla came and leaned on the basket edge beside her. "It's beautiful."

Emma looked at her briefly and worked hard to resist the urge to tell her to piss off. After another moment, she nodded. "The jungle is a monster, but she hides her fangs well."

"Most monsters do." Camilla half-smiled, but her eyes held a quizzical expression. "You never told me how you feel coming back again?"

Emma turned to lean her back against the basket edge. "I'm conflicted—part elation, but scared shitless."

Camilla snorted. "Sounds like my first marriage." She continued to stare down at the canopy top. "If we do ever find Ben, I mean, *when* we do, do you think he'll be happy to see you?" She tilted her head. "What do you think he'll say to you?"

Emma's teeth ground for a second or two as she started to get what the woman was after. It didn't matter her motives now; they were well on their way. Over her shoulder, once again, her cameraman filmed them.

"I would think he'll be overjoyed, relieved, disbelieving..."

"Yes, maybe disbelieving." Camilla's smile fell away.

Emma's brows drew together as she looked down at the smaller woman. "Why did you come? Really?"

Camilla brightened again. "Looking for clues, señorita. I am a journalist; it's what I do." She turned to lean her back against the basket railing as well. "My apologies if I seem...intrusive."

"*Intrusive*?" Emma snorted. "Yeah, well, you do what you gotta do, and I'll do the same." She went to push off the basket railing but paused. "You don't believe me, do you? About where we're going and what we'll experience." Emma smiled grimly. "You're in for a surprise, lady." She went to stand by Drake.

She watched as Fergus worked the burners while Brocke manipulated the vents and flaps that could be opened and closed with a series of cords. This allowed him to inflate or deflate the canopy, or just expel air from one side or the other that would cause the balloon to be gently pushed in the direction they wanted.

The modern balloons also had something akin to a trap door in the top that allowed for rapid drop if needed. In the past, balloons would land, and in strong winds wouldn't stick the landing, instead getting tipped and dragged. The vent-trap meant they could release a large volume of the hot air quickly and either drop themselves fast and stick, or totally deflate the bag.

Drake turned. "Looking good."

"Yep," Emma said. "Took us more than a day to traverse this first part."

"We just did it in under three hours," he replied, and then pointed. "I think we're headed in the right direction."

In the distance, there was a line of clouds, low and so dark they looked purple. They could just make out the flashes of light within them as lightning was being discharged. It reminded her of those science pictures of electrical impulses within a human brain. Just the sight of it gave her a tingling in her stomach. *This is where the shit gets real*, she thought.

"Looks like thunderheads," he said.

"Only looks like it. But it's something else entirely," she mumbled in return.

They scudded onwards, moving with the zephyrs and at the time, only a few hundred feet above the treetops.

Emma looked upward and past the enormous, bulging sack of air above her. Where they were at that moment, it was a cloudless, azure blue and seemed empty. But invisible to them within that atmosphere, it was like an ocean with different currents, rivers of air movement, and eddies that swirled in place, dropped or shot upward, and all depending on your height.

There were highways, laneways, and hidden alleys, and if they failed to gain enough traction and forward movement in one lane's river of moving air, they could simply rise or drop until they found another more suitable stream.

For now, they were headed in the right direction, and with the warm sunlight, calm air, and without even the noises of the jungle below, it was a luxury they needed to soak in, and also gather strength for the ordeal she knew was coming.

Emma looked at each of her team members, and suddenly felt a pang of, *what*, guilt?

The soldiers looked formidable enough and she was glad they were here. But she had coerced Andy and Helen into coming. She needed them, and though she had told them what to expect, she had never really tried hard to impart the full horrors and dangers involved.

Maybe I'm the monster now, she thought, and let her eyes move to

Camilla and Juan. They had bullied themselves into coming, so she felt less concerned about them. In fact, given the direction Camilla was taking with her questions right now, she couldn't give a shit about the woman.

Besides, even if she had told them what to expect, she bet they would have come anyway. Andy had also told her that some of the questions Camilla had been asking them bordered on being intrusive, and some were even directed more at whether they were worried about Emma, more than where they were going.

Because I'm the monster, remember? She laughed softly, and then turned away to look over the side.

Emma looked down and noticed the treetop canopy had opened out a little. There, *finally*, a landmark—a clear stream like a sparkling ribbon threaded its way through the green. Colored birds looking more like exotic, tropical fish darted in and out of the branches. It had to be the *river of paradise* she remembered from their last expedition. And maybe, if it truly was, they were making very good time.

She continued to stare, her mind taking her back to that last time— their sense of joy at finding a place that was Eden-like in such a dangerous jungle. There were green meadows, clear streams full of plump fish, birds, flowers, and clear air, before they then headed into the miasma of a stinking bog. It was like the Promised Land that also came with a warning—*Go no further*.

But they did anyway.

Her mind then took her to the plateau, and those last few moments all those years ago when she went over the lip of the cliff edge and left Ben behind. They had no choice; the thing that pursued them was going to kill her, and the last glimpse of Ben had shown her his face creased with fear and worry...not for himself, but for her.

She screwed her eyes shut. *Please be there, Ben*, she silently prayed. She opened her eyes and dispelled the memories, but none of the guilt. Emma breathed in the warm-scented wind of the jungle. *Focus*, she demanded.

More hours passed, and it was only when the sunshine dimmed did Emma become conscious of the change in the atmosphere. There was also a slight breeze now that ruffled their hair.

The broad scents of fragrant jungle blooms, rotting vegetation, animals, and brackish water were replaced with hints of ozone, as if lightning had just made jagged forks through a night sky. She noticed that the hair on her arms stood on end.

"Look."

Drake's voice jolted her out of her reverie. He held up a compass, and she saw that the arrow floated inside and never stayed on true north.

"GPS is gone to shit as well," Ajax yelled.

"Like you said," Drake observed. "The magnetic effects have distorted all our electronics."

"It's beginning," she breathed, feeling her own heartbeat quicken. "Now, we get to use what we were born with—eyes, ears, any other senses we can call on to help." Emma straightened. "But I think it's pretty clear which direction we need to head."

In the distance, the cloud was changing, growing, and now looked like a chaotic explosion as a column of cloud swirled like a tornado and now reached high into the atmosphere. Within that dark column, lightning crackled non-stop and forked downward, sideways, and even up into the sky.

"What the hell is that?" Fergus said, his mouth continuing to hang open.

"The finger of God," Juan said. "Reaching down to the earth."

"Or maybe, the devil, reaching up from Hell," Camilla added.

Juan turned and raised an eyebrow. But Camilla just clung to the small crucifix around her neck and gave him a half-smile. "Don't mind me." She turned away.

The swirling cloud began to spread out, not into the upper atmosphere, but lower like a fog that crept over the land, and at its center, the huge purple column over just one area of the jungle.

"Well, whether it's the finger of God or the Devil, it's pointing the way," Andy observed.

"Yup." Drake lifted binoculars to his eyes. "Don't like the lightning inside it; not good if we get a strike. But it has a low ceiling, and that's what we want." He lowered the glasses. "Provided the wind doesn't get too high, we'll need to rise above it soon."

"The column won't last, but the cloud will." Emma turned. "The wettest season is here. We better get everyone ready."

CHAPTER 23

Once again, Ben had covered himself head to toe in greasy mud. He belly-crawled forward and kept his eyes as slits as he lifted his head over the plateau's edge.

At this time in history, the future flat-topped mountain was only just beginning to have the surrounding jungle weathered down around it. Over the millions and millions of years to come, the jungle would sink, while the harder granite would erode more slowly, making it seem to rise like an island into the sky. But now, it was just a slightly raised area in a vast primordial jungle.

Ben knew there was something different about this raised area. Just like the surrounding jungle, it was home to all manner of creatures, hunters and the hunted. But it was also home to something that was vastly more deadly than any two-legged, razor-toothed theropod.

He glanced up through the trees and saw the thick cloud swirling above him. *It's started*, he thought, as a thrill of excitement and impatience ran through him.

The cloud was also starting to drop, creating a misted atmosphere on the plateau, and though slightly cooler, it was still dripping with humidity. He also knew that at its center, the cloudbank would break and rise. But right now, as the comet, Primordia, approached, everything was thrown into chaos—the atmosphere, the weather, the magnetic orientation of the Earth, and even time and space, as a portal or doorway to another reality was opened.

For Ben, that doorway would be to the future, his home. And in that future, the reality was a pathway to right here and now. The plateau itself was only a few square miles. The surface of that tiny landmass was thrown forward or the future backward, but only for a little over 24 hours. And at the end of that period, when the comet pulled away and the time distortion ended, the two realities went back to being ordered once again. And anything left behind on the plateau would find itself back here, just like he did.

He moved his head slowly, no fast movements, scanning the undergrowth before him. He let his eyes move over the dense jungle, the broad and fleshy leaves and bulbous hanging fruits. There were the tangling vines, some with hooked barbs that tore at the flesh, cycads, and tongue-like ferns. There were massive trees that climbed into the clouds, some recognizable as being primitive pines, ginkgos, and redwoods. Many had fungi, like flatbread growing out from their trunks, and their lower branches had what looked like strings of green pearls hanging from them.

There were also trees he was now familiar with but had no idea what names to call them. The ones with bark-like course hair, or plated scales, or even a surface that looked like popped rice.

He was horribly familiar with all of them, but he was still as much an alien in this world, as if he had crashed here in a spacecraft from another planet. Tiny, soft little human beings didn't belong here, and when their time came to rule, it would only be because the land giants had all departed into a fossilized history.

Ben licked dry lips. He knew time was his enemy now. If Emma was coming, he needed to find her quickly. But where would she be? She was a climber, so the odds were she would be coming up over the cliff edge, *somewhere*. And from there, he'd have to make some educated guesses, and try and get in her head and think like her.

Perhaps she might decide that a good place to start was somewhere they both knew—the site of their first entry. It was a familiar place and somewhere they could rendezvous. *If there was a chance she was there, then that's where I'll be too*, he thought.

It was all he had, but he couldn't help the excitement creeping back into his gut.

Ben crept up over the rim, and then scuttled in amongst the fern stems. *Slow down—no fast movements—stop and look*—he had a long way to go, but he couldn't afford to let impatience cloud his judgement.

Right now, a sixth sense made the back of his neck tingle, and he paused and hunkered down. A twig snapped behind him.

Ben spun; spear up, just as the hunter landed on his chest, crushing him flat.

The seven-foot-tall theropod had warty, pebbled skin, small eyes, and a large boxy head. It also weighed as much as a linebacker and hissed like a steam train as its dagger-like claws penetrated his flesh.

Ben felt the weight pushing the air from his lungs—one three-toed foot was on his chest, the other on his shoulder where the scythe-like daggers on its feet penetrated his flesh. He began to panic, as he knew that this would be the scout, and others of the pack would soon follow.

He stabbed upward with his spear, using his last reserves of energy. The spear dug into the creature's shoulder, but not deep enough. The hunter reached down, grabbed at it with its rows of serrated teeth, and bit right through the pole, cutting it in two. The old blade fell to the mud.

Ben had nothing left.

I was so close, he thought. *Sorry, Emma.*

CHAPTER 24

Full Comet Apparition

Comet P/2018-YG874, designate name, Primordia, was now at its perihelion or maximum observable focus as it had now reached its closest point to Earth.

The magnetic distortion had also reached its peak, but now the field generated a form of stability. The hurricane-like winds that had been roaring above the top of the plateau ceased, and the boiling clouds dropped to become a mist that moved through a primordial forest.

Torrential rain fell on the surrounding jungle, but now on the plateau top it first eased to a warm rain, then stopped, and at its center, sunlight broke through.

The season of Primordia had begun.

CHAPTER 25

"Hang on." Drake grabbed the edge of the basket and planted his legs as the balloon swung in the furious wind.

Camilla screamed and Andy threw an arm around Helen to hold her in place. Emma gritted her teeth and turned. "Drake?"

"I know." The big man nodded. "Gonna try and rise above it."

The clouds had thickened and visibility was down to around 50 feet. In addition, below and above them there was nothing. The danger now was that with the wind becoming stronger, and therefore the balloon accelerating in the air, flying blind was suicide. For all any of them knew, the plateau edge was right in front of them, and at the speed they traveled, if they collided with it, they'd either be tossed out or snagged up on a rock face.

Drake yelled at Fergus to give them some more burn, and the redheaded Special Forces soldier cranked up the propane gas burners to produce a strong jet of near colorless fire that increased the fill of the bag. In seconds, he felt them start to rise.

The balloon swung again, and he saw Emma's fingers dig into the wicker railings. The commercial balloons were great fun in less than five-mile-per-hour winds, exhilarating in five to six, but once you got over ten, they became damned dangerous.

Drake knew sensible people didn't usually go up in anything above eight. He also knew that sensible people didn't try and balloon into a prehistoric world in the middle of a cyclone.

"Fergus, *more burn*!" Drake yelled.

"You got it." Fergus shot another drought of hot air into the canopy, and their rise began to accelerate.

"Ease up," Drake called, and Fergus slowed the rate of hot air delivery. He kept his eyes on Drake, his hands on the controls. Brocke and Ajax also watched, their hands on the flap ropes, waiting for orders to tug on one or the other. But for now, they lifted, and also sailed ever northeastward—toward, he hoped, what was the top of the plateau.

The wind eased a little, but they were still trapped inside a murky whiteout. Drake bared his teeth, feeling his patience run out. "No instruments, so don't know if we're at two hundred or two thousand feet. Hard to judge rate of climb without landmarks." He scoffed. "We could be right up against the cliff edge and not even know it."

"*Quiet!*" Andy hissed.

"*Huh?*" Emma turned.

The young paleontologist held a hand up to them. "Just...quiet. *Listen.*"

He and Helen were leaning far out over the side of the basket, their heads turned. Inside, everyone was frozen now, listening.

Then they heard it.

"What the hell is *that?*" Ajax's brows snapped together.

Camilla nudged Juan, who lifted his telephoto camera and held it ready.

The sound came again—a scream, or maybe a screech. No one was able to identify it, and even Helen and Andy just looked at each other, confusion creasing their features.

Emma leaned far out of the basket, her head turning one way then the other. She spun, her face a mix of both relief and worry.

"Follow it," she yelled. "It's coming from the plateau top."

Drake pointed. "That way; Brocke, give me some starboard vent, in 3, 2, 1...*now.*"

The man pulled on a cord, and gas vented from the opposite side of the balloon. Fergus needed to give the burner some juice to compensate for the loss of hot air, and the balloon moved sideways toward the sound of the screams.

The cry came again, but this time so close it made everyone cringe back in the basket.

"I do not like this," Juan mumbled and crossed himself.

"Me either." Ajax pulled his rifle from over his shoulder and held it ready.

"Hold fire." Drake had his hand up. He cocked his head as he concentrated on tracking something.

"There's something out there," he said, and closed his eyes to concentrate.

Out in the mist, something flapped; big, heavy and leathery sounding. And it was close by.

"Oh shit." Emma turned. "*Quick!* Get us up, get us up!"

"What the hell?" Ajax pointed his gun, but there was nothing to sight on. "Can't see shit."

Drake drew his handgun and listened, trying to get his bearings. Out in the murkiness, something that sounded like a sail flapping in a strong breeze continued. It came from one side, then the other—it sounded like it was circling them.

"Fuck this," he said. "Let's get above this crap. Fergus, take us up a few hundred more feet—give me a ten-second burn...*now*."

The redheaded man twisted a knob and pushed a lever forward to the max on the burner, expressing a flame and jet of hot air. The basket immediately grew heavy beneath their feet as they shot upward.

Whatever was out there flapped again, and this time it was so close that it threw a massive shadow over them. Camilla shrieked and backed away, bumping into Fergus who elbowed her aside so he could concentrate on his job and watch Drake for instructions.

"Eyes out, boys." Drake held his gun loosely, and Brocke and Ajax did the same, the barrels pointed out into the swirling cloud beyond the edge of their basket.

"What are they?" Juan asked.

Drake shook his head. "Dunno; but they're big whatever they are."

Helen's eyes were on Emma, and she pointed. "You know, don't you?" The woman tilted her head. "Are they what I think they are?"

Emma had her own gun drawn and turned to look out into the impenetrable cloud. "We never got close to them. But we saw them in the skies. Pterosaurs."

"Terror-what?" Ajax yelled back, his lips curled.

"Flying dinosaurs," Andy replied. "Well, flying reptiles actu—"

"They can fucking *fly*?" Ajax just shook his head, and everyone turned back to the cloud.

"Why does the cloud suddenly seem creepier now I know that?" Brocke said, chuckling nervously.

"How big are they? Will they attack us?" Drake asked, trying to see through the billowing mist.

"They were undoubtedly territorial," Andy replied. "And some of them were very big."

"Bigger than a condor or albatross?" Brocke asked.

"Well, the sea-going albatross has the largest wingspan of any living bird today," Andy began. "They can spread wings up to twelve feet, tip to tip. But they usually only weigh in at under twenty six pounds."

Helen turned. "But there were species of pterosaur that were literally flying giants. They weighed in at seven hundred pounds, and one of them, the *Arambourgiania*, had a wingspan of over forty feet, and on the ground would have stood taller than a giraffe."

"Okay, so big then," Brocke stated, nodding.

"Good. 'Cause, the bigger they are, the bigger the target." Ajax grinned cruelly.

And the bigger they are, the more damage they can do to the balloon, Drake thought. He spoke over his shoulder. "Fergus, give me another ten-second blast. I don't want one of those flying giraffes crashing into us."

It was too late. An enormous shadow came out of the swirling mist and materialized as a leathery vision from hell. It hit the side of the basket and clung there like an obscene bat. A massive wedge-shaped head, furious red eyes, and a beak three feet long lined with backward-pointing teeth lunged inside.

Screams, yells, and the screeching of something from Earth's dawn caused a chaotic panic in the crowded basket.

It's a man in a Halloween mask, Drake thought insanely. For the first time in decades, he felt the electric jolt of pure fear run through him. It looked like a giant man in a leathery suit and weird ugly mask that was clinging to the side of their basket. And the bastard must have been heavy as it dragged down one of their sides.

"Out of the way!" Drake yelled as he ducked and weaved, gun up, trying to take a shot.

Juan screamed as the beak opened and snapped shut on his arm, and then tugged. His feet came off the ground, and Brocke dived and grabbed one of his ankles. Emma did the same to the other leg and a tug of war ensued for a few seconds.

"Hit the deck," Drake yelled.

Camilla, Helen, and Andy dove to the floor, and gunfire rang out as Ajax, Brocke, and Drake poured dozens of rounds into the thing. Blood spurted, the screech turned to a scream of pain as the massive creature let go, and Juan fell back to the floor of the basket, wailing and gripping a torn arm.

Emma jumped up and peered over the side in time to see the huge body fall away in the swirling cloud.

"Jesus Christ," Fergus yelled. "A fucking monster."

Drake still had his gun pointed out at the boiling fog as more huge shadows began to loom.

"Fergus, get us out of here, *now*."

Fergus pulled hard on the throttle lever, and gas jetted out like a dragon's roar. The balloon jerked upward so fast it made the group hunker down to maintain their balance.

Emma gripped one of the ropes to stay upright and also had her M4 carbine under her arm and her legs braced. Between Drake, herself, Brocke, and Ajax, they had all four quadrants covered, and in another few moments, the looming shadows were left behind.

"I see sky," Fergus yelled.

"Thank the Father, Son, and Holy Ghost," Camilla stammered.

Emma saw she was holding a cloth against Juan's arm that was already stained scarlet. Her lips moved in silent prayer.

"Let me help." Helen scooted over and peeled it back. "Okay." She pulled out the first-aid kit.

Emma knelt beside her. "Bad?" She saw underneath the man was a growing stain of dark blood on the basket's wicker flooring.

"Gonna need stitches, and…" she rummaged, "…yes, we have a needle and thread in the kit."

Helen went back to feeling up and down the lacerated arm. "Doesn't feel like a break, so that's a good thing. Hold your breath." She liberally poured iodine onto a cloth and wiped it over the gashes.

Juan grimaced and sucked in a breath.

"Can you move your fingers?" Helen asked.

The cameraman wiggled all five and nodded. "Yes."

"That's good; also means there's probably no tendon damage." She held a cloth on the wound and lunged forward to grab Camilla's hand.

"Here, keep your hand pressed down here." Once again, she rummaged through the kit. "Damn, no morphine, so…"

She held out three oxycodone to Juan. "Take these. I'm going to have to stitch it and wrap it tight. You're losing too much blood."

"Yes, please, go ahead." He threw down the tablets dry and swallowed several times to force them down. Juan then tugged the remains of his now tattered and very red sleeve up as high as he could manage.

Helen expertly threaded a needle with nylon twine, and then eased Camilla's hand away. She squeezed the folds of ripped flesh together, pushed the needle right through, and then began to sew, pulling the ragged lips of the wound tightly closed as she went.

Juan's brows came together and his lips pressed so hard they went white, but to his credit, he never made a sound.

In another few moments, she had bandaged it and then rubbed his shoulder. "Now that's a scar with a story behind it."

Juan held out his arm so Emma, Helen, and Camilla could pull him to his feet. He patted the bandage and wore a devilish smile. "I'm going to be famous." He staggered for a moment. "Oops."

"Easy, might be a little shock setting in." Helen hung onto him.

Juan gripped her arm to steady himself. After a moment, he looked up into her face. "Thank you." He held on, and the corner of his mouth turned up. "You are a very good woman. Are you single?"

Camilla groaned. "He's back to his old self."

Helen slapped his shoulder. "I'm sure it's just the oxy talking. Let me know if it gets itchy or the pain increases. We don't know what that big guy might have left behind when it bit you."

Blue sky opened above them, and sunlight streamed down on top of the balloon. Drake took one last look around, and then reholstered his gun. He eased forward to look out and upward, feeling the dry sunshine on his face for a moment, before facing down. As he did, he slipped a little on Juan's blood on the basket floor. First chance he got, he'd clean that up. If Emma was right about there being big predators on the plateau, they didn't want fresh blood spread over their home base.

Drake also saw that Juan was up cradling his arm, but his face was still pale. He came through it okay and didn't think shock would be a problem. The Special Forces soldier looked over the side and down again—below them, the thick clouds were like a field of purple cotton. And within the boiling, angry mass, lightning forked to light up portions as though there were Christmas lights hidden in there somewhere.

"No way we're dropping back down into that," Ajax seethed. "Freaking nightmare."

"What put you off?" Fergus grinned. "The zero visibility, high winds, or flying monsters?"

"Fuck you," Ajax fumed.

"He's right," Drake observed. "Can't chance dropping into that cauldron again." As he watched, the entire mass slowly rotated, like dirty bathwater circling a plug.

"There." Emma pointed.

Drake saw it. "Fergus, Brocke, 10 o'clock."

All other heads turned to where Emma was pointing. The dark and slowly turning clouds seemed to dip into a sort of vortex. Fergus and

Brocke opened and closed flaps, expertly maneuvering the balloon closer. It took them another 30 minutes until they edged over the vortex.

"Ho-*oooly* shit." Andy grinned. "I think I can see jungle down there...and a lake. But it's sort of ...distorted, oily."

"I expected that," Emma said. "I believe there's some sort of barrier, like a partition layer, magnetic waves or something, between our time and the past. It's probably what stops those pterodons from flying away. We'll need to pass through it."

"Cool," Andy said and turned back to hang over the basket's side.

Drake leaned further out and held his binoculars to his eyes. "No clearings for landings that I can see." He looked to Emma. "Were there any you can recall?"

Emma bobbed her head. "The only open spaces we encountered were at the jungle's end—right on the plateau edge."

"That's where you said it ended up becoming like a hurricane?" Ajax threw in.

"That's right." Emma turned. "Hopefully, we'll be gone long before then."

Drake was looking down through the binoculars again. "It's not a huge plateau to search, so the plan is we're in and out quickly."

"Not too quickly," Andy said.

Drake saw Emma turn away. *She's hiding something*, he thought. He didn't like it. *Lack of information on a dangerous mission got people killed.*

"We're over the center, boss," Fergus intoned. "What are your orders?"

Drake looked to Emma. "Okay?"

She nodded.

"Take her down, Mr. O'Reilly."

"Aye, aye." He opened the top bag vent and let out some hot air. Immediately, the balloon started to drop in the air. "And, going down."

"*Hoo-wee*. Next stop, ladies stockings, haberdashery, and freaking dinosaurs, man." Ajax grinned ear to ear.

*****

Emma gripped the edge of the basket hard as the balloon dropped into the funnel-like vortex in the clouds. Her heart hammered in her chest, and even though she had been mentally preparing herself for a decade, now that she was actually doing it, a growing ball of nausea in her stomach told her she was fooling herself to believe she had it all under control.

She also knew that once down there, it wasn't the plateau at all. In fact, it had seemed more like a tiny slice of an entire world, not ours, and so ancient as to be unrecognizable to tiny, soft, and modern creatures like us.

"Alright, ladies and gentlemen, would everyone be ready for a fast disembark when we hit the ground?" Drake said. "We don't know what we might encounter, but as we'll be coming down big and slow, if anything looks up, we might be perceived as some sort of big fat bird coming in to roost."

"You mean like something's big fat dinner?" Camilla asked.

Drake just shrugged, but Emma knew everyone got the point. Backpacks were checked, loaded, and zipped. The civilians' weapons were holstered and anything not secured was strapped down. The soldiers rechecked their weapons and held them ready.

The balloon approached the oily film-like layer that almost seemed like a cap over the land below, and as the basket touched it, it actually slowed in the air as though it was a type of membrane. Helen reached over and stuck a hand out as the basket settled through it like they were sinking into it.

"It's sort of like…thick oil. But it's dry." She wiggled her fingers in the air as the basket eased down through the layer, a little like it had landed on the ocean and was now slowly sinking.

"More like some sort of distortion layer," Emma said. "Between our time and theirs."

Helen frowned as she leaned over. "I can hear something."

The balloon settled further down into the layer by another few feet.

"Sort of like, *um*, whistling." Helen looked up. "Or howling."

"Howling?" Drake's eyes widened. "*Wind.*"

They dropped all the way through the membrane layer, and then all hell broke loose.

The balloon and basket were grabbed by hurricane-force winds that acted like a mighty hand pulling and tearing at them. Immediately, the bag of the balloon was dragged down, and the entire basket went sideways. Bodies slid and crashed to the side, and equipment also skidded, smashing into them and also some bouncing and then disappearing over the side railing.

Juan yelled in despair as his camera case bounced once, twice, and then sailed into space.

"*Hang on!*" Drake yelled over the roar of the wind.

Emma screwed her eyes to slits and hung onto one of the basket's ropes as she tried to remain upright. The wind was like a living thing; it was loud, had a physical presence, and seemed goddamn angry.

It became obvious that the strange distortion effect over the land not only separated the two worlds, but also had a layer of super agitated air between them, like the very planes of reality were rebelling against each other.

In the next second, Andy lost his grip on the basket's railing, fell, and then slid into Fergus' legs, knocking him over. As the soldier's hands were knocked away from the burner, the jet shot up to its maximum three-foot flame.

The envelope of the balloon was treated with significant flame retardant, so they didn't catch fire like the Hindenburg Airship. But that doesn't mean they can't burn—they can, but instead of catching fire, they melt, and to Emma's horror, she watched as a four-foot hole was seared through the side of the balloon.

Gas heaved out, and the bag began to rapidly deflate as the wind continued to pummel the huge floating sack, squeezing even more of the hot air from it.

The balloon immediately dropped a hundred feet, as people yelled, screamed, and tried to hang on. Eventually, the balancing act between lighter-than-air travel, and gravity, is always won by gravity.

The upside was they passed out of the wind agitation layer, but they were coming down now at a rate of about 10 miles per hour, and as the balloon continued to deflate, they accelerated, going from balloon rate, to parachute rate, to falling at a rate that was going to mean serious injury, or death.

Drake struggled to his feet. He dragged himself to the basket's edge and peered over.

"*Coming down…!*" and then, "*…on water!*"

Oh shit, no, Emma thought.

"Bra-*aaace!*" The big man bent his knees.

The basket struck hard, and it was like a bomb going off, as they were all crushed flat to the bottom of the basket.

And they bounced. Bodies, equipment and supplies lifted and

dropped again. Juan, who could only hold on with one arm, landed on top of Emma and his elbow smashed her lip, cutting it.

They were all thrown to one side of the large basket, and it immediately caused it to tip. Water began to pour over the side as they settled.

Emma pushed the big Venezuelan off and climbed to her feet. They were toward the middle of a lake, *the lake*, and she quickly looked one way, then the other to get her bearings.

"Out, out, out." She grabbed Juan and dragged him up. "Swim, swim…" She pointed to the closest bank. "Drake, to the shore, *there*. Fast."

The soldiers were tossing packs over the side, and also helped in pushing people out. In another few seconds, the basket was inundated and beginning to sink.

She went over the side and found herself next to Drake. "Well, we're here, and at least we're alive," he said glumly.

Emma's head spun left and right. "We've got to get out of the water."

"We will." He trod water beside her. "But we need our equipment."

"No, you don't understand." She grabbed at him. "Something…" She coughed out some water. "…lives in here."

Drake stared for a second or two before he got it. "*Jesus Christ*; everyone goddamn *swim!*"

He yelled as he watched the balloon start to sink. "Hurry, get away from the bag when it starts to go down. It'll snag you and take you with it."

Drake trod water for a moment as he watched his men set off, pushing packs before them, or stroking one-armed. Andy and Helen were already swimming away strongly. But Camilla was struggling and looked like she barely knew how to keep afloat let alone swim.

Emma headed for her, but Drake headed her off. "I'll get Camilla, you get to the shore. You're bleeding. *Go.*"

She felt her lip, and the sting of the cut there—blood in the water—bad news. She started to swim, now feeling vulnerable in the open lake. The sun shone down strongly, but below her, there was nothing but a deep, dark blackness. Added to that, it was brackish and warm—*blood warmth*, she thought morbidly.

They were strung out in the water, separated now by a good 100 feet. Some of the soldiers were close to the bank, and in fact, it looked like Brocke had already clambered up and dropped off his package.

She was mid-way. Behind her, the balloon was just a colored lump at water level, already being dragged down by the basket. Debris littered the surface.

Well back, she saw that Drake now had Camilla on his back. The woman had her arms around his neck and the big man breaststroked with her along for the ride.

"Dammit." Emma hovered in the water. Even further back, Juan splashed, only just staying above the surface. He held his bandaged arm up, as though trying to keep the already-soaked bandages dry. But even from where she floated, she could see that the gauze was leaking red.

"Just damn swim." She grimaced, and then turned about, indecision wracking her. She was about to try and swim over to get him, when she heard splashing behind her. Emma spun, eyes wide.

Brocke grinned and motioned with his head. "Head in, Emma, I got this." He winked. "Used to be the state swim champ."

She felt relieved, and before she could even thank him, the young soldier put his head down and powered on.

"Keep moving!" Drake yelled to her, spitting water as he tried to keep himself and Camilla afloat.

Emma nodded and was about to turn back, when she spotted the large, dark lump on the surface. She felt a shock run right through her body.

She prayed it was something that came down with them and had floated away but knew that was a lie. She froze, and all she could do was watch.

The thing was big, and she had no idea what was still below the surface, but the one thing she was sure of was that thing didn't come from their balloon and sure as hell wasn't there when they came down.

Emma continued to stare, and her chin began to tremble even though the water was like a warm bath. Then, to her horror, the small island began to sink, ever so slowly, and just as the lump vanished, it was immediately replaced by the familiar V-shaped water pattern of something moving just beneath the surface. And its destination was clear—straight at Juan.

"He-*eeey*!"

She forced her body to unlock, and then launched herself high in the water, waving madly to Juan and to Brocke. Everyone else was on the bank now and could only watch. Drake caught up to her and turned.

"It's going for them," she spluttered.

Drake pushed the woman off his shoulders and Camilla immediately latched onto Emma. The soldier then dragged his M4 rifle off his back and hung in the water, arms up and the gun pointed.

"Goddamnit, *no shot*." He turned to Emma. "Get to the bank, we can't do shit here." Then he spun to his remaining men on the water's edge, yelling so loud it echoed across the lake.

"Give Brocke some cover. We got company."

*****

It both heard and felt the impact through the water. It sensed the thing that struck was large, so for the first few seconds, it slid below the surface to hide.

The freshwater mosasaur was a smaller variety to its giant sea-going cousins, but was still nearly 40 feet long, squat, and powerful. It had four paddle-like flippers that were the last vestiges of limbs, plus a scythe-like tail akin to that of a dolphin. It was a powerful water hunter, and an expert ambush predator.

It knew that the thing that landed would be either a threat or food. And as no attack came, it decided it might be prey instead of predator.

Then it began to feel the thrashing of smaller creatures on the surface, and gently rose up to investigate. Though the huge lake had many varieties of fish, it supplemented its diet by also taking the land-based animals that wandered too close to the water.

It saw the thrashing bodies, strung out in a long line, leaving a large mass behind. Its long tail thrashed and propelled it forward, with just the top of its head showing. As it approached, it moved into attack-ambush mode and dropped down another foot, so the only telltale sign was a V-shaped wave on the surface as it closed in.

When it was within 50 feet of the creatures, it then smelled the blood in the water—rich, salty, and nutritious. The things *were* edible. It selected its target and began to accelerate.

*****

Brocke reached Juan and pulled the man close. "Gotcha, big guy. Gotta get outta here now."

Juan held up his torn hand and arm, still spluttering. "Can't swim, can't."

Brocke grabbed him and immediately saw the idiot had one of his huge cameras still hanging around his neck. He grabbed it and ripped it up and over his head, tossing it over his shoulder where it splashed and vanished.

"*Hey*." Juan's eyes widened.

"*Shut up*." Brocke grabbed his shirt. "Listen, there's something in the lake. You swim, and you don't look back. Understand."

"Something in the water?" Juan's brow furrowed and his head snapped around. "Shit."

Brocke pushed him at the shoreline. "*Just swim*."

Juan threw one arm over, and then the other that resulted in a shortened deformed stroke from his wounded arm, but at least he was moving. Brocke hung back for a moment, letting his face sink to nose level and his eyes just on the surface. He looked along its top, scanning about. He couldn't see anything. He knew that might not be a good thing.

He felt his testicles start to shrivel and knew there was nothing but deep, dark water underneath them.

"Fuck it, I'm outta here." He started to swim as well.

He kept his head above the water as he stroked this time. He didn't want to outpace Juan, but he also wanted to see and hear what was going on. Maybe, he hoped, the thing was spending its time investigating the balloon as it sank. Maybe, he hoped even harder, it got caught up in the rigging and was being dragged down to the bottom.

He looked ahead to Juan who was now only 10 feet in front of him. The man's wounded arm was still bandaged, and the blood that had soaked it had now washed away…into the water.

Please, I hope whatever this thing is, it's not like a shark who can smell the blood in the water, he prayed.

There was something about being a soldier that had seen active service, and in extreme hot zones, that seemed to heighten the senses to danger; call it a soldier's sixth sense. And right now, those sensory alarms were screaming in his head.

There was clear and present danger, and a pending attack. Brocke felt a calm come over him and he stopped and trod water, bicycling his legs to keep his upper body above the surface. He drew his M4 from over his shoulder.

He spun, and not six feet away, the thing's head surfaced. It was like a smooth alligator, but bigger, *so much bigger*.

From where the eyes sat toward the back of the skull, he could just make out about six feet of snout and jaws. The thing turned a little, regarding him with one large, predatorial eye.

Any normal man would have been frozen in fear or been reduced to a screaming pile of insanity. But instead, Brocke kicked hard in the water and launched himself high. As he lifted, he pointed his weapon and yelled a battle cry that carried right across the lake.

The creature also lunged, perhaps stirred by the activity. It became a test of which killer would be quicker.

Brocke never got to fire a shot.

*****

On the shoreline, they watched with a mix of horror and fury. Helen had hands up on each side of her head, and a small sound escaped her lips like that from a tiny, frightened animal. Camilla sat down and turned away, her lips moving rapidly. But Andy was riveted.

Drake, Fergus, and Ajax had waded back into the water, guns tight to their shoulders, but the attack was too far out for them to do anything but watch, teeth bared in impotent rage.

Emma stared as the animal surged and then jaws that were longer than the man sprung open and closed over Brocke, snapping shut with an audible *clack* like a bear trap closing. The massive beast's momentum took it upward and its huge body lumped in the water before diving again. A tail as long as a Buick flapped in the air, and then in only a few more seconds, the surface of the lake returned to calm.

Drake lowered his weapon and let his eyes drop to Juan who was nearing the shore. He half-turned to his men.

"Get him out."

"What the fuck was that?" Ajax's voice was high.

"Freshwater mosasaur," Helen breathed. "Probably."

"They're usually sea-going creatures, and those guys can get to seventy feet." Andy stared out into the lake. "But they also lived in large bodies of fresh water. And grew pretty big there as well."

"No shit," Ajax seethed, and then spun back to the lake. "Fu-*uuuuuuk*!" He continued to roar his curse as he fired a long burst into the water, throwing up a zipper of sprays out to where Brocke had been taken.

"*Stow that!*" Drake yelled.

The young soldier spun to Emma and jabbed his finger at her. "She knew. She fucking knew that thing was in there."

"Shut it." Drake showed his teeth. "In case you hadn't noticed, we're not in fucking Kansas anymore."

Ajax still stared from under lowered brows. "If we had—"

"*Nothing,*" Drake cut him off. "So what if she did? We crashed, remember? We weren't supposed to be anywhere near a goddamn lake."

Ajax continued to glare as Fergus helped Juan up onto the bank, and his jaws tightened for a moment before he marched over and jammed the muzzle of his rifle into the Venezuelan's stomach.

"Why didn't it take this fat piece of shit? He's the one bleeding and probably attracted it."

"So are you," Emma said softly.

Ajax looked down his body to see blood seeping through his pants. He slapped the wound hard. "Fuck it." He turned away, cursing even more.

Drake looked down at Juan who was now up onto the bank and lying down, breathing hard.

"Brocke, our brave soldier and friend, died doing what we were designed to do, what we were bred to do—protect people." He looked up into Emma's eyes. "That is our lot." He turned to Fergus first, who nodded, and then to the sullen Ajax.

Emma looked around, trying to get her bearings. It was the same, and it was different to how she remembered: *alien.*

Huge trees launched up into the sky, but between them, there were stands of strange plants that looked like 30-foot-high green pompoms on sticks. Spiky-looking cycads spread wide on the ground, in between ferns with strappy or broad, pulpy fronds, and stuff that looked like hanging beads that might have been fruit, seedpods, or maybe even insect eggs, for all she knew.

Emma sighed. "We need to move. And we need to be silent. There are hunters everywhere."

"Equipment and supplies check, *everyone,*" Drake said, and the group quickly looked over what they managed to salvage.

Emma looked back out to the lake. A few packages, boxes, and assorted flotsam and jetsam bobbed there. They might as well have been on the far side of the moon, as no one was going to get them.

Fergus squatted by his packs, forearms on his thighs. "Good ammunition for the M4s, we've got a dozen grenades for the launchers, and a few spare mags for the SIG Sauer; not so bad." He looked up. "A defensible ordnance. Not enough to make war, but enough to stand our ground."

Drake grunted. "Good. We only need to do that for twenty-four hours."

Andy and Helen sorted through some other packs. "A bottle of water each, water purifiers, and some protein bars." She sighed. "I've got some personal medical supplies, but the medical kit wasn't stored away after Juan, so…"

"So it's lost." Drake exhaled through his nose. "Okay, overall, could have been a lot worse."

Ajax scoffed. "Jesus, man, are you missing the fucking elephant in the phone booth here?" His face was flushed and eyes wide. "The balloon's gone; you know, that big fucking thing we were gonna fly out in?"

"We climb down," Fergus said evenly.

"Oh yeah, how? If Ben really has been here ten years, why didn't he climb down then? He was top-notch Special Forces guy. If anyone coulda done it, he could have."

"You don't get it, do you?" Emma stepped forward. "If Ben had climbed down at any time other than when the portal was open, he'd be climbing down into the world as it was a 100 million years ago."

"So he needs to try it now?" Andy queried.

"Exactly," Emma replied. "Now that the two time zones have been thrust up against each other."

"Now?" Helen repeated, her gaze flat. "Now, when the plateau is as high as the top of the Empire State Building."

Emma turned, her voice quieter. "We'll find a way."

"Oh, we're fucked." Ajax threw his hands up and walked in a circle.

"We're alive. So I think you just won the lottery," Emma said. "Coulda been worse…just ask Brocke."

Ajax's eyes bulged for a moment, but he kept his mouth shut.

"We gotta move," Drake said. He turned to Emma. "You think Ben might have tried to get to the cliff edge? Where you scaled down?"

She nodded. "It's where I'd go."

"Then that's where we try first. How far?" Drake asked.

Emma pointed. "Miles, I don't know. This isn't part of the jungle we went through. But it took us about four hours to get there. We followed a stream…but that was a mistake."

"Why?" Helen asked.

Emma turned. "Because that was where the snake found us."

Helen stared. "The snake, *our* snake?"

Emma nodded.

"Oh Jesus." Helen rubbed her face.

Andy put his arm around her shoulders. "This is crazy, but I want to see it, and I also *don't* want to see it. I can't help it, I'm a scientist."

Helen gave him a horrified look. "Not sure I do now."

"Trust me; you *don't* want to see it either," Emma said, sounding wearied.

Andy looked around and saw everyone's expressions. "Okay, yeah, well then let's avoid following the river."

They loaded up, Drake checked the group, and then ordered Fergus to lead them out. Emma stood staring back out over the water, and he came closer.

"I was going to go back for Juan," she said. "But Brocke took my place."

Drake exhaled and nodded. "Well then… I guess it was just his time, and not yours." He turned to her. "Five minutes in, and we're already one down," he said softly. "I don't intend to lose any more."

She half-turned to him for a moment and studied his face. After a few more seconds, she just grunted and turned back to the water. She bet he didn't intend to lose Brocke either. *This place makes the decisions, not us*, she thought bleakly.

"Come on, let's catch up." She headed into the jungle.

CHAPTER 26

Drake crouched and scanned the undergrowth. Jungles were crap places to make war. There were so many potential places of concealment that it rendered the human eye next to useless. As a Special Forces soldier, he was trained to identify shapes—heads, faces, human forms, even if those shapes were fragmented and broken up by camouflage. But in here, that's not the type of adversaries they were trying to avoid.

In jungles, human camouflage was reaching new levels of sophistication thanks largely to technology. He heard that the next thing to come off the production line was real invisibility tech that grabbed surrounding landscapes and projected the images onto a uniform. The result was that you didn't just blend into the environment, you became part of it.

But evolution, not technology, ruled in this place. Things had evolved to hide, and wait, and not be seen while they were doing it. Drake had been in jungles all over the world and witnessed how some creatures were able to change the colors of their skin, use weird body shapes to merge with their surroundings, and even pretend to be something else entirely.

He'd read Emma's report. And basically, right here, right now, there were animals that had that ability, except were a hundred times bigger and meaner. And that worried the hell out of him.

He looked down again at the print in the mud—three-toed, many inches deep, and had to be close to six feet long; whatever made it weighed several tons.

Drake turned to the group; all had eyes on him bar Camilla and Juan. The cameraman was sitting down and looking flushed in the face. Camilla was holding a water bottle to his lips. The guy had lost plenty of blood and now was being asked to push himself beyond his limits—*tough*; there was no other option.

Drake clicked his fingers to get Helen's attention and waved her over. Emma and Andy came with her.

He pointed to the mud. "Like your expert opinion here."

"Jesus." Helen touched the print gently with the tips of her fingers.

"Big theropod carnivore." Andy rested on his haunches. "*Aucasaurus*?"

"*Hmm*, no, I think bigger," Helen replied.

"*Carnotaurus*? That bad boy was a local down here and grew to thirty feet in length. Stood nearly ten feet tall and weighed in at about three tons." Andy raised his eyebrows.

"Look; this is hard soil, and check again the depths of the print." Helen turned to look at her brother. "Think even bigger."

"Oh wow," Andy breathed. "*Giganotosaurus*."

"Okay, I only got the first part of that." Fergus crouched beside them. "But I'm betting anything with the word *gigantic* on the front of it has got to be bad news."

"The baddest," Andy replied. "It was the biggest shark-toothed dinosaur that lived in these parts during the Late Cretaceous Period."

"Shark-toothed, *huh*?" Fergus' mouth twisted. "Well, that sounds fucked up."

"Yeah, and I hear it only ate redheads." Drake raised a brow at him.

"Ate everything," Andy said. "Had an oversized head and jaws, giving it massive bite power, plus ten-inch-long serrated teeth."

"*Jesus*." Fergus ran a hand up through his sweaty hair and Andy went on.

"Walked on two large and powerful hind legs, small three-clawed arms, and was up to forty feet long, fifteen feet high." The young paleontologist made both his hands into three-fingered hooks. "And even though it weighed in at about thirteen tons, it was extremely fast and agile."

"Yeah, well that motherfucker is going to be even faster when it gets a grenade up its ass. Let's see it run fast with a three-foot hole in its gut." Ajax grinned down at them like a death's head.

"Were they solitary hunters?" Emma asked.

"We think so," Helen replied. "The mega alphas tended to be territorial, so they pushed anything else out, even their own kind. Mating season excluded."

"Good." Emma looked up. "The big guys were a nightmare. But it was the smaller ones that hunted in packs that were the real threat. They moved like greased lightning. Hard to outrun them."

"That fast?" Fergus asked.

"Think of a cheetah crossed with an alligator." Emma gave him a humorless smile.

Fergus turned to Drake. "Thank you for inviting me."

Drake scoffed. "This from the guy who said he missed the action only six months back." He looked across to Emma. "Anything else you can tell us, based on your experience?"

Emma thought for a moment. "Their colors are more striking and varied than you can imagine."

"Like you said about the *Titanoboa*?" Andy queried.

"The what?" Ajax asked.

"The snake." Drake frowned. "You read Emma's report, right?"

The huge soldier just shrugged. "Some of it."

"Good prep, soldier. Since when did you start going on missions without doing your homework?" Drake glared.

"One, this ain't a mission, and two, who thought any of this shit was actually going to be real?" He glared back.

"In this place, reality comes at you fast," Emma said dismissively, and then turned back to Andy. "As for body markings, mostly striped or blotched with colors ranging from brick red, to shades of green and brown."

"If they're motionless in dappled light, they'll be invisible," Drake said.

"Until you walk right into them," Andy said.

"I read Emma's notes on the snake. Is it as big a threat to us as she says?" Fergus stared hard at the young scientist.

Andy took in a deep breath. "The *Titanoboa* was the largest snake that ever lived. Its fossil remains were found right around these parts. They were deep in a coalmine. At this point, we don't know if it was down there due to sedimentary settling, it lived there, or just crawled down there to die." He rested on his haunches and picked up a stick. He cleared away some dirt and began to draw.

"One of the biggest snakes alive today is the Asiatic reticulated python. Grows to about thirty feet in length and can weigh in at five hundred pounds." He had drawn a stick figure of a man, and a squiggly line, the snake, next to him. The snake was enormous and five times the size of the human. He looked up at Ajax. "About twice your body weight I'd say."

"Big sucker," Ajax replied.

"It certainly is…today." Andy grinned up at him. "But it's an earthworm compared to what existed in our primordial past." He began to draw again. "Those fossils the scientists discovered in that mine just a few years back had paleontologists estimating its length to be well over fifty feet. But here's the kicker, they had no idea whether the specimen found might even have been representative of the largest of its kind, so they could have grown bigger, *much* bigger."

Andy finished his drawing and looked up, brows raised. "Imagine, a snake fifty, seventy, feet long?" He dropped the stick. "They called the snake *Titanoboa*; the name says it all. And it wasn't just long, but solid muscle that was as thick around as a small car."

Fergus rubbed his face hard, and Ajax seemed to be brooding as he took it all in. The picture now showed a monstrous snake; thick, powerful, that made the stick figure look like a bite-sized toy.

"One more thing," Emma said. "It wasn't slow moving. It was quick, *very* quick. For something so big, it moved like lightning."

"And thus ends the motivation session." Drake checked his weapon and cradled it in his arms. "We need to do our jobs, and then work on getting the hell home. Any questions?"

Andy got to his feet and wiped his hands off. "I still want to see one." He looked at Helen. "Just a glimpse...but from a distance." He smiled crookedly.

"*No*," Emma said. "Just forget it. If you see it, it means it'll have already have seen you. And then you're dead."

"Well, maybe," Andy said, and his eyes gleamed. "But just imagine a snake that big."

"I don't need to imagine," Emma shot back.

Andy continued to beam, and Fergus nudged Drake with an elbow. "Jesus, look at this kid, will ya? He's lovin' being here."

"Beats working in a museum." Andy waggled his eyebrows.

Drake sighed. "Come on, move out."

CHAPTER 27

Ben slithered through the undergrowth and stopped to rest as his head spun from dizziness. The wounds on his chest felt like they were on fire. Three deep gauges, and he was sure he had fractured ribs from that big bastard landing on him.

But just as big fish ate small fish, it was also true that big fish got eaten by even bigger fish. While Ben was being mauled, and he thought his number was finally up, something had burst from the jungle and scooped up the seven-foot-tall theropod standing on his chest like it weighed nothing. The others of its pack had fled screeching in panic back into the undergrowth.

Ben didn't wait to hand out thank yous, but instead ignored the pain and ran between a pair of clawed feet that must have been six feet long. One thing he'd found out about being in the vicinity of a big carnivore was that everything else headed for the hills. So the jungle had been empty on his blind run.

But now, he had other priorities. Wounds festered, and even a minor cut could mean blood poisoning if not attended to.

He slithered on, finally seeing what he was looking for. He pulled himself into the patch of thick grasses, choosing the greenest stalks and carefully tugging them from the damp soil. He was careful not to dislodge the bulbs as they came up. He quickly shelled one the size of his thumb, and then stuck it in his mouth, grinding the bitter plant root down to pulp, and then spat the mush back onto his hand.

Maybe one day the plant would evolve into an onion or garlic. But as he hoped when he first found them, whatever it was, it was close enough to contain a potent chemical called allicin that was a powerful natural antibiotic.

With his vision blurring from pain, Ben smeared the salve into the chest wounds, feeling the agony as he rubbed the bitter mush into the torn flesh. The extra bonus was the odor of the root masked the smell of open wounds. He chewed some more, his jaw working slowly as he made sure to liberally coat all his wounds. He then finally tugged up some more bulbs and stuck them into a sack which was the last shred of his shirt that had long given up as a garment of wear.

Ben's head swam, and he crawled and dragged himself under a

huge palm frond, hoping he was concealed as he spun away into unconsciousness.

CHAPTER 28

The trek was slow, arduous, and hampered by the thick tangle of vines, bracken-like fern fronds, and the occasional hooked thorn that punctured even their tough jungle clothing. It was also slowed by their caution, as Drake would ease through the tangle, rather than hack his way.

Fergus was taking his turn out at point and was first into the clearing. "Ho-*oooly* shit." He turned and pointed out the obvious.

"This is bullshit." Ajax's lip curled as he also stared. "This doesn't make sense; there were people back then? I thought that evolution stuff told us humans didn't appear until only a few thousand years ago."

"Millions actually. In fact, 4.4 millions," Andy added.

Fergus turned to Emma. "This can't be real."

The building was ancient, massive stone blocks, columns and mighty carvings, but now eroded and beginning to crumble.

"I'm guessing it can and it can't be," Drake said. "Just like us being here can't be real."

"He's right," Emma agreed. "The way we climbed up originally began in a secret passage in a structure like this. The locals, perhaps the Pemon's ancestors, knew about this place and the wettest season. We think they'd been coming up here for hundreds or maybe even thousands of years and feeding the creatures."

"Magnificent," Helen remarked. "Of course they'd feed them, by sacrificing themselves to them. But in their minds, they were honoring them. And if they built this, even the hardest of stones would weather down to nothing by the time it became our present time."

Once again, on each side of the doorway was the coiled behemoth strangling another mighty creature.

"The gargoyles—the snake and the beast," Andy said. "Their god of gods."

"So where are they now?" Ajax asked. "The people, I mean."

Emma snorted softly. "Ever heard that expression about feeding the crocodile, in the hope it'll eat you last?" She turned to him. "I'm betting it finally got around to eating them."

"Are they the same as the ones you encountered on the jungle floor?" Drake asked.

Emma nodded slowly. "The same basic form; the same Amerindian style, part Aztec, part Mayan, part Olmec. But there were also glyphs and carvings that were nothing like either." She narrowed her eyes. "But these statues are a little more rough-hewn, and that might be because they were constructing them in an environment a million times more hostile, and so might have been a little rushed."

Helen nodded. "It's not really my field, but I'd bet money on them being the same."

"Good," Drake replied.

They peered out from behind their curtain of foliage across the clearing. Hidden insects buzzed, chirruped, and hummed in the undergrowth and also in the thick canopy overhead. Bars of sunshine threw down columns of light between the trees, and the occasional leathery-winged creature darted from tree branch to tree branch above them.

Drake and Fergus used their binoculars to get a close-up view of the temple structure, while Ajax watched their backs. Emma did the same, but Drake noticed she seemed to be more interested in scanning the treetops.

The Special Forces soldier looked for unusual shapes, colors, or anything out of the ordinary. The problem was, to his modern brain, everything in this place was out of the ordinary.

"I got nothing," Fergus said, and he did another sweep.

"I don't like it. Why don't we just go around it?" Ajax said over his shoulder. "Stay low, stay in cover. We ain't here for sightseeing anyway."

"What? No way we don't look." Andy looked appalled.

"We're going to check it out." Drake lowered his glasses.

"Is it safe?" Camilla asked. "I mean, I'm professionally curious, but have we got time for this?"

"We don't have time to *not* investigate it." Drake turned to Emma. "You said that the ruins on the jungle floor had a secret cave that led up here. Do you think there's a chance at all that these ruins have a similar cave vent that leads back down?"

"Maybe, why not? For all we know, the Pemon found other ways to the top of the plateau and built their temples over them." She hiked her shoulders. "But I'm not the expert."

"That's good enough for me," Drake said. "Finding Ben is our mission objective. But staying alive and getting home takes precedence over anything else. So we check it out."

Something slammed into the treetops over their heads. Guns were immediately pointed upward, and the suspects were flying things that could have been bats that skimmed awkwardly from treetop to branch. *Could have been bats*, in that their wings were noisy, and they landed clumsily. But that's where the comparison ended, as they were emerald green, and had long heads with a knob on the back to balance out a long serrated beak in front.

In addition, they didn't sing or even squawk. These varieties made a *tock* noise that sounded like metal on a hollow log. They turned their heads sideways to regard the humans with interest, and maybe a little hunger.

"They're not birds," Andy said. "Smaller cousins of the thing that attacked our balloon." He grinned up at them. "Probably scavengers."

"I bet they taste like chicken," Fergus said.

Suddenly, the constant background noise of the jungle was shut off as completely as if someone had flicked a switch. The group turned about.

"What just happened?" Fergus slowly lifted his weapon.

"Not good," Helen spoke softly in a silence where even the insects had gone quiet.

Drake scanned along the jungle's edge, trying to see in past the first long line of foliage. The group started to bunch up, like a small herd of animals pulling in close to the pack.

At first, Drake could hear or see nothing, but then he began to feel it—like the jungle was suddenly holding its breath. He'd been on a mission in the Congo, when a big cat started to stalk them one night. Same thing happened. It was like the creatures of the jungle shut down, all hoping that it was the other guy being stalked and not them.

"Predators in the vicinity," Helen whispered.

"Oh, fucking great," Ajax spat. "I've changed my mind; I think we should take a look in that temple thing after all."

"No, not yet." Andy's eyes were round. "Let's wait and see if whatever it is just passes us by."

"And if it doesn't, we're exposed as all hell out here," Fergus countered.

"I think defensive cover would be a bonus right now." Drake pointed. "We should also change Juan's bandages. He's leaking."

Juan looked down and saw that his arm was stained a dark red-brown again. "It itches."

"Yeah, that's a good sign," Ajax said, chuckling.

"Means it's healing?" Juan asked, hopefully.

"*Nah*, means it's probably infected," Ajax scoffed, but then grinned. "But don't worry; we have the skills to perform a rapid field amputation if necessary."

Juan paled and gripped his arm.

"Shut it, Lieutenant," Drake said with a scowl.

Ajax continued to laugh cruelly as he turned back to peer at the temple ruins.

Emma also looked at the man's arm with concern, and then back at him with her lips pressed flat. Drake bet he knew why—the smell of his blood would draw predators like flies to crap.

"We move." Drake eased his head around. "On my word; Fergus, ten feet forward, left flank. Ajax ten feet, right. Everyone else, close in tight, single-file up the center. I'll bring up the rear. We stay low, fast, and quiet."

A single twig snapped just a dozen feet out to their left. Then some tree branches shook a little on their other side.

Fergus eased his gun around. "Boss, we're about to be surrounded."

"Yep, time's up. Focus on the temple, nowhere else." Drake took one last look around. "3, 2, 1...*go!*"

Fergus and Ajax shot out to the left and right, guns up. Everyone else was in the center with Drake behind.

As Drake sprinted, he could sense the eyes on them. He hoped they were nothing oversized but couldn't help feeling this was like a kill box. Then the jungle exploded around them.

What he at first thought were muscular ostriches came bursting from the jungle on three sides. Except instead of feathers, their skin looked warty and rough, blotched with green, brown, and some red. Their legs were heavily muscled and small arms ended in talons. They were only about six feet tall, but dozens were piling out and moving faster than they were, making a weird hissing rattle in their throats.

"Move it!" Drake yelled.

He turned and let loose a short spray with his M4—his bullets pumped into two of the hunters and they immediately went backward, blown off their feet. The others just accelerated.

"*Engage!*" he fired again.

Fergus and Ajax lay down controlled bursts, the professional soldiers never missing. The hissing rattle got louder as the theropods closed the gap.

They were still 50 feet out from the wide-open temple doorway, and Drake began to doubt they'd all make it. They were heavily outnumbered, and he turned again, and noticed the creatures were now only a dozen feet behind him. They ran like roadrunners, necks pointed arrow-straight at him as they leaned forward with their whip-like tails pointed out behind them for balance.

Their small red eyes were almost luminous with excitement, and their open mouths showed backward-curving teeth like a band saw. Drake wondered what the bite would be like—would it shred flesh and rip it from the bone, or would the bite be powerful enough to simply sever an arm or leg?

He turned, running sideways, and took out two more that had been so close. He could even hear their ragged breathing. At just 20 feet from the doorway, he turned to fire again, expecting to see them basically at his neck.

Drake slowed. "What the hell?"

The creatures had veered off and given up the chase. His group were now safely inside the temple, and Ajax and Fergus took a position up on each side of the doorway.

Drake stood on the front steps, breathing hard. The pack of carnivores melted back into the jungle. He jogged up the steps, and he turned at the doorway again, gun up and pointed back the way they'd come. Nothing followed them.

Weird, he thought. They basically had them and gave up. He looked inside and saw his people lying on the stones, sucking in deep breaths.

"*Yeah.*" Ajax grinned. "We kicked their ass, man." He whooped and lifted his gun. "Don't mess with modern man, you fucking big-ass lizards."

Drake let his eyes drift to the walls of the jungle. "I don't get it. They had us dead to rights. But they gave up."

"Superior firepower tends to do that to an enemy." Ajax fist-bumped Fergus.

"They're not our enemy," Helen said. "They're just doing what nature intended."

"Something spooked 'em," Drake said.

"Us," Fergus added.

"Hey, maybe they're superstitious." Andy laughed softly, and moved further inside, pausing at carvings, crouching to examine something here and there, or just marveling at the architecture.

Drake watched him for a moment before examining the arched doorway. Then he noticed what was scattered about on the ground.

"This opening had a door once, I think."

On either side of the framework, huge blocks were tumbled away. Also, what looked like to have once been wooden logs. There were signs in the rotted wood that they had been lashed together, but they fell to dust when he touched them with his boot.

Emma crouched. "I don't think this was a door. More like a barricade."

Ajax snorted. "A barricade? Well, didn't work, did it? Whatever they tried to keep out just came on in anyway."

"Last stand," Fergus said ominously.

"Yeah, well…" Drake attached a flashlight to the barrel of his M4. "Whatever went down happened a lo-*oooong* time ago."

"There are no remains," Helen said. "Maybe they got away."

"Or maybe they got eaten, whole," Ajax replied.

"Those blocks have gotta weigh at least five hundred pounds each. Whatever pushed them in probably wasn't the size of a brush turkey, right?" Fergus said. "Or even the size of those things that took a run at us."

"Yeah, had to be something real powerful," Drake agreed. "But the doorway isn't that big."

"Maybe not big, but long," Andy said from the dark interior. "Look."

Everyone turned toward him.

"They worshipped them," Andy said, standing before a statue in an alcove.

"Jesus Christ." Drake felt a chill in the pit of his stomach.

The statue was of a giant snake, 10 feet high, leering down on them. Its eyes glittered green in the light of their flashlights.

"Hey, shit, are they emeralds?" Ajax crossed to the statue and stared up at it. He pointed, grinning. "I think they're emeralds; big as damned golf balls, man."

"Leave 'em," Drake said.

"The hell I will." Ajax pushed his gun up over his shoulder and drew his blade. He turned. "Hey, Fergus, gimme a leg up."

"*Nah*, man. I'm superstitious. Leave me out." He turned away.

"Fuck you then; more for me." He went around the back and scaled up the body of the snake and crawled on the neck out toward the head. He pulled his blade from its scabbard and reached forward to dig into one of the eye sockets for a few seconds. The gem popped free and fell to the ground. He did the same with the second eye.

Camilla picked one up that had rolled toward her.

"That's mine," Ajax said quickly as he slid off the statue and dropped to the ground.

"You're welcome to it." She held it up, turning it in the beam of her flashlight. "I've got good news and bad news." She faced the young soldier. "The good news is, it *is* a gemstone." She tossed it to him. 'The bad news is, it's not emerald. I think its aquamarine, and quite common in South America. It's a good one though."

"So, worth something then?" Ajax refused to be put off.

"Sure; the big ones, I'm guessing a few hundred dollars, maybe even a few thousand."

"Damn." He shrugged. "Better than nothing." He tucked them into a pouch on his leg. "At least I'll have something to show from this hell jungle."

"One person's heaven is another person's hell," Andy said, staring up at the carvings in the wall. He turned. "The natives found a way to ascend to heaven, here, to pay homage to their gods."

Emma joined him. "In the previous temple we found, it depicted human sacrifice. I think they were trying to buy these creatures off."

Andy nodded as a few of the group crowded around. "This temple is already thousands of years old and looks abandoned for maybe that much time again. But just imagine it." He scoffed. "Them finding this place. It would have confirmed all their prayers, legends, and fears."

"And nightmares," Helen added. "The Mayans, Aztecs, Olmecs, many of the ancient races of this area had sophisticated calendar systems. They would have been able to predict when the time was *right* to ascend." Helen folded her arms. She turned to them. "One more thing. A lot of these ancient races also thought Heaven was *down*, and Hell was up. So maybe it wasn't gods they were trying to appease."

"But demons," Andy added softly, staring up at the wall. There were images of small figures kneeling on the ground. A monstrous snake was bending to consume one. Andy blew air between his lips.

"I'm guessing here, but it looks like at first, they gave themselves over willingly."

"Perhaps it was an honor," Emma said.

"Some honor. Poor saps." Andy frowned. "I'm happy just getting a participation ribbon in the 100 dash."

The next image showed the figures setting fires and the beasts being driven back. "The beautiful relationship came to an end."

"Feeding them just brought more to the dinner table," Emma observed. "So they finally decided to keep them out of the house. Or try to."

"Then they must have tried to seal the entrance; tried to stop them coming into the temple." Drake turned back to the tumbled blocks. "But they got in anyway. And when they did, looks like they were pissed."

"They walled themselves into their own tomb," Camilla mumbled. "So sad."

"Maybe not," Emma said, as everyone turned to her. "Maybe they were just trying to protect their way home."

"So this *could* be a way home?" Ajax grinned.

"I didn't say that," Emma added quickly. "But it's possible."

Drake turned again to the front door. "Okay, ladies and gentlemen, we got work to do. *Fergus.*"

"Yo." The redheaded man's head snapped around.

"Watch the door. Helen, take a look at Juan's arm and redress it. Emma, you know what we're looking for in the shape of some sort of escape hatch."

"Vent or what we call a chute," she replied. "Could be just a crack in the floor or wall. Might be air movement." She sighed. "But basically, we're looking for anything that looks like a natural opening."

The group spread out, and Helen sat Juan down. The Venezuelan man held his still seeping arm and grimaced—not a good sign, Drake knew. She began to unwrap the bandages.

Drake went and put a hand on Fergus' shoulder at the doorway. "You see anything move, even a freaking bug, you let me know. If there's no other way out deeper inside, then this place..." he said evenly, "...is either a fort or a kill box."

"Got it, boss." Fergus kept his eyes on the jungle outside.

Drake joined the group as they began to investigate the ink-black interior of the temple. There were dark alcoves, doorways with heavy slabs of stone lintels, and carvings of all manner of great beasts, some he recognized walking on two titanic legs, all head and teeth, and others on four with long necks. But the dominating theme, and that must have been their preferred deity or demon, was the giant snake.

There were also more images of men and women, some bound by the wrists and neck. Some of the people were tied to stakes, and all presented as offerings to the snake god. To be close to one of these monsters would have been gut-wrenching, but being lashed in place, knowing you were going to be eaten alive by the beast, would have been a terrifying way to have your life ended.

"Bastards," he muttered.

Drake shone his light inside one of the vestibules and then entered. The room was filled with stacked urns, and shining his light inside one of them, he saw a brownish crust in the bottom—*blood*? he wondered.

"Hey!" Andy's shout brought his head around.

Drake backed out of the room. "Where are you?"

"*Here*." Andy stepped out of a room on the other side of the temple. "Got steps leading down inside."

The group crowded in, and they found a room only about 30 square feet, this time with statues of warriors seeming to lunge from the walls. At its center, there was a dark square.

Andy stood at its edge. "Goes down to another floor, I think."

"Down is good," said Ajax. He lifted his gun and placed a foot on the first step.

"Wait." Emma crouched by the dark entrance.

Ajax frowned down at her. "What?"

Emma turned to Helen and Andy. "Smell that?"

"Yeah, it stinks; probably some goddamn mold," Ajax said. "So what?"

Helen settled beside Emma. "I smell it." She looked up at her brother. "Snake."

"Yeah, snake musk," Andy agreed. "Don't know how I missed it."

"Ah, fuck." Ajax backed up off the step.

"I've smelled it before. Last time I was here. Like heady cat's piss; a mix of body odor and ammonia." Emma backed up a step. "We need to get out of here."

"We do," Drake said. "But we also need a way down. And if this is a possible way down, then we need to check it out."

"You know what I'm thinking?" Andy asked.

"No, but let me guess; you're scared shitless." Ajax grinned as he stared down into the dark.

Andy chuckled. "Yeah, I absolutely sure am. Anyone with a brain would be. But I'm thinking that the reason that pack of theropods outside stopped chasing us and peeled off was not because we overwhelmed them with firepower, but because they smelled something that scared them off. Something coming from in here."

"Or they already knew what lived in here," Emma said.

"Well, that doesn't spook me at all." Drake shook his head. "To hell with it." The soldier reached into a pouch and pulled out a flare.

"Everyone stand back. Ajax, on my ready." He punched it down onto his thigh and ignited the pyrotechnics. Immediately, a brilliant red light illuminated the room, making everyone squint or hold up hands in front of their faces. He tossed it down the steps.

He and Ajax crouched, guns up, waiting for a moment, seeing if anything made an appearance. After another full minute when there was still no movement, the pair headed down.

Emma half-turned. "Stay here." She followed them.

*****

Emma marveled at how the Special Forces soldiers moved: walking forward, legs braced and guns up, sweeping the barrels left, then right, up, down, and then back again. They seemed to move like machines and miss nothing.

The flare cast a hellish glow over the interior of the room. Underfoot things crunched and though now the room was filled with the smell of burning chemicals from the flare, she could still detect the vinegary sourness of the snake. It made the hair on her neck stand on end.

Drake turned and saw her and waved a hand forcefully, indicating she stay behind them. She had no problem with that. She held the SIG Sauer handgun in a double-handed grip, tight, and as she'd spent countless hours training with the weapon, she trusted it more than any other.

She swallowed, her mouth now bone-dry. It was a labyrinth down below, and the further they moved down a dark corridor, the further back they left the light of the flare. Underfoot things still crunched and looking down, Emma now understood why.

"Guys…"

"What?" Drake hissed over his shoulder.

"That isn't gravel we're walking on."

Drake looked down, and then half-turned to Ajax. "Bone fragments—this must be their nest."

"Kill room," Ajax muttered.

The soldiers continued to move forward and Emma followed closely. They turned into a large room, and she noticed that the doorway had been abraded on either side. Drake reached a hand to it, running his fingers up and down along the smoothed edges.

"Something big passed by here, often; wore it down," he said. "One guess."

"Jesus, this doorway is six feet wide." Ajax grimaced.

Emma felt it first—the breeze on her face—and she straightened. "Something up ahead."

"Hey, what are those things?" Ajax pointed his barrel light into the corner where there was a jumbled pile of objects that looked like leathery footballs, all broken open.

"Exactly what they look like—eggs," Emma said.

"All hatched," he replied. "But they look old." He nudged one with his boot and it fell to pieces. "Very old."

At the far end of the room, there was a coal-black hole in the wall, with a carved surround.

"There," Drake whispered.

They eased cautiously toward it. The surrounding stones had been ornately carved with glyphs, and what could have been letters or words, but were impenetrable to the trio.

"Wish we could decipher it," Drake said, lifting his barrel light a little higher to shine inside the portal.

"I know what it says," Ajax said, chuckling. "It says, this way home."

Just past the ornately carved surround, they could see that the worked stone was only on the outside; inside, there were raw stones and a dark shaft leading on well beyond their light beams.

"A natural cave mouth, and there's airflow," Emma said, feeling her spirits soar. She sniffed. "But also might be home to something."

The large portal was also abraded, and the ground smoothed by the constant rubbing of something big.

"Wanna take a look?" Drake asked.

"Not really," Emma replied, chuckling nervously. It was her turn to pull out a flare and followed Drake's example by jamming it down on her thigh—it freaking hurt.

"Put it further in," Drake whispered.

Emma nodded and then leaned in to launch it in through the portal. The flare sailed in and never even got to bounce as the snake that was lurking just inside burst out at them like it was on a spring. The foot-wide head and glinting eyes caught the glow of the flare as it shot forward, making them blaze like it was a demon rising from Hell.

Emma screamed and fell back. But Ajax and Drake stood their ground and responded with the calm reactions of professional killers. They fired long bursts into the head and body.

The M4 rifle's medium-caliber shells punched through the armored scales, but the snake still managed to rear up, ignoring the dozens of punctures. It started to pour into the room and the two soldiers continued to pile it on before finally they shredded the neck, nearly severing the head until the thing thumped down dead at their feet.

"*Fuck you*," Ajax said. "We're king of the jungle here."

Drake held out a hand and Emma grabbed it, hauling herself up. "Jesus, that just scared ten years out of me."

"You and me both." Drake turned back to the dead snake. Then gun back up, peered past it into the portal where the serpentine body disappeared for dozens of feet. "You're right, these guys are huge."

Emma looked down at the length. The head was a foot wide, the body thicker around than hers. But given its girth and how quickly it was tapering inside the hole, she bet it was about 30 to 35 feet.

"A juvenile," she said.

"Say what? It's just a freaking kid?" Ajax's mouth dropped open and he kicked at it. "Thing's gotta weigh a thousand pounds if it's an ounce."

Emma looked into the hole. The flare still glowed and she could see the remains of bone fragments, plus the tell-tale sign of the white, chalky packages of their droppings.

"The nest." She looked back at the eggs. "Don't know how many are in there. Or whether Mom is home." She shook her head. "Shit."

"What?" Drake asked.

"That might be our way down." She leaned in a little further and turned her head, trying to listen for movement, but all she heard was the hiss of the flare. She took a chance and leaned in a little more, reaching for Drake's flare. Her fingers extended, and she had the unsettling sensation of being watched.

Emma grabbed it and then tossed it in even further than her own. She looked up and froze. Eyes, lots of eyes, glinted red in the dark. "Guys…" She eased back. "I think…" She backed up and out of the portal opening. "We need to get the hell out of here…*now*."

Suddenly, the airflow stopped, and she heard a sound coming up from deep down inside the cave—it was something heavy and coming closer.

"Oh crap; I think its Momma." She grabbed Drake's arm. "Let's go, move it!"

"Oh yeah?" Ajax loaded a grenade into his M320 undercarriage launcher. "How about I give this asshole an enema—clean 'em all out at once."

"No," Drake said forcefully. "You might collapse the tunnel or bury us all." He grabbed the young soldier's arm and backed up. "Right now, we poked the hornet's nest, and the hornets are angry. We'll make a plan and finish this later."

The three of them backed up to the steps and ran up to meet the group. Drake led the way.

"Okay, people, we are leaving."

"Find a way out?" Andy asked.

"Maybe," Emma said. "Just one problem—there was somebody home."

Juan groaned and Camilla wrung her hands as she knelt beside him. "I don't think we can travel much more. He's sick."

"Leave him here, then," Ajax dictated.

Camilla got to her feet. "Can we both not stay, and maybe…" She looked at each of the soldiers. "…maybe, Fergus can stay and guard us."

Emma walked toward her, her eyes hooded. "Still think it was me that killed Ben? Still think I made this all up now?"

"I never said that," Camilla pleaded.

"You didn't have to." Emma's jaw clenched. "If you stay behind, you'll be dead within the hour. Your call."

"No, they come. Get him up." Drake motioned to Juan, and Ajax went and dragged the Venezuelan cameraman to his feet.

Drake joined Fergus at the door. "Anything out there?"

"Nada. Everyone's gone home." Fergus turned. "You guys got a bit noisy down there—all good?"

"The residents didn't like us poking around in their bedroom. So we're giving 'em some space…for now." Drake let his eyes run over the green wall and then pointed. "2 o'clock; that space between the two big tree trunks. That's our entry point."

"Got it." Fergus watched the jungle.

Drake turned. "Okay, people, let's clear out."

Emma joined him. "We'll need to come back."

He nodded. "But not right now. We can't fight these snakes in a small space; we'll need to draw them out first." He put his hand on her shoulder. "Don't worry, I have a plan. First, let's find Ben."

Emma nodded. "That's what we came here for."

"Damn right." Drake looked past her. "Okay, people, same as before, my men will take flanking positions, everyone else stay in the center and keep up. We move hard and fast." He turned back to the jungle, taking one last look. "On my 3, 2, 1…*go*." He sprinted out.

CHAPTER 29

The rest of the day was spent darting, hiding, crawling forward a few feet at a time, and then scurrying to the next place of concealment. The humidity and heat sapped their strength as much as the constant tension and fear sapped their mental acuity.

At one point, they emerged from the miasmic jungle into a vast open area of primordial forest. Emma recognized the smell, but not the shapes. "Like pine."

"It is. Or will be one day," Helen observed.

The stand of huge pine-like trees had waxy, flaking bark, and large, heavy wood cones. It was like a land of giants as everything here dwarfed their tiny bodies. Later, they also had to skirt around a herd of brightly colored and crest-headed dinosaurs, that each stood about 12 feet at the shoulder.

"Hadrosaurs," Helen said.

"We suspected they fed off the pinecones." Andy grinned. "And now we know for sure."

Fergus scoffed. "Jesus, how the hell do you eat a pinecone? Like eating a freaking rock."

"Dinosaurs like hadrosaurs, which we know as duckbill dinosaurs, had unique jaws with thousands of rows of teeth adapted to grind up the tough cones. Think of the cones as super big and hard nuts," Andy said. "In these Cretaceous forests, marshlands, and swamps, everything is food."

"Including us," Ajax said over his shoulder.

"Got that right." Emma wiped her face, feeling the grime. There were twigs in her hair, and the odd tiny bug wriggling in the rivulets of salty water pouring from her.

They'd need to reapply their repellent soon. It was an odorless form of DDT—supposed to keep *everything* at bay, but Emma wondered whether it being odorless to them was the same as being odorless to things that had the sense of smell of bloodhounds.

"It'll be sundown soon," Fergus said and swigged from his canteen.

"So what?" Emma shot back. "We continue to search all night. We can sleep when we're home."

Drake turned. "I agree. We're on the clock, so we continue the search. But we'll need to recharge, so we'll be taking rests every three hours. If there was ever a place where we need to be sharp, it's right here, right now."

"Another hour," Emma shot back.

"No, we need to rest *now*," Camilla said softly. Beside her, Juan's face looked like it was shaped from wax, and his bandage had already turned several different shades as his arm now seeped a yellow fluid.

Emma grunted her annoyance. She knew Drake was right. But, so was she. They only had a small window to find Ben, and then get the hell out. She'd just make sure the rest stops were as short as possible.

"Fine; rest, eat, drink, recharge, and then we continue." She turned away.

"Anyone else hear that?" Ajax asked. He lifted some glasses to his eyes and scanned the foliage.

"Insects," Andy said.

"Yeah, there's always insects, you putz. But not like this...*listen*." Ajax turned back.

Emma focused; there *was* something over and above the constant background hum, click and chirrup of the Cretaceous bug life—there was a constant drone, like one of those kit airplanes the enthusiasts fly in the park on weekends.

"Flies," Drake said. "Lots of them."

"Yep, and that means death," Fergus added. "Just up ahead, I think." He turned to Drake. "Take a look?"

"Not all of us," Drake said and turned. "Emma, we'll do a quick scout."

She nodded and turned back to where the noise was coming from. The ancient conifers were smaller here but tightly packed together.

Drake set off, rifle ready, and eased around and between the spiked limbs and trunks. Emma followed as he burrowed through the living barriers of young pine, bracken stalks, and eased around the odd hairy tree trunk. In another few minutes, the buzzing became loud enough to drown out everything else.

"There." He pointed with the barrel of his gun.

"I see it," Emma whispered, even though she didn't need to.

There was a cloud of insects swirling madly over something on the jungle floor. The surrounding ferns and grasses had been trampled into a mat, and many of the larger remaining fronds were splashed and shining—blood, and not old blood—as it still retained some hues of glossy scarlet. It was these fresh areas that excited the vermin.

"Last few hours. Fresh kill." Drake eased upright. "Stay here."

He walked slowly forward, crouching, his eyes never stopping as they moved over the jungle. Emma took her M4 off her shoulder and covered him.

She knew that the hunters had camouflage and an ability to remain motionless that rendered them nearly invisible. Plus, they were fast, and deadly. If one attacked, she might have time for one shot, so she needed to be ready.

She watched as Drake stood in amongst the remains of whatever had taken place there, and then he craned forward as he spotted something in the ground. He darted forward to retrieve it, and then took a few more seconds to examine the area, looking in along the jungle line.

Emma couldn't make out what he had found, but after another moment, he rose, quickly looked about again, and then backed away, returning to crouch beside her.

His expression was grave as he grabbed her arm. He then held the thing out to her. "I'm sorry, Emma."

She stared—it was an old rusted knife, lashed to a broken stick. She continued to stare, her brain at first not understanding what the implication was.

Drake continued to hold her arm. "Something was killed there within the last few hours. There are no remains, but plenty of blood, and *this*." He turned the knife over. "That's a military-issue jungle knife...or used to be." He sighed heavily. "Like the type Ben Cartwright would have been using."

She got it then. "No way." She shook her head, violently. "*No way.* You think that Ben would survive ten years in this hellhole place, and get himself killed the damn day we arrive? *No. Fucking. Way.*" She glared, and was too forceful, she knew.

Drake just looked away for a moment and sighed again. "We can talk to the group. But I think you have to face the fact that our mission might be over." He let her arm go. "Come on."

The hell it is, she thought.

*****

They pulled back from the site of the massacre and rejoined the group. Drake told them what they had found and showed them the broken spear tip.

Fergus picked it up. "Was a Ka-bar—high-carbon, non-reflective black blade, with epoxy powder-coat; it's why it survived with only a little rusting." He looked at Drake. "Yeah, it'd be his."

"He got attacked, put up a fight, but…" Ajax shrugged. "…it went bad."

"But you said there were no bodies." Fergus' forehead creased. "Come on, we know Ben Cartwright; that guy could take down an elephant with his bare hands. He would have gutted at least one of them. Where were they?"

"Two things," Drake said with resignation. "Maybe the Ben we knew could have. But maybe not the Ben Cartwright that's been trapped here for ten years. It'd wear any man down."

"Bullshit," Emma spat. "Half a Ben would have been enough to fend them off."

"Yeah, maybe," Drake responded. "But there is one other answer to why there's no bodies. These things eat their own; all meat is good meat here; nothing is wasted."

"Then we're done here," Ajax said.

Fergus grimaced. "Gotta agree. I think the evidence points to the fact he put up a fight but didn't win this one."

"Bullshit," Emma spat. "Until I see the body, I'll never believe it." Emma folded her arms.

Helen stepped in front of her. "There'll never be a body, Emma. Even if it wasn't a big predator, these creatures even consume bones; you know that."

"Sorry, Emma, but she's right," Andy said, but wouldn't meet her eyes for a moment. He finally looked up. "For what it's worth, I vote we stay a little longer. Just to be sure."

Thank you, she mouthed.

"I see what you're doin'," Ajax sneered. "He's only saying that 'cause he wants to do more looking around to satisfy his egghead curiosity."

"Egghead?" Andy's brows shot up.

Ajax grinned back at him. "Well, the vote is in and the ayes have it. We go home."

"Fuck you, fuck all of you. I'm not leaving here until I find some proof he's dead. Until then, he's still alive." Emma bared her teeth.

"That's your decis…hey, wait a minute." Ajax scowled. "If you don't come back, we don't get paid."

She rounded on the big soldier and couldn't help tears of frustration welling in her eyes. "The money is already in your account, you chicken shit. I transferred it the day we left."

Ajax's anger flared, and he went to step forward, but Drake reached out one big arm across the man's chest. Ajax gripped his wrist, hard. The younger man glared at Drake, and the older soldier returned the gaze with unflinching confidence.

"Listen up. We're all tired, all on edge, and all a little beat up. We take a few minutes to rest our feet, have something to eat and drink, and then plan our next move." Drake pushed Ajax in the chest, making him back up a step. "Agreed?" He looked at each of them, and then faced Ajax dead on. He raised his voice a few decibels. "*Agreed?*"

"I guess," Ajax grumbled.

The others nodded, or simply sighed, shrugged, and waited for the next move. Drake found them a patch of ground that was hidden and less sodden than the rest. They sat, chewed hard protein bars, and sipped water that was as warm as blood, while they all became lost in their own thoughts.

Emma tried to think through what she would do if the group decided to leave. She was resolute, and it only took her a few seconds to choose a course of action; she would stay and continue to search. She hadn't waited all this time, and come all this way, to give up so quickly.

She turned to look at the team. Fergus, Ajax, and Drake were in a huddle and talking quietly. Andy and Helen had finished eating and now examined something they had found interesting in the soil. Camilla seemed withdrawn, pale, and stared at the ground between her feet, while Juan lay back, shivering slightly. He was fevered, and she knew that if anyone needed to bug out, it was him.

The Venezuelan cameraman lay flat on the ground, eyes screwed shut, and looked to have passed out. *Needs his rest more than any other*, she thought. His arm was wrapped in new bandages, but already she could see the seep and swelling; it looked damned bad. The last time Helen had rebandaged him, they all got a whiff of the sweet smell of corruption. Without a doubt, either the pterodon had a bacteria-laden bite, or there had to have been some sort of venom at work.

Emma had read about the bite of the Komodo dragon that was so laden with bacteria, wounds festered quickly, and could result in blood poisoning and toxic shock in hours.

She rubbed her eyes. Maybe Ben *was* dead. And maybe it was time to get the hell out. She sighed deeply.

They'd already lost one good man when Brocke was taken. Juan was getting sicker, and she knew what everyone was thinking; now was the time to cut and run. It'd be so easy to do.

Her problem was, she just didn't *feel* that Ben was gone. For some insane reason, or some sixth sense, something was telling her he was still alive. She knew he was one of the most resourceful and tough men she knew. She smiled dreamily; they say love is blind. But she knew it was also deaf, dumb, and sometimes, just plain stupid.

That's me. She sat straighter. *And I'm not ready to go yet*, she thought determinedly. Her only decision was whether she, in good conscience, should try and keep the team with her or send them home.

She'd been here before, and lived through it, *just*. But how long would she survive by herself? she wondered. And how long would the group survive without her, the only person here with any experience in this place?

She looked across to them—Ajax noticed her looking and nodded with a smirk. Andy and Helen continued to place things in tiny sample bags, and Camilla still looked like she was suffering from post-traumatic stress.

But it was Juan that worried her—she wanted him gone. The guy would be an anchor soon, doing nothing but slowing them down. She hated herself for being so mercenary. *But I'm different now*, she knew.

She narrowed her eyes as she stared at him. The man was still lying flat out, but oddly his body jerked and jumped as though he was having a restless sleep…*very* restless. He had to be bone tired, and his fever would have sapped any remaining energy, but the ground he was on was muddy and damp and can't have been that comfortable.

As she continued to watch, she saw that the soil under him seemed to have been churned, no, *was churning*. Then to her horror, something eased up from the earth, just below his thigh, at first looking like a long rubbery penis before two long pincer-like limbs opened from the end and clamped onto his flesh, dug deep, and then tugged the muscle downward toward the soil.

"Juan?" Her mouth worked as she stared, her eyes now wide.

Another revolting pipe came up from the soil, affixed to the man with its pincers, and started to burrow into his flesh.

"Juan! *Get him up, get him up*!" Her voice was loud enough to snap everyone's head around, to first her, then to the cameraman. Even Camilla was roused from her zombie-like trance.

Drake and Fergus were at the man in an instant and each grabbed an arm and tugged—but he wouldn't budge. Both the Special Forces guys were hugely muscled, and though Juan was overweight, they still would have outweighed him by 20 pounds each.

They tugged again and heaved. The man came forward, and Camilla screamed. Like hoses, there were several blood-red pipes extruding from his body. Emma's first thought was his organs had somehow spilled from his back.

"Jesus; there's something stuck to him!" Fergus yelled.

Then she saw those two hooks, or claws, or teeth, or whatever the hell they were hanging on, so the thing's head could remain attached and eat at his flesh like a lamprey.

And then the nightmare began—the grotesque worms fought back and tried to drag Juan back down. They wanted him close to the ground so they could continue their feast in private.

Ajax leaped forward and unloaded a dozen rounds into the soil underneath him. Immediately, the worms disengaged and snapped back below the earth like a man slurps up strands of spaghetti. Fergus and Drake quickly dragged Juan away, but his head lolled forward loosely onto his chest.

"Lay him down," Helen said. "On his stomach."

"What the hell were they?" Emma demanded.

The men laid Juan down and ripped open his shirt. There were circular holes in his body and several on his wounded arm that probably attracted the revolting things in the first place.

"They were feeding off him," Emma observed. "They're below us." She turned in time to see a rubbery head emerge from the soil where there was a splash of the Venezuelan man's blood. "There." The pincers opened, and the head was exposed—the thing was little more than a mouth on the end of a long muscular pipe.

Ajax fired again, and the thing vanished.

"If I had to guess, *Websteroprion armstrongi*, from the polychaete family, I think." Andy stared, his eyes going from the soil to Juan's wounds.

"They're a very ancient species of giant bristle worm, what've been around since the Paleozoic, 500 million years, give or take. They were scavengers, but because of their size, we think they could have been opportunistic hunters."

"Well, consider that fucking theory confirmed," Ajax spat.

"Yes, yes," Andy said distractedly. "Fossil records had them at ten feet long. But they could have grown bigger. We've found evidence of them from oceans to swamps—basically, places like this."

Helen looked up at them. Her hands were red to the wrists, and she had patches of bandage over a dozen places on his back, arms, and legs. The man groaned and his eyes were rolled back.

"He's lost a lot of blood. *Too* much blood," she agonized.

"He's fucked," Ajax said.

"Don't say that." Camilla glared at the young soldier, but her eyes now looked haunted and dark shadows circled them.

Ajax just smirked. "Oh, okay, he's fine. My bad."

Drake rested on his haunches beside Helen and rubbed both hands up over his face He exhaled. "Chances?"

She wiped her hands. "Without a transfusion? Plus, his body was already weakened from whatever infection he got from the pterodon bite?" She shook her head. "One, maybe two out of ten if he gets care in the next twenty-four hours. Zero out of ten if he doesn't."

Ajax laughed. "Darling, do you remember where we are? Even if we got him down off this prehistoric hell, somehow, we're still smack in the center of the biggest jungle on the planet."

"Lighten up." Drake glared up at his man before turning back to Helen, and then fixing his eyes on Camilla. "I don't like his chances, but don't worry, no one is going to get left behind."

Camilla pressed her hands together. "Thank you."

Emma walked a few paces away, letting her mind run. She turned. "Drake, got a minute?"

He stood, brushed his hands off, and joined her. "What's up?"

Emma faced away from the group. "The blood."

He sighed. "Yeah, yeah, I know."

She faced him. "No, you don't. Maybe you're starting to get it, but blood draws the hunters. And there are things here from your worst nightmares."

"I know what you're saying, what you want, and I won't do it." He looked at her from under lowered brows. "If it was you injured like that, would you want me to dump your ass?"

She didn't blink. "Yes." She walked in even closer to him. "Juan's already dead. We drag his blood-soaked body with us, and he will cause more of us to die with him." She motioned back to the group. "Look."

Drake turned for a moment before facing her again. He folded his arms.

She continued to stare hard at the Special Forces soldier. "Which ones are you willing to sacrifice? Because I'll tell you right now, one or more of them will be killed, probably badly, if we bring him with us. Like Ajax said; he's fucked."

Drake shook his head, baring his teeth. "You are one ice cold bitch, lady."

"No, I'm someone willing to put the group over the individual." She stood her ground.

"We're leaving," he said evenly.

She nodded. "I know you are. I won't try and stop you."

He exhaled and ran a hand up through his hair. "Jesus, Emma. Come on. You know in your heart that Ben can't possibly be alive. Don't goddamn sacrifice yourself."

"That's not my plan. I'm just going to do what I came here to do. What I've waited ten years to do." She grabbed his wide shoulders and stared into his eyes. "And in my heart, I know he's alive. I have *zero* doubt of that."

"You're crazy brave, or just plain crazy." He hugged her, stood back, and gave her a small salute. "Good luck, and may God walk with you." He turned and rejoined the group.

PART 3 – THE PAST IS THE FUTURE

"*Any truth is better than indefinite doubt*" – Arthur Conan Doyle

CHAPTER 30

Emma watched them go with a feeling of resignation and relief. And for the first time, she felt something else that she loathed: self-doubt.

Fergus drew the short straw and had the near comatose Juan hanging from his side. Andy was on the other side, but the soldier basically carried the weight, and Andy was just there for balance.

Their plan was to head back to the temple, and maybe fight their way in, or hope they could somehow evict the occupants. She really hoped they were successful, and not just for the wellbeing of her colleagues. But also because when she found Ben, that's where she'd be heading, and if time was short, she wanted to be able to make their way straight to the base of the tepui before the doorway snapped shut again.

Emma walked a few paces toward the edge of the clearing and stared in the direction of the plateau edge. She inhaled, smelling the damp green, the sap, rotting earth, and leaf detritus. There was also the oddly sweet smell of weird blooms, and a unique muskiness she knew came from dinosaur shit.

She checked her sidearm and took a sip from her canteen. Emma took a look at her watch, an old wind-up analog Seiko with a crystal face and demagnetized steel casing that she knew would keep running no matter what the comet threw at them.

It was 5pm; time was growing short. She was now alone, but knew in her heart that this was how it was always going to end up. She gritted her teeth and headed in.

*****

Drake led them through the dense jungle, retracing their steps where they could, and making detours around areas that sounded occupied.

Once they came across a gargantuan creature that was like a giant hippopotamus, except it had a longer neck and a small head. On its back was a row of large triangular plates that moved and changed angles like solar panels to catch rays of sun. A twig snapped and the thing froze. The plates on its back turned from an iridescent green to a drab khaki, and it melted back into the jungle.

Drake was about to lead them on, but Helen reached out a hand. "Wait. Get down."

They squatted, staying under cover, and in just another few moments, they heard something treading heavily, and a huge intake of air as a creature sniffed deeply. Then from the jungle came a beast from their nightmares.

On two colossal legs, the thing materialized from between the giant jungle tree trunks. Two almost-deformed-looking front arms were held stiffly forward and its body was a deep orange with black stripes on its back. But the colors broke up its shape in the dappled light.

Its massive clawed feet eased it forward, slowly, as it was obviously stalking. It was attempting to be silent, even though the monstrous beast must have weighed in at about 15 tons.

"*Giganotosaurus*," Helen breathed.

The monster lowered its head and inhaled again, this time directly over the place where the plant-eater had occupied only moments before. It picked up the trail and slid into the jungle, following the big vegetarian.

Drake didn't even realize he was holding his breath until his lungs began to burn. They waited another full five minutes until the sounds of the jungle returned.

"Jesus." He turned, looking back the way they'd come. Never in his life had he cut and run on anyone or anything. But he'd just dropped Emma on her butt, while they held most of the firepower. He felt like a complete asshole.

"Okay," Helen said.

Drake stayed low and called everyone in. "New plan."

"Say what?" Ajax scowled.

"Going back for Emma," he said matter-of-factly.

"No, we're not," Ajax shot back.

"I know *you're* not; you're to continue on to the temple. Clear it out. You can either give us another six hours, or not, your choice. Either way, you're to get everyone down and out of here."

"Bullshit, man." Ajax paced away for a few steps and then spun back. "No, no, no, you're not going either." He looked panicked. "We need your firepower."

Drake shook his head. "You'll be fine." He turned to Fergus. "You're in command."

"You're not fucking listening. *You're staying.*" Ajax's voice was suddenly dead calm.

"Shut it and get back in line, soldier," Drake said over his shoulder.

"Don't make me do this, Drake." Ajax's voice now had a menacing edge.

Drake turned slowly to see the big man holding his sidearm loosely in his hand. Drake came to his feet. "What do you think you're doing?"

To the side, he saw Fergus look like he was about to charge in, and Drake held up a hand to him. He turned back to Ajax.

"Not a good time to be losing it, son."

"It's not me that's losing it, *sir*." Ajax's eyes were wide. "We all stay together. Mission is over, you know that. Priority now is getting *us* home." He lowered his brow. "Anything else is command negligence in the field."

"I see." He nodded toward Ajax's weapon. "Put the gun down before you hurt yourself."

Ajax straightened to his full height. "Your behavior leaves me no choice. I'm assuming command."

"Bullshit you are," Fergus growled.

Ajax momentarily pointed the gun at him. "I know you agree with me." He swung back to Drake. "We're all going to head to the temple." The gun was at his side again.

Drake could see the man was agitated, knew he was impulsive. Right now, he was unpredictable. Worst outcome was one of them killed the other. Ajax was right about one thing—they needed *all* the firepower they had.

"So what's the plan?" Drake lifted his chin. "You disarm me and take me hostage? How's that gonna work?"

"This is stupid," Andy said, peering around from behind the young soldier. Andy tried to sidle around him, and then reached out, just touching his elbow. "Ajax…"

"Fuck off," Ajax half-turned and growled, his gun hand coming up.

Big mistake, Drake thought. He moved fast, stepping in close, grabbing the young soldier's wrist, pushing down and to the left. Then, before Ajax could fully react, Drake snapped his other elbow back to the right and along the man's jaw. The crack of elbow tip on bone was like a gunshot going off as Ajax's teeth clacked together.

Ajax dropped his gun but lowered his head and recovered fast. He threw out two rapid blows, both aimed at Drake's face. But they were slow due to his disorientation and Drake easily blocked both. He then flattened his hand and struck at Ajax's exposed throat. His fingertips dug in at Ajax's Adam's apple.

Drake pulled the blow; if he wanted to, he could have crushed Ajax's windpipe. As it was, it still would be a painful blow and cut off his air for a few moments. Drake wanted the fight over, but he didn't want him dead or even permanently incapacitated.

Ajax's eyes bulged and he gripped his throat. Drake finished him with another blow to the cheekbone. Ajax went down onto his hands and knees.

He stayed down, one hand gripping his throat as he made coughing noises.

"Take it easy, son. Breathe in slowly through your nose." Drake retrieved his gun and stood over him. "Feel better now?"

Ajax coughed again and his head stayed down.

"Fergus will assume command in my absence. Got it?" Drake stared down at him.

Ajax finally nodded. Drake held out a hand, and Ajax reached up and gripped it. Drake pulled the man in close, almost nose to nose. "When the other guys lose their heads, we keep ours. We are sanity in chaos. Got it?"

Ajax nodded again. "I just wanna—*cough*—get the fuck outta here."

"Yeah, we all do." Drake handed him back his gun, and Ajax took it, but Drake held onto it for a second, looking into his eyes. "We good?"

"Yeah, yeah, sorry, boss. Won't happen again." Ajax reholstered his gun.

Behind Ajax, Drake saw Andy fist pump. Drake turned to the entire group. "Like I said, I'll be going for Emma and Ben. In six hours, I hope to be back. You can wait for me or not—your choice. Fergus will take it from here."

"*Ah*, shit." The redheaded soldier shook his head.

"Whatever; long as we get to bug out," Ajax said.

"I'm staying too," Andy said.

"What?" Helen rounded on him. "No, you're not."

The young paleontologist tilted his head. "Helen, you know they'll need my expertise. Besides, you're the only one of us with medical experience, not me. You need to look after Juan. Without you, he's dead." He shrugged. "Sis, my mind's made up."

"Your funeral," Ajax said.

Fergus didn't look happy, but gathered himself in. "Boss, six hours, be there, or we gotta be on our way."

Drake saluted then turned to Andy. "You don't need to come. In fact, best if you don't; you might just slow me down."

"Don't you worry about me; you provide the brawn and I'll provide the brains. Together, we might just find her."

Drake chuckled. "We got six hours, Mr. Brains; so let's go to work."

He and Andy melted back into the undergrowth.

CHAPTER 31

Ben jerked upright, spun one way then the other and quickly rubbed his face to full wakefulness. He tried to judge the time by the lengthening shadows—it had to be late afternoon. He only had tonight, and maybe a few hours tomorrow morning to find a way off the plateau and back to his own time, and maybe also find Emma if she was here.

He felt the breath catch in his throat at the thought that she might actually be on the plateau right now, somewhere out there, maybe even looking for him. He wanted to yell. He wanted to cup his hands on each side of his mouth and call her name. But he knew instead of bringing Emma, he would only bring the hunters. Making noise invited death.

Ben tried to get in her head, to think like her—if she were here, she would search for him. But where would she start her search? He smiled; she would be trying to think like him, just as he was trying to think like her. Would she start at the last place she had seen him? He knew both of them didn't have too many times they could guess wrong—he either found her, or he missed her, and this time, it'd be forever.

He decided. *As good a guess as any*, he thought.

Ben struggled to his feet and worked hard to stifle his groans. The salve had worked to keep his wounds clean and they were already scabbing. But the pain on and in his chest was like being wrapped in white-hot iron cables.

He waited a few more seconds until the throbbing eased. He needed to find her, and quickly. She'd been here before, but there was much she didn't know. He'd found out things about the plateau that he needed to tell her and warn her about.

CHAPTER 32

Ajax watched as Fergus had lain Juan down at the trunk of a tree. The guy was like a boneless sack, and though he still breathed, raggedly, he was just dead weight.

The big soldier peered between hanging vines and three-foot-wide tongue-like fronds that dripped with moisture. Helen and Camilla crowded in behind him. The light was fading fast, and he knew that in less than an hour, it'd be dark.

He looked back at the even darker portal that was the open doorway of the temple. He didn't want to go back in there, as every Special Forces alarm was ringing in his head. But then again, he didn't want to be out in the open in this godforsaken place either.

He knew it was a *Morton's Fork* decision—two choices, both of them shit. But one at least had a chance of escape, so…

"See anything?" Helen whispered.

"Nothing," he said without taking his eyes off the ancient stone building.

Fergus had his binoculars up to his eyes. He half-turned. "Okay, stage-1, we go in, clear the main floor, and then do a quick recon. Stage-2, we secure the environment, defend our position, and lay low until Drake gets back."

"Nah, not happening," Ajax said. "We're not waiting. We don't know how long it's going to take us to kill those snakes, or to climb down, or to even make sure we're climbing down the right tunnel." His mouth turned down. "My gut feeling is we won't be seeing Drake, or anyone else again."

"Drake asked for six hours; he's still got five more. We can give him that." Fergus lowered his glasses.

"I second that," Helen said. "We wait."

"I vote for leaving now," Camilla said. "Look." She pointed at Juan. "He needs emergency help. I'm sorry, but we cannot wait."

Ajax snorted. "Yeah, well, I gotta tell you, lady, your buddy is pretty much a freaking corpse already."

Camilla's mouth snapped shut and her eyes blazed.

"We're taking him back," Fergus said.

Ajax's grin fell away. "You mean *you're* taking him back. You're in charge, so you can be in charge of him." He turned away. "We've been paid, so I don't plan on putting my life at risk for some asshole I don't know from Adam." He jerked his thumb toward Juan. "Just remember, these two nobodies muscled their way in on our little adventure. Serves 'em right."

Camilla gathered herself up. "I'll have you know—"

"Shut the fuck up, you whiny bitch." Ajax rounded on her. "Or I'll leave you *both* right here."

"Hey, what's your—?" Fergus grabbed Ajax's arm.

"*Don't.*" The big young soldier just scowled. "I am *not* in a good mood right now." He motioned to the three civilians. "As far as I'm concerned, they're expendable."

The Venezuelan woman looked like she'd been slapped. Ajax scoffed and then turned left and right, scanning the undergrowth for movement. "Can't see any of our leaping lizard buddies, so we go hard and fast for the front door. Helen, you'll be going in first, me next, then you two can bring sleeping beauty."

Fergus' jaw clenched, but he seemed to bite it down.

"On my ready." Ajax pulled his M4 and held it tightly. "3, 2, 1, *go.*"

Helen took off across the clearing, Ajax following with his gun up, and Fergus and Camilla dragging the now limp form of Juan.

In just a few minutes, Helen got to the doorway, paused, and then darted in, followed by the rest. Fergus lay Juan down and snapped his flashlight onto the barrel of his M4.

"I'm taking right flank." He started to scan the temple's main room to the right side.

"Yo, got it." Ajax did the same at the other side.

Helen and Camilla tended to Juan, but there was nothing they could do now, as they couldn't even get the near-comatose man to sip water.

Both of the Special Forces soldiers met at the dark entrance to the downstairs rooms. Fergus crouched.

"I still think we should wait for Drake and the others. If he comes back with Ben, I want to be here for that."

Ajax nodded. "That's fine; I'll head on down. But while both of us are here and armored up, the first thing we need to do is clean those fuckers out of the caves, right?" He raised his eyebrows. "You gotta admit, it's certainly gonna make it easier for everyone, if when the guys arrive and if they're short of time, that they don't have to try and fight the dragon then, *huh*?"

"Yeah, there's that." Fergus stared down into the dark. "We can't use explosives."

"Yeah, I agree we can't deploy grenades when we're in the tunnels. But if that thing is as big as we think it is, we might need those explosives. The M4's might do little more than piss it off."

"We need to lure it out then," Fergus observed.

"Yup." Ajax rested on his haunches, staring down into the darkness. "When I was a kid, we used to go fishing for moray eels on the rocks at the seaside. One of us had string with some meat tied on it, and he'd dangle it just outside the eel's home, while another of us held the spear ready. When old Mr. Eel smelled the meat, out he'd come, mouth open, those razor-sharp teeth ready." He laughed cruelly, as if relishing the memory. "What he got instead was a five-pronged spear in the neck—we never missed."

Ajax stood. "So, to draw out our giant eel, we need some bait."

"We go hunting?" Fergus asked.

"Nope, I got a better idea. C'mon." Ajax went and crouched by Juan, and looked at both Camilla and Helen. Fergus stood behind him.

"Ladies." Ajax saluted with two fingers and smiled warmly. "Listen up; to get home, we're going to have to flush that big bastard out of his, *our*, cave. When it comes, we'll need every ounce of firepower we got—that means you two ladies blasting away as well."

"You mean downstairs, in the dark?" Camilla's voice was small.

Ajax nodded slowly.

"I'm ready," Helen said.

"That's the spirit." Ajax looked down at the comatose Juan. "And your boy's gotta play his part as well."

"What?" Camilla frowned. "How?"

He looked up and into her eyes. "Well, we need something to tempt the snake out of its hole. Juan's the only one that can't fire a gun right now, and…" He grinned. "…won't run away if something makes a lunge at him."

"You…want to…use him as *bait*?" Camilla's eyes were wide, and she began to shake her head. "What kind of monster are you?"

"The kind that wants *you*, and all of *us*, to live." Ajax continued grinning, his silver tooth glinting in the fading light. "Do you have a better plan?"

Camilla put her hands to the side of her head. "No, no, not happening."

Ajax twisted his features into mock concern. "Oh, so you want to take his place? Are you sure?"

"That's enough," Fergus said. The redheaded soldier leaned his head back for a moment. "Look, it's a shit option, but it's the best shit option we got. We can protect him."

Camilla spluttered, and Helen turned to the men and spoke through clenched teeth. "I don't like it either."

"Me either," Fergus said. "But it'll probably work. And we'll be there to blast the shit out of anything that comes out. It's the only way to maximize our firepower while the snake is focused on something else—I think we'll need to try it."

The group fell into silence for a few moments, and then Ajax looked at each of their faces. The half-smile was still on his lips as he spoke.

"Good, team meeting over. Help me get our boy up so we can begin."

They dragged Juan up, and between he and Fergus, they carefully pulled him down the steps. Helen and Camilla followed, guns drawn, but Ajax thought that both of the novices would more than likely shoot him or Fergus than hit the freaking snake no matter how big it was, so they were instructed to keep their weapons pointed down, and not to fire until told.

But what he really needed the women for was to add to the noise and confusion when the thing came out. All he needed was for the monster to be disorientated for two seconds—enough time to line up a kill shot. Also, having four targets for the snake to potentially attack meant the odds of him being killed went from 50-50 to one in four—much better.

They crept down, just using their flashlights. It was how they remembered the large room, with the portal opening at the end. The rocks were polished smooth by something about eight feet wide continually rubbing against them.

"Keep your eyes on that freaking hole, man," Ajax said to Fergus.

"You got it," Fergus replied.

Ajax grabbed a large block of stone and dragged it about 15 feet to be right in front of the hole. Then he took Juan and slid the unconscious man across so he was sitting up with his back against the stone, facing the dark hole in the wall.

"Just like he's home watching football on television," Ajax said, sniggering.

The man's head lolled, but he stayed in place.

"And now, we ring the dinner bell." He pulled out a flare, holding it tight, but turning first. His grin had fallen away. "You ready for this?"

Fergus nodded, the stock of his rifle in tight against his shoulder. Helen and Camilla were too frightened to even speak.

"Let's boogie." He jammed the flare against his thigh and waved it inside the tunnel.

"Hey!" he yelled. His voice echoed away into the stygian depths. "*Hey*!" he yelled even louder and waved it twice more. "Come and get it."

Ajax then dropped the flare between Juan's feet, and they all retreated back into the shadows, guns pointed at the large hole in the wall.

Ajax licked his lips. "Hold fire until that big asshole comes out."

They waited, with just the sputtering noise of the fizzing flare and its infernal red glow. Ajax wished the stupid flare *was* silent as it masked the approach of anything from within the cave-tunnel. But at least it lit up the first 10 feet of the interior, so as a trade-off, it was justified.

He'd positioned himself the furthest back of the group, and he tried to visualize how it would play out. He saw several scenarios; one of them, unfortunately, was the snake coming out fast and overshooting Juan. Then, either Camilla or Helen would probably start firing wildly as they tried to follow it with their guns. That'd mean they'd probably be firing across at the opposite side of the room, where Fergus was. Being at the back, he put himself behind that. He hoped.

Ajax looked briefly over his shoulder, reconfirming his bearings. He'd also put himself close to the stairs in the event everything went to shit. He wanted to be the first one out. Live to fight another day was his motto.

He looked across to Fergus. He was the only guy he could count on to score a hit every time. The man had his gun in hard at his shoulder and his eye down on the barrel. If Ajax could take one person with him down the chute, Fergus would be the guy.

Ajax planned on letting the others pepper the thing with the SIG Sauer's standard bottleneck rounds, and hope they did the required damage. But he knew if it pushed through that and came outside of the portal, then boys and girls, cover your fucking ears, 'cause he was going to lay down some fragmentation shit and end the argument right there and then.

He waited, his nerves begging to stretch. He looked up off his gun sight. "Hey, maybe no one's home," he said.

"Maybe," Fergus replied. "But we don't know how deep it goes."

The flare sputtered down and then went out, leaving them in total darkness. Four flashlights came on as one. Camilla's beam was shaking like she was having convulsions, and Helen's wasn't much better.

Ajax grabbed another flare from his thigh pouch. "Last one, then we're going in." He ignited it and tossed it in front of Juan again.

The room bloomed with the Hadean red glow once again. The group waited, their nerves stretching to breaking point, and their eyes focused hawk-like on the smoothed portal opening.

After another few more moments, Ajax ground his teeth and cursed. It should goddamn be working; they had a body, still alive and warm. The light and heat from the flare should have drawn any hunter in the area. It should *fucking-shit-goddamn work*.

No choice now, he guessed. They were going to have to go in. Ajax sniffed, his eyebrows coming together. Just floating over the top of the flares pyrotechnic stink, he thought he could detect other scents. Something more acrid. *Was it here when they came down?* he wondered. *Musta been.*

He sniffed deeper this time. It was a bit like cat's piss, musky, old meat, and maybe something that smelled like old gym socks.

Ajax clicked his fingers and Fergus turned to him. But his comrade in arms froze as he stared—but not at him—at something just past him.

Ajax felt the hairs on his neck rise, and he spun around.

"Contact!" Fergus yelled as Ajax threw himself to the side.

Stopped on the steps leading down to them was a vision straight from Hell. The triangular head of the snake was as wide as a small car and filled the entire tunnel. Its unblinking eyes reflected the dying glow of the flare, making them dance like twin infernos.

Both he and Fergus opened fire and piled dozens of rounds into it. Camilla screamed and just went to her knees. She grabbed the crucifix from around her throat and held it up as some sort of talisman. Helen fumbled with her handgun, finally getting off some shots that struck the walls and ceiling.

The snake came down the steps like molten death. Its massive, muscular body seemed to be something from mythology and not of some flesh-borne world.

Ajax ejected his magazine and jammed in another. His last. In the blink of time it took for the task, the snake was right in front of him.

CHAPTER 33

Emma watched the stream for many minutes, losing herself in the clear water as it burbled over stones and surged around fallen logs. Along each edge of the waterway were fronds, palms, vines hanging like bead curtains, and huge trunks reaching thick roots into the dark, compost-rich soil.

The light was nearly gone now, but the edge of a huge moon was just starting to show through the tree canopy. It lit up the stream like a ribbon of silver. She knew if she followed the watercourse, it would take her to the plateau edge. She also knew that tracking along the streambed or its bank would mean she was under less cover, and it was exactly what she had warned the group to avoid.

She wondered how they were getting on. *Fine*, she bet. They had Drake with them, plus a truckload of weaponry. She was the dumbass who headed off by herself.

She sighed and looked up to the sky, spotting the huge lunar disc as it became visible—a hunter's moon, Ben had called it once. She knew why. There were always nocturnal hunters, but a huge moon meant that the daytime hunters could double their chances of a kill by hunting on through a moonlit night.

Speed or safety? That was her choice.

She squinted as she continued to look upward. To the west, there was a tiny streak of silver—*Primordia*—the comet was starting to veer away from the Earth. Time was running out.

Dammit, she thought; *it had to be speed then*. She was up against a wall and needed to find Ben or pick up his trail in the next few hours, and then leave more time to get back to that temple. She prayed that the team would be able to clear out the horrors that lived in there. And she doubled down on praying that it was a chute that took them all the way to the ground.

She pulled the night scope from her pack and slid it over her head—it was as heavy as she remembered. She flicked it on and then turned her head slowly. She panned back and forth, and then craned her neck to look upward at the overhead branches. Thankfully, everywhere was all empty and all quiet.

She checked her watch; 10 hours remaining—*still doable*, she hoped.

Here goes nothing, she thought, and eased down the bank, her feet skidding in the mud. She sucked in a deep draft of humid air, and then set off.

CHAPTER 34

"Keep up," Drake said over his shoulder before turning back to the tell-tale signs of passage on the ground—tiny flattened stems, indentations in the soil, and almost imperceptible grazes on rocks. It had to be Emma; no other thing living on this plateau would be this clumsy, unless it weighed several tons and didn't give a shit.

He looked briefly back at Andy again—the young scientist grinned in the near darkness. He wore his night vision goggles that made him look slightly robotic and geeky, and more than a little like a kid at a birthday party.

"I hoped I'd get a chance to use these; I love them," he whispered.

"Fine," Drake said. "They're yours. Now stay close so you get home in one piece to enjoy them."

They had to clamber over some fallen tree trunks; the massive boughs were about five feet around, but sagging in the middle as they weren't like real wood, but more like some sort of soft fibrous material, a little like that of the trunk of a tree fern.

Drake slid down over one stump with Andy dropping softly beside him. The soldier held up a hand to halt, and then took off his glove. He crouched and placed his hand on the ground, and then half-turned his head and concentrated—he could feel it under his fingers then; the tremors.

"Something big on the move."

"Coming this way?" Andy flipped the goggles up and stared into the darkness for a moment and then flipped them back down.

Drake concentrated a little more and felt the tremors again, each a second or two apart; they were growing stronger, as if from the gait of an enormous beast.

"Yeah." He looked around. "We need to get under cover."

"Do you know what type it is?" Andy leaned closer.

Drake snorted. "Listen, kid, my expertise in dinosaurs extends to watching Jurassic Park." He grabbed Andy's shoulder. "But that's why you're here, remember, Brains?"

"Oh yeah." Andy grinned and thumbed over his shoulder. "Those tree trunks; I think one was hollow."

Drake took one last look around. "Then that's where we're going.

Lead on."

He followed as Andy turned and crouch-ran back the way they'd just come. They found the massive tree that had fallen and over time broken into pieces. A 15-foot section lay at a slight angle to the rest, and at one end, Drake could see what Andy had previously spotted— the trunk seemed to have a four-foot hollow section within its six-foot girth.

As he quickly shone his light inside, he now felt the tremors beneath his feet. Whatever was coming was now pretty damned close.

"In we go." Drake folded himself in, with Andy sliding in next to him.

"Tight squeeze," Andy said, lying up against Drake.

"Doesn't mean we're engaged," Drake said.

Andy chuckled.

Drake elbowed him. "Quiet."

The footfalls were big enough and close enough now to be felt right through the tree trunk and their asses. Dust and debris rained down on top of them, and Drake also pulled his night scope, slipped it over his head, and flicked it on.

Inside their hiding place, the trunk lit up in the usual phosphorescent green of the night vision. He saw there were a few weird-looking toadstools, mounds of leaf debris, and what could have been flat rocks like hubcaps, embedded inside the hollow trunk with them. Drake and Andy remained still and silent, as whatever moved around just outside came right up to where they were hiding.

They heard deep sniffing as something huge inhaled droughts of air; it was either tracking them, or hopefully following the scent of something else entirely.

Drake looked along the trunk and out into the darkness that was now lit green, just as a foot, like that of an ostrich except hundreds of times bigger, came down on a tree trunk segment right next to them. The soft and fibrous trunk compressed down almost flat, and Drake prayed the next foot didn't come down on them.

At worst, they'd get crushed immediately. At best, they'd have to make a run for it, and then one of them might get chased down and eaten alive. *No*, he thought, *that one* was the worst scenario.

The snuffling came again from outside, but a little further away. Drake breathed out, and then sucked air deep into his lungs, conscious of his racing heart hammering on his ribs. On the next intake, he smelled something weird that he hadn't noticed before—bitter almonds, and it was getting stronger.

He turned and leaned in close to Andy. "What the hell is that?"

"Not reptilian," Andy said and looked down the length of the log. "More like…"

Drake followed his gaze. Some of the things he had thought were flat stones embedded in the tree trunk's inner walls, suddenly lifted up on eight pincer-like legs.

Oh fuck no, Drake whispered, trying to slowly reach down to pull out his gun.

"Holy shit; *Pulmonoscorpius*," Andy whispered as he backed up and into Drake. "Don't move a muscle," he said, and kept backing up all the way past the soldier.

"Thanks," Drake said, pointing his gun.

The thing was three feet long, and it lifted two claws before it that were larger than human hands. From behind it, a long, segmented tail extended and for now at least, the sting on its tip was straight-out flat.

Drake stared—it was shiny, like hard plastic, and segmented like it had been assembled from different pieces. It turned toward the open end of the trunk and took a few steps, but then stopped. The sounds outside hadn't quite abated, as whatever the monstrous thing was out there still poked around. The insectoid thing obviously changed its mind and turned. Toward them.

It stopped again, seeming to balk at heading down toward the two men, and froze, watching, glossy eyes like dark buttons fixed on them.

"Early scorpion," Andy whispered as he peered around Drake.

"Venomous?" Drake asked.

"Probably. What's the point of having a stinger without venom? Even if it's not highly toxic, with the size of that guy, the amount it pumped into you would probably kill you anyway." Andy nudged Drake's arm that held the gun.

"Don't shoot; that big predator outside will react."

"Right, so I'll just give that giant scorpion a good talking to." Drake shook his head.

The massive scorpion began to scuttle toward them, and it knew they were there as its tail went from straight-out behind it, to curling up and over its back.

"*Ah*, shit. Not good," Andy whispered.

Even in the dark, Drake could see that its sting-tip was as large as an apple with a barb like a hypodermic syringe pointed straight at them. Drake knew at this range he couldn't miss, but Andy was right; if he took out the scorpion, he might bring the thunder down from that big mother outside.

Andy tapped his arm again. "Get your knife ready. Follow my lead."

Drake pulled his long hunting blade. Then Andy carefully moved to the other side of the log and lay one hand on the ground, palm up, and started to wiggle his middle finger. He continued to slide his other hand and arm along the inside of the trunk.

With the glass-like eyes of the scorpion, it was impossible to tell if it sighted the wiggling finger, but its head moved a fraction.

"Come on, just a nice worm for you. See, it's wiggling, and ri-*iiight* here."

One of the giant scorpion's legs rose and came forward, then another, and in an almost mechanical motion, it began to creep forward. The huge claws opened, intent on grasping and holding the moving finger so it could deploy its stinger.

"Re-eeeady," Andy breathed.

The scorpion rushed forward, hunger overtaking any caution. Andy swept his other arm across and grabbed the foot-long tail just under the bulbous stinger. The massive claws reached up for Andy's hand.

"*Now.*"

Drake swept his blade across, just under Andy's hand, and severed the chitinous appendage. The massive scorpion went mad, scrambling and skittering. In another second, the thing vanished in a blur of thrashing legs out the other end of the log.

Andy tossed the barb out after it. He turned with a big kid-like grin splitting his face.

"And that, Sergeant Brawn, is why you need me."

CHAPTER 35

The stream turned into a broad, shallow river, and then turned into a swamp.

"*That's just great,*" Emma seethed.

There was no more riverbank, no path, just a lot of water that was probably shallow, but as it was ink-black, it could have been bottomless for all she knew. To add to the eerie setting, there was a mist hanging listlessly over the dark water. And its surface wasn't still; there were ripples, pops of bubbles, and the signature V-waves on the top as things moved about in the depths.

She'd seen enough of the lake to know that things took advantage of water, and the more water, the bigger the creatures were that made it their home.

Emma flipped her goggles from light-enhance to amplify and immediately the green fluorescent landscape became enlarged. She turned slowly—there were mangrove-type roots up on stilts, numerous palms, ferns, fronds, and things that looked melted or rotted with decay. The humidity was all-encompassing, and everything was wet, dripping, and smelled of sulfur and methane.

In amongst the trees, she could make out the massive column-like legs and rotund bodies of enormous creatures, their heads lost in the dark foliage canopies way overhead. They were near motionless, and the only sound came from the occasional gurgle of bellies and bursts of gas she assumed were dinosaur farts.

She breathed a little easier, if not through her mouth. One of the things she'd learned was that if the plant-eaters rested easy, then predators probably weren't close by. She turned, scanning the swamp, and then in the direction she needed to try and get to.

"Maybe," she whispered. Just over the other side of a stretch of water was what looked like dry ground.

She crouched, scanning along the banks, and then the water, looking for places to cross.

Dumb, dumb, and dumber, she thought. She'd done her homework and researched what she could potentially run into in this time period—and there was plenty to fear in the waterways, swamps, and generally boggy areas.

There were the ancestors of massive eels, snakes, heavy-jawed fish, and the crocodiles. Monstrous things like the *Deinonychus* that reached 35 feet in length, and probably chowed down on other dinosaurs. She'd be a tasty morsel to something like that.

But then again, those big plant-eaters wouldn't be looking so chilled out if there was a 10-ton, 35-foot croc hanging around.

She plotted her path—down to the water's edge, and then leap to that first large flat stone, and then to the next. Finally to leap off and sprint the rest of the way—if it was as shallow as she hoped, she'd be over the other side in an instant. The key tactic was to stay out of the water as much as possible.

Emma stood, wiped her hands on her pants, and walked down to the water's edge and looked in—nothing. She had zero chance of seeing the bottom. She looked out to the first flat rock about 10 feet hence, and then backed up, five, 10, 20 feet.

Emma exploded forward, sprinting, and then leaping from the water's edge to the flat stone. She came down and tried to stick her landing, but oddly the stone sank a few inches.

"*Shit.*" She kept her balance and leaped to the next, even larger one that had to be 10 feet around. This one had a slight upward curve and she landed easily, going into a crouch. But again, within seconds of her touching down, the entire rock moved.

"What the fuck? Hey, stop that." On one side, something lifted from the water. It was about two feet wide, and then the thing swiveled.

"*Jesus.*" It was a head, *a goddamn big head*, with a long downward-curving beak. It glared and made a hoarse rattling noise deep in its throat. She remembered there was one more thing to look out for—giant freshwater turtles.

"*Oops*, sorry, buddy." She stood, arms out like a surfer, and then ran up its back to leap off, and land on another smaller one that also sunk—*probably its young*, she thought. But this time she kept going, clearing a few more and landing on the bank.

She turned. The eyes of the turtles glowed like headlights, and she could imagine what they were thinking—*what a rude little creature*, they undoubtedly thought.

Emma grinned and saluted them. "Thanks, guys." She then turned back to her path and saw that the water was shallowing into puddles here, with a few remaining boggy areas.

She began to jog to the jungle edge. Her feet sloshed, first to the ankles, and then to her calves. Then, her feet sunk, deep, and she fell forward. Her hands struck the oily slickness, like porridge, and nothing to grab onto. It was all around her, and in the seconds it took her to realize where she was, she had already sunk to her waist.

It hadn't been a puddle at all. *But just a thin veneer of water over quicksand*, she thought with horror.

She remembered what she needed to do: relax, try to lay flat, and float. However, her legs wouldn't come up as the glutinous mass was low on water and high on silt, and the layer on top was brackish swamp-slime, and below that a sucking bog. It was more quickmud than quicksand.

In seconds more, she was in it to her chest.

"No, no…"

Emma grimaced, and turned one way then the other. *This is where I yell for help*, she thought insanely.

She looked for something, anything, she could use. She spotted a tapering log, just at one end of the pool she was in, and she reached out for it. Her fingers fell a foot short, and she stretched again, with little forward motion.

She needed to be closer or she needed longer arms. As she wasn't able to move back or forth, so, longer arms it was.

She sunk a little more—*now or never*, she thought and reached down to undo her nylon clasp belt and pull it out of her belt loops.

She wrapped one end around her hand and concentrated—the log had a skinny end and was hard to see clearly in the darkness.

Emma pulled her smallest blade from her belt and stuck it right through the nylon webbing until it reached its hilt. She held up the miniature grappling hook and began to swing it back and forth a few times before launching it.

"Shit." She missed.

And the motion caused her to sink another few inches. She grinned at the lunatic thought that popped into her head; she remembered the mysterious print from the museum with the weird indentations they thought might have been a human footprint.

If they thought that was a mystery, then what would they make of a human skeleton dug out of some prehistoric petrified bog in 100 million years time? she wondered. *I'll be a sensation*, she answered herself.

She reeled her belt in, and once again swung it back and forth a few times, and then this time gave it more slack. The belt and its blade hook slapped down on the log end, hooking it.

The log was immediately whipped away with an angry hiss like a steam train. Emma froze.

Then the diamond-shaped head emerged from between the fern fronds about 30 feet away.

"Oh, for fuck's sake."

The snake was big by modern standards, but smaller than the monsters she had seen on the plateau. The head was a foot across, and she bet its body was as thick as her waist, and given where the head just appeared, would have been 30 feet long if it was an inch. *Small*, she knew, but easily big enough to make a meal out of her.

Emma stuck a hand down into the mud and fumbled for her SIG Sauer handgun. She lifted it free from the glutinous mess she was stuck in, aimed, and pulled the trigger—there was a grinding sensation, but nothing happened. She pulled again and again with the same result.

The guns were extremely reliable, but she guessed they drew the line at being gummed up with gritty silt.

She dropped the gun, and instead grabbed at her longest blade, drew it, and held it up. The 10-inch metal tooth was a feeble defense against something this size, but it was all she had.

She knew the snake would have hundreds of backward-curving teeth in two rows that were used for gripping. If it got hold of her, she'd never get herself free from the mouth.

She knew what to expect—it would rear up and then lunge, using its muscled body to strike out, hit her hard, and bite down, embedding its teeth in her flesh. Her knife would probably never even penetrate the armored scales. The one chance she had was to stick her knife into the softer palate—inside its open mouth.

Emma could have wept; the odds of her pulling that off were about zero.

Stay focused and stay alive. She tried to think through its attack, how it would come, and what she would do.

She bared her teeth. One thing's for sure—she'd die fighting. Emma raised the knife. She knew how to use it.

The snake glided forward, but instead of coiling itself back, loading its muscles for the impact strike as she expected, when it got to the edge of her scum-covered pool, it simply slid in below the surface.

"Oh, no, no, no."

It was going to come at her from below.

Emma became frantic and swiveled one way then the other. Her screwing back and forth forced her lower into the slimy water.

The snake entered the pool and for all she knew was right below her now. No, she bet it'd do one thing first…and it did. The huge head rose a few inches from the water, sighting her, before easing back down.

Fuck it, she thought.

"*Help!*"

She tried to swim backward but was stuck in place.

"He-*eelp!*"

She lowered her head and shoulder into the water and sliced the knife back and forth. Emma couldn't resist the urge to open her eyes, but the gritty blackness did nothing but fill her eyes with slime and grit. Coming back up, she screamed again.

"Goddamn it!" Frustration boiled over.

"*Emma!*"

She spun, her stinging eyes held wide.

"*Help me…snake…in water.*" She sputtered a little. "Stay back…quicksand."

Drake edged forward, with Andy holding onto him from behind by his belt. The soldier had his rifle pulled back tight into his shoulder. He fired several rounds into the water—spraying one side, then the next.

Andy let Drake go and quickly ripped a length of rope free from his pack and tossed the loop to her. She grabbed it, feeling her groin tingle at the thought of the snake still being down there.

As the pair of men began to haul her out, Emma felt something touch her thigh and she kicked at it, feeling the scaled resistance of its muscular body. She jerked her leg away and in another second, she was sliding backward in the mud.

Drake came and crouched beside her, and she clung to him, feeling her emotions boil over. She kept her face buried into his shirt for several more moments before using it to wipe the grime from her face and out of her eyes.

"Thank you." She leaned back and gave him a crooked smile. "I'm having a real bad day. How about you?"

*****

The massive *Giganotosaurus* lifted its head, listened for a moment more, and then sniffed deeply. The cry of a distressed animal was irresistible to it.

The cry came again, longer this time, and not far away. It sniffed again, inhaling the breeze as it tried to pick up the spoor trail.

The huge 30-ton body turned, its tail flattening ferns, tree trunks, and palms as it tracked the sound. The darkness didn't bother it, and in fact, as well as having a highly developed sense of smell and excellent hearing, it had nocturnal vision.

The sound had been close, and the huge hunter lowered its head and stiffened its thick tail out arrow-straight behind it as it pushed through the thick jungle growth. It was a massive battering ram of muscle and teeth and could run at 30 miles per hour if needed.

It picked up the trail and moved further up toward the center of the plateau.

*****

Ben's head shot up, and he froze, listening.

Then the cry came again, longer this time. Could it be?

"Emma?"

Ben's eyes widened in both shock and exuberance. He hoped and prayed she would come, *knew* she would come, but hearing her voice, any voice, was still a shocking sound after 10 long years.

It *had* to be her; who else would or could it be?

And she was close.

And she was in trouble.

It took all his willpower to stop himself going madly crashing through the jungle. He'd found out too many times that predators were always there, always waiting. Even the plant-eaters, the great cows of the prehistoric times, were so huge that he could be crushed underfoot, gored by a horned head, or obliterated by one swing of a clubbed tail. This was not a place for soft mammals, and wouldn't be for many, many millions of years.

Slow down, slow down, he kept repeating, trying to turn it into a mantra to ensure he stayed alive. His chest still burned and felt tight from the scabbing. Plus, breathing was a minute-by-minute agony, but all of it was forgotten as Ben burrowed and darted around a forest of dawn redwoods, massive trees that vanished into the darkness hundreds of feet above him and had trunks easily 20 feet around.

Thorned cycads, spread wide like massive starfish, and from some lower branches and ferns hung things that looked like huge wasp nests.

Ben slowed as he passed underneath a particularly large and angry-looking one, and recognized them as not insect nests at all, but instead some sort of fungal parasite that showered spores when they were disturbed. He guessed the objective was that if an animal brushed past them, they'd end up covered in the fungal spores and then it would lumber off, taking the seed of a new generation of fungus with it, so they could propagate over a larger area.

The problem for Ben—and one he'd found out the hard way—was if the spores touched human skin, they generated an angry immune response of a blistered rash, itching, and then weeping sores for weeks afterwards. And if they got in your eyes, forget about seeing anything for a while.

He then moved through a stand of hanging vines and bamboo-like stems, so closely packed he had to squeeze through sideways.

In the center of the thicket, he paused and cocked his head, listening some more. Ben desperately wanted Emma to call again, or give some sign, but he also wanted her to shut up. A noise in the dark attracted the hunters in an instant. And even in darkness, there was no hiding from most of them.

He swallowed down a small ball of tension in his gut, because he knew up here, there was one predator that could see in the dark, knew which way you went from a single handprint on a tree trunk, and could also see your body heat flaring like a beacon in the darkness.

They were all at risk. And now that Ben was totally disarmed, he was more vulnerable than ever. And then.

"*Goddamn it!*"

Ben heard her again, very close now. He gave in to his impatience and worry for her, and his limbs took on a will of their own. He barged through the jungle toward her voice.

*****

Drake looked over Emma's weapons; he ejected the magazine, popped out a few rounds, and then sighed.

"All I can salvage is the ammunition. The gun needs to be broken down and cleaned. That grit and silt has jammed everything up." He handed it to her.

Emma took the handgun back and reholstered it. "Yeah, well,

that's not going to happen, is it?"

He chuckled. "Not as bad as it sounds; we find some clean water and I can break it down and rinse it out real quick. I'll also need to eject and repack the rounds, but it'd all be done in maybe ten minutes."

She half-smiled. "When we find some clean water, and when we have better light, and when we have a spare ten minutes." Her smiled widened. "The sand in our hourglass is running down, Drake."

He nodded. "Yep." He tilted his head, looking at her. "We came to find and help you. So what do you want to do?"

She checked her watch and blew air from between pressed lips. "We surely can't be far from the clearing edge now. We give it another couple of hours, and then…"

"And then we decide what comes next," Drake answered. "And we make that decision clinically, and without emotion, right, Emma?" He stared hard at her.

She turned back to the jungle, spotting Andy examining something on the lower branches of a massive tree. He smiled as he picked something from one of the limbs. *At least he's enjoying himself,* she thought.

She turned back to Drake. "Yeah, sure, another couple of hours. Then we decide what comes next."

*****

Andy collected a few strange insects with horns on their heads, or had multiple legs, but claws on the end of each limb, like they were test models in some sort of evolutionary game that Mother Nature was playing. He tucked them into tubes or bags, sealing each. He couldn't wait to compare notes with Helen when they caught up with them.

He held one up, admiring it. Andy knew he could spend months, years, a lifetime here, investigating plants, animals and species never before seen. Evolution was a game, and it rolled the dice on creativity sometimes. Added to that, fossilization was just as much a crapshoot. Even the most optimistic experts knew that the further back in time you went, the lower the chance a species makes it into the fossil record.

Andy sighed; there were exotic things here that no one had seen, would see even as a fossil, and perhaps could even imagine in their wildest dreams.

While Drake and Emma talked, he guessed he had a few more

minutes, so he lifted his search to the lower branches. He was about to turn away from one hanging limb, when he spotted the bulbous papery-looking sack hanging from the branch.

Drake had warned him about using his flashlight, so he flipped his night vision down over his eyes. The first thing he noticed was that the papery-looking sack was cold, meaning it wasn't an insect hive, or at least an occupied one. Even though bugs themselves were room temperature, a group moving together generated a lot of heat, and a hive would have been warm.

There was a hole in its bottom, and he doubted it was a fruit, as it seemed to just be attached to the limb as opposed to growing from it. *As it wasn't part of the tree, then maybe it was some sort of parasite?* he wondered.

Andy ducked down, but the flaring green night goggles didn't help. He looked over his shoulder at the still-talking pair. *One or two seconds of real light couldn't hurt,* he thought.

He lifted his goggles away from his face and pulled out his slim flashlight and moved in closer. He still wore gloves and so had no qualms about touching the thing.

He reached out for it and flicked on his light just as he grabbed the bulbous sack and lifted it toward himself, planning on shining his light inside the hole.

Immediately, there was a reaction—the sack compressed and *exhaled* exactly like a lung with a sound like an old man wheezing. The particle dust or whatever it was blew outward with some force and covered Andy's mouth, nose, and both of his eyes.

Then the excruciating pain set in.

"Jesus…" He dropped his light and backed away. "*Ouch, ouch.*" He rubbed at them, shaking his head. "*Drake.*"

In a second, he felt a strong hand on his arm. "What happened?"

"Thing on the tree, farted on me. Spores, I think." He grimaced. "It's in my eyes. Stings like hell."

"Stay still," Emma said.

Andy felt hands on his head, tilting it back.

"Open your eyes," she said forcefully.

He did as he was told. He could see nothing, but felt warm water being poured over his face. He immediately felt relief from the pain, but his vision stayed blurred.

"How's that?" she asked.

"Better." He blinked. "But still can't see a damn thing." He cleared his throat and spat. "Must have been like some sort of puffball fungus. Covered me."

"Anyone else remember being told not to touch anything?" Drake said with little humor.

Andy still hung onto him. "Yeah, but I'm a scientist. I know what I'm doing."

Drake chuckled. "Yeah, I can see that now. But in reality, you're now disabled, in a prehistoric jungle, at night. Great timing, son."

"Leave me," Andy said, feeling dumb and resentful at the same time. "Pick me up me on the way back."

Emma shrugged. "Okay…"

"*No.*" Drake cut across Emma, glaring at her. "How long would he, or you, stay alive in this jungle if you were blind?"

Emma just crossed her arms and looked at him from under her brows. Drake turned to Andy. "Take off your belt."

"*Huh*? Why?" the paleontologist asked.

"Do it, quickly," Drake said. "I'm going to have to put you on a lead. When I say duck, you duck. When I say left or right, you do as I say. You'll need to use senses besides your eyes until your vision comes back. Got it?"

"Sure, sure," Andy said, still feeling guilty for putting this extra burden on Drake, but relieved he wasn't staying behind.

Drake took the belt and looped one end around the back of his own belt. The other end he tied around Andy's wrist.

"There." He turned to Emma. "Okay, let's do this. In two hours, if we don't find anything, we head back."

"Two hours." Emma simply turned away, moving in the direction she expected was the plateau edge, and Ben.

*****

Emma felt her anger and impatience begging to burn within her. She had the germ of a feeling that kept trying to grow within her about going home with no Ben. The comet, Primordia, would leave, the wettest season would end, and the portal, gateway, or whatever it was, would close again for another 10 years.

Did she have the drive to try again in another decade? Would Ben even be alive? Was he even alive now?

Fuck it, she spat into the darkness.

They had to cross over a fissure in the landscape. It was only about seven feet wide, but a good 20 deep and it narrowed at the bottom. Hopefully, there was a fallen tree over it for them to ease across.

They reentered another stand of ancient pine trees, and she accidentally kicked a cone the size of a small football, the heavy seedpod hurting her toes and then lifting off and bouncing away. It threw up twigs as it bounced, and then settled. But after it had stopped, instead of silence returning, there came the soft crack of a branch. But about 50 feet further in.

Emma raised an arm and held her position. Then she felt a hand alight on her shoulder. "We got a problem." Drake kept his voice soft and calm.

Emma froze, just letting her eyes move over the primordial landscape. The clouds opened a little, throwing down a few more slivers of moonlight, and the black-on-blackness of the night jungle forest was illuminated enough to make out shapes.

There were endless trunks of the massive primitive pines, standing thick and mighty and seeming to reach the sky. But in amongst them, there was another shape—just as mighty—but this one had a large boxy head the size of an SUV, an upright stance, and colossal legs of raw power.

Emma felt her stomach flip. The creature also seemed frozen, and if she wasn't where she was, she might have believed it was some sort of giant mockup, and they were at a fun park looking at a Disney model.

But it was real, and the only reason it was rooted to the spot, was that perhaps their non-movement had meant its eyesight built for tracking moving prey had temporarily lost them.

"What is it?" Andy whispered from behind them.

Without turning, Drake gently shushed him, and then leaned ever so gently back toward Emma.

"We can't outrun that monster over open ground. If it attacks, we need to get somewhere it can't follow."

"Yep," she whispered back. By the look of the carnivore's size, it must have been the *Giganotosaurus* that they had seen previously. It was larger than a *T-rex* and one of the biggest theropod carnivores to have ever lived.

Emma tried to keep her eyes on the massive beast while talking to both men. "Remember that crack in the ground we passed over a while back? Think we can make it?"

"Maybe deep enough. And we'll damn well die trying," Drake said. "We're gonna have to run for it. I'll let Andy know the plan."

She heard him whispering, and then she saw the massive creature take a careful step. The way it eased its foot forward, bird-like, and then placed it gently down in front of it, it told her it was beginning its stalking…of them.

"It knows we're here," she said. Emma looked at the coiled power of the thing and started to doubt they could stay in front of it.

"On the count of three, we're gonna go for it," Drake said.

"Wait," she said. "Need a diversion." She reached for one of her flares and held it for a moment in her hand.

"Now count."

Drake began. "3, 2…"

She punched the flare down on her thigh, and it immediately turned their jungle a brilliant red. The *Giganotosaurus* bellowed, and the sound was a physical force that battered their senses and made Emma's heart race. It charged, and the ground shook beneath them.

"*1!*" Drake grabbed Andy and they ran for their lives.

Emma tossed the flare at the thing as it bore down on them. She didn't wait to see if it struck, but the sound of trees being pushed aside, thumping footfalls, and thunderous roars, ceased for a moment. Even if the flare only gave them seconds, it might just be enough.

She ran almost blindly, praying she was heading back to the crack in the Earth. She also hoped it was as deep as she first thought. Up ahead and just to her right, she could just make out Drake dragging Andy along, trying to guide the young scientist around, over, and under obstacles. He fell, and Drake roughly dragged him back to his feet.

Behind her, the ground-shaking pursuit started again. The flare was still burning as the glow still emanated from behind her, but it had obviously lost the attention of the huge meat-eater.

Worryingly, she was catching up to Drake and Andy. She knew that together the two men were a larger target. They were also moving slower.

Behind her, she began to hear the deep huffing and drew her shoulders up and pulled her head down as though the inch difference might make the monster miss her when it reached for her.

"Run…*faster!*" she yelled, as she was about to overtake them.

And then they both vanished into the ground. Emma didn't slow, and in fact accelerated to where they had disappeared. She saw the small crevasse and dove into it.

Where they landed, the fissure in the ground was only about seven feet wide, but a good 20 feet deep. Emma pinballed from one side to the other as she fell to the bottom. Drake immediately grabbed her and pulled her in close to the wall where he and Andy hid.

Soil rained down as the ground shook from the gargantuan footfalls, and then they stopped, and the huffing of huge breaths came from just above them.

The silvery moon was directly overhead and they pressed themselves back into the shadows where there were mounds of fallen bracken, rotting logs, and rocks. From beside her, something the size of a small dog with too many legs scuttled out to investigate, and she batted it away with her fist. She had bigger problems.

Then the moon glow seemed to shut off, as a massive boxy head leaned out over them. It inhaled, deeply, sucking up huge drafts of air. She was bathed in sweat, and she bet the two men were the same—she knew they probably stank to high heaven, and the great beast wouldn't need super senses to know exactly where they were.

Seemingly satisfied, it turned its head sideways as eyes that seemed too small for the oversized head turned toward them. It seemed to bulge slightly like the lens of a camera focusing, or that of a bird that regards you from behind the bars of its cage.

The massive body lowered, and the head reached in. It had to turn sideways to fit in, but the head on the powerful neck craned downwards as the heavy back end of the animal gave it balance and the monstrous powerful legs braced, like the ballast of a crane.

"*Shit*," Drake hissed. He held up his rifle; the barrel was bent, and he'd obviously landed on it. Instead, he pulled his handgun and held it against his chest as he stared upward. Emma lunged across and grabbed at Andy's holster, taking his gun and doing the same. But she knew the 9mm guns would be like shooting peas at a thing with a skull that had to be many inches thick, plus a hide that was tougher than hardened leather.

"It can't reach us," Drake whispered. He looked up and down the crevice, and then back up at the great beast. "And this is the widest point. I think we're okay here."

The head was lifted back out, but it stayed above them.

"One problem," Emma said. "We can't wait here until it gets bored and gives up."

Drake turned to her. "Sure, but I think we can afford to give it just a few more minutes, right?"

She bet he grinned in the dark.

"I guess." She hunkered down as soil rained heavily onto their heads. "Now what?"

Emma looked up just as a single three-toed foot that had to be as wide as an industrial shovel began to rake at the dirt. "Look out." She leaped out of the way as a large rock was dislodged and rolled down into their crevasse. She seethed. "That big bastard is going to try and dig us out."

Like a monstrous dog, the *Giganotosaurus* raked with one massive foot and then the other. After a few pulls, it'd stop and lower its head again, checking on the width. In a few more moments, it had already widened the top of the fissure by several feet.

Emma looked up and down the crack in the ground. "Move." She crouch-ran a few dozen feet along the crevasse floor. Drake pulled Andy along after him as he followed. She stopped and flattened herself back against the wall again. The beast followed them, and immediately began its raking again.

"Shit," she hissed.

"We can't stay in here," Drake said.

Emma looked at the walls on either side of her. There was no way to climb out quickly. And even if they did, they'd be back out on the thing's turf. Frustration boiled within her. She spun, lifted her gun in a two-handed grip, gritted her teeth, and fired half a dozen quick rounds into its face.

The head pulled back, and she was sure she hit it, perhaps every time. But after a few seconds, the raking began again directly over them. The huge head leaned over and reached down again, and then inhaled deeply. This time, the head angled and the mouth opened and the jaws snapped shut again, so close she actually saw the broad, flat tongue inside the mouth.

It was only *just* too far away, but it was getting closer. Emma held her breath as she smelled the vile carnivore stink emanating from its gaping mouth. She'd seen her friends disappear into mouths like those, and she was damn sure she'd never let that be her fate.

Once again, the head pulled back, and the raking started again, and once again, the trio scurried another 20 feet further along the crevasse. But it was like a dog enjoying a game; the great beast followed them, to immediately rake again.

Emma groaned. The problem for them was that the further along the crack they went, the shallower it got. A few more sprints, and the monster would only need to dig a few feet to reach them.

She turned to see Drake looking at her. He grinned and shrugged. "This has been one helluva a trip, Ms. Wilson."

She couldn't help smiling in return. "It'll sure be something to tell your kids about."

"That's first prize," he said. "Second, is just staying alive to tell anyone."

Andy leaned around Drake and lifted one side of the bandage over his eyes. He blinked myopically, and then ripped it off. He kept blinking, and then looked upward, seeing the massive boxy head reaching down.

"Jesus." He ducked as the massive head thundered down into the gap. 'Please tell me it's just my screwy eyes making me see that."

"I wish," Drake said, also hunkering down even more. "Maybe you should put that back on, buddy."

Emma grimaced. "Welcome back."

The head smashed down again, and Emma contemplated another scurry along the trench. But she saw that it became too shallow. They'd be dug out in an instant, if the beast even had to dig. The other option was to try and rush past the head and get to the other end of the fissure—where there were already huge holes now dug in the edge of the crack.

"Lie down flat," Drake said.

You mean, lie down and prepare to die, Emma thought grimly.

The claws raked and raked some more, and stones tumbled down on them, adding to the fear and chaos. Emma could hear its breath quickening as it started to tire, she hoped, but more likely it was becoming excited at the prospect of soon being able to reach its prizes.

To hell with that. I'm not lying down and not staying here, she thought. *I'd rather die trying to get away than be picked off like some piece of fallen fruit.* The moonbeams shone down again, illuminating the end of the crevice. It shallowed out, but even at its end, was still around seven feet high; too high to jump and run, and scaling meant she was vulnerable even for the few seconds it might take her.

Her mind computed the distance, the speed she might need, and her odds—*low*, she knew. She also knew by herself she might make it, *might*. But if all three of them tried, then they'd bunch up and potentially get in each other's way.

She sat up, just as there came the thump of something striking the opposite wall of the crevasse. There came more, as more of the things rained down. A few struck the *Giganotosaurus*, and it roared its displeasure or shock.

More things rocketed down, and she heard the hard objects striking the head of the great beast with a solid crack of wood on bone. One of the items rolled close by, and she scurried over to reach for it.

"A pinecone thing." It was larger than the variety she knew, and the size of a small football. The cone's scales were closed tight, and it was damn heavy, several pounds at least, and hard as a rock.

The cones continued to shoot down, striking the *Giganotosaurus'* head, neck, and flanks. It finally screamed its rage, and turned, looking for something to confront.

Emma looked up to see the beast's tail hanging over the edge of their crevasse, as the thing must have been facing away from them now. She got up, hunched over, trotted to the end of the crevasse and jumped up, catching the lip with her fingers and pulling herself up to peek over.

She saw the massive theropod snap at the air and take a few thunderous steps toward the huge primitive pines, but it could find no assailant. All the while from high up in the branches, the heavy cones sailed down, striking the infuriated beast over and over.

Drake lifted himself up beside her, and she turned to him. "Jesus Christ; who's doing that? Is it Ajax?"

"Unlikely he'd even think of coming back for us," Drake said. "Plus, the guy can't climb for shit."

The animal bellowed a few more times and lowered its head. More accurate strikes cracked down on the huge skull again and again, and finally, the thing lumbered off in amongst the pine trees. They listened as the heavy footfalls got softer and softer.

It seemed that a head full of lumps changed an easy meal into something not worth the trouble.

"Round one to our pitcher," she said.

Drake took out his binoculars. "And looks like we're about to find out who they are."

A figure scaled down the tree and jumped lightly to the ground. It was a man, with hair to his shoulders. Though underweight, his body still bulged with sinewy muscle and the frame was still broad.

He was near naked save for the remains of a tattered pair of pants covering his groin and one thigh. There was also a woven sack over his back.

He looked around slowly, and he lifted his head as though sniffing. Seeming to be satisfied, he turned back and walked confidently to the edge of the pit. He stared down at the trio, and then his face broke into a broad smile.

"What kept you?"

Emma fell back into the crevasse.

*****

Ben had tracked the sound of Emma's voice and then followed the trail of the massive theropod. He'd seen the group disappear into the crevasse, and given he had no weapons, he had to rely on the one thing he retained—experience.

The big carnivorous beasts had hard heads but small brains and were easily confused and distracted. He'd used the ploy before to see the smaller ones off, and the large, heavy pinecones made ferocious missiles.

He climbed well above the beast's reach and began his attack— one strike, a dozen, 20, 40, before it had finally had enough. He stayed in place, watching its head and shoulders muscle back in through the tree growth and move away down along the waterway.

It might be back, but for now, it would lay low for a while and nurse its headache.

He walked to the edge of the fissure, seeing the heads now poking up. The moon had vanished and he could only just make out their shapes. Each step closer he went, he felt his heart swell to bursting.

Ben tried not to run, but his steps quickened anyway. Would his voice crack? Would he mumble, not being used to talking to anyone but himself for years and years.

He crouched, spoke just a few rusty words, and Emma fell back into the crevasse.

"*Huh?*" He jumped in after her, and a body immediately fell on top of him.

"Only a guy like you could survive in this place for ten years,

Cartwright." Drake threw an arm over him, while Ben tried to help Emma sit up. He brushed the hair from her grimy face.

She burst into tears and reached out for him. "I knew. I knew."

He hugged her close. "You came." He couldn't say any more, as he felt hot tears running down his own face.

"Ho-*oooly* shit," a young man said from just behind Drake. "He actually survived. How? What did you see? Where did you go? I have so many questions." He tried to burrow in closer, but Drake elbowed him back a pace.

Drake reached out a hand to Ben's shoulder. "Captain, we need to bug out, like *right now*. The walls are closing in."

Ben stood, pulling Emma up with him. He kept his eyes on hers the whole time. "Roger that; and I'm certainly not staying here another ten years." He grinned, wiped his face, and turned to his friends, really seeing them for the first time.

"You got old." He grinned.

Drake grinned. "Oh yeah, wait until you see your first mirror after a decade, buddy. And get a haircut, you hippy."

The four of them climbed out of the crevasse, and Ben turned his head to listen for a moment. "That big guy will be back."

"Then we need to be *far* away," Emma said and hung onto him tightly.

The four of them huddled in together, and Ben looked down at Emma, then to Drake. "Do you have a plan?"

"We ballooned in, and we were gonna go out the same way. Unfortunately, it got ripped apart coming in," Drake answered.

"But we think we know another way down," Emma added. "We're not sure if it's viable, but there's another temple built over a chute. I think it leads to the ground."

"First prize, we climb all the way down, and then keep going," Andy said, and stepped in closer. "Captain Cartwright, *Ben*, what did you see? Where did you—?"

"Not now," Ben said and pushed long hair back off his face. "There's one problem; the reason I moved off the plateau and stayed far away is because it's owned by the snakes. And most of the big nests are underground."

"Of course," Andy said. "That's why we found the fossilized remains of the *Titanoboa* deep in a coalmine. It wasn't sedimentary settling, but that's where the thing lived." He snapped his fingers. "And

I bet being underground shielded them from the worst effects of the meteor strike extinction event."

"Then the snakes will definitely be in the temple," Ben said.

Drake snorted. "Yeah, we found that out. Don't worry; Ajax and Fergus will clean them out by the time we get there."

Ben laughed softly. "You talked them into coming along as well?"

Drake shook his head. "Not me, your girlfriend. And Brocke came as well. But we crashed into the lake, and…he bought it there."

"Fuck." Ben's mouth flattened into a line momentarily. "He was a good guy."

"The best," Drake added.

Ben reached out and took Drake's hand, shaking it. "Thank you, Sergeant; you've done a good job. This place is Hell." He pulled Emma in closer. "You're all mad, you know."

"Hell to us, but not to the creatures that live here," Andy added.

Emma looked up at him. "And we're not supposed to be here."

"True." Ben hugged Emma again. "So let's go home."

CHAPTER 36

Eventually, hunger overcomes caution, fear, and pain. The *Giganotosaurus* turned and then headed back to where it had tried to catch the small sweet-smelling creatures in the ground.

It avoided the same path it had come before, not wanting to suffer the same bombardment. But upon returning to where it had dug at the crack in the ground, it found they had fled.

But their scent was still strong. It moved quickly to where the fissure narrowed and smelled that they were on the other side of it. The great beast turned away and trotted about 50 feet from the eight-foot-wide crack, then swung back and accelerated quickly, its massive legs pounding down on the hard earth. When it was a few feet out, it leaped across the fissure to land on the other side with a thunderous impact.

The huge carnivore then traced its way back to where it detected the small things had climbed out. It followed the scent trail, huge nostrils flaring wide and sucking in the odors—they'd moved into the jungle. It began to follow.

CHAPTER 37

"What was it like, Ben? Please, I *must* know," Andy persisted. He was like a small satellite as he stayed at Ben's shoulder. "You've got to tell me what you saw."

"It was Hell." Ben sighed. "And what did I see?" He turned. "I saw a place that people should not exist in."

"Ruled by tooth and claw, *huh*?" Andy pushed.

"Ruled by hunger, and without mercy—eat or be eaten," Ben replied.

"I want to see it," Andy said. "I want to see it all."

"There's a price." Ben turned. "I stayed alive because I lived below the ground, in caves, only foraging at night, and staying out of sight. Being seen meant inviting death." He grinned like a death's head. "If I was a cat, this would be my last life."

"Yep, I get it." Andy nodded. "Working with fossils all my life means having to use my imagination to construct what dinosaurs must have looked like when they were alive. But being here, I've seen *living* dinosaurs. The colors, the way they move, even the sounds they make, *un-bel-ievable*." He grinned.

"Yes," Ben said. "They're faster than we ever imagined. The hunters display pack behavior, just as the plant-eaters move in herds. And some of the pack hunters are smart, even smarter than dogs. They can work things out, problem solve, and they learn real quick." His eyes narrowed as he remembered. "Makes me wonder what the world would be like if they hadn't all become extinct."

"They'd rule the world," Andy said, beaming.

Ben snorted softly. "The ones in the ocean were the same."

"*What*?" Andy grabbed Ben's arm and stopped them both. "You *actually* made it to the *ocean*?" His mouth gaped.

Ben nodded. "Several weeks' hike, always moving at night. Spent months there living off the land and sea."

"Oh God." Andy let him go. "I want to see it," he whispered.

Ben shook his head and began to walk ahead. "The price is too high." He stopped and turned. "Things...*people*, die horribly here."

Andy nodded, but kept his head down.

CHAPTER 38

They entered the swamp half an hour later, about the same time the weird mist started to settle around them. Ben stopped them to crouch by a particularly viscous-looking pool. He dipped a hand into the soft mud and started to liberally apply it to his shoulders, underarms, face, and neck.

"Insects?" Drake asked.

"Keeping insects off is for comfort," Ben said. "But mainly it's to mask my body heat and scent. And that's to survive." He held out a handful. "I suggest you all do the same. After ten years of not seeing and hearing another human being, I can tell you one thing—you smell." He half-smiled. "Not in a bad way, it's just that I can smell you. And if *I* can, the hunters *certainly* can." He finished and stood. "Not to mention the snakes. They'll see you in the dark." He looked at Emma. "Remember?"

She nodded. "They can see our body heat." She held out her hand. "Pass me the cold cream."

Andy and Drake looked at each other, and Ben pointed to the mud. "I'm serious. You don't need to strip down, but coat your clothing and all exposed skin." He looked up at the sky for a moment and saw that the moon had vanished. "Em, how much time do we have?"

Emma checked her watch. "Four hours. It's three until sunup." She turned to Drake. "I'm thinking a good hour and a half to the temple."

"By then, Ajax, Fergus, Helen, Camilla, and Juan should have all scaled down. Or maybe waiting for us," Drake said. He crouched, scooped some mud, and lathered it on his neck, cheeks, and up through his short hair.

"That's quite a team. But more people, more risk," Ben said evenly.

"Yeah, most I hand-picked," Emma said. "Ass kickers like Drake, but also some scientists. Camilla and Juan are press, and managed to barge in on a, *take us or else* proposition."

"Frankly, I'll be happy if they're all gone," Drake added. "If not, we'll get an update on why." He exhaled. "I only hope, if they are there, it's not because it's a dead-end…or something worse."

Drake, Andy, and Emma were lathering the mud on their faces,

194

ears, and began to cover their clothing. Drake stopped for a moment. "And before you ask, we don't really have a Plan B."

"Yeah, we do." Emma tilted her head. "The mist made me remember when we scaled up, and I scaled down the last time. We seemed to pass through a distortion layer of air."

Ben nodded. "You think maybe that was what separated our two time zones, and our worlds?"

Emma nodded. "We know the magnetic effects of Primordia are localized. So maybe that was as far as the time distortion effect reached. So our Plan B is if the temple's chute is deep enough, maybe we can drop below the distortion line. So once Primordia moves on, we can climb back up, and be...back." She shrugged. "It's a theory."

"I like it." Ben nodded. "And I never even thought about that."

"Or we could climb back up, and still be here," Andy said, not looking worried by the prospect at all.

Ben grinned at Emma. "But, I believe in miracles."

A wind began to rustle the treetops, and Ben looked up again. "And so it begins."

"Or ends," Emma said softly.

CHAPTER 39

12 Hours Past Comet Apparition

Comet P/2018-YG874, designate name, Primordia, was pulling away from the third planet to the sun to continue on its eternal elliptical voyage around our solar system.

The magnetic presence that had dragged at the planet's surface, caused chaotic weather conditions, and created a distortion in time and space, was lessening in intensity by the seconds, and in just a few more hours would vanish completely.

The clock was ticking down, and soon there would be another 10 years of calm over the mountaintops of the Venezuelan Amazon jungle.

CHAPTER 40

"So, what's the first thing you're gonna do when you get home, big guy?" Drake walked at Ben's shoulder.

Ben turned to smile at Emma, who nodded in return.

"Yeah, *after* that," Drake said, chuckling.

Ben had lived it in his mind too many times. He grinned in the darkness. "Ribs."

"*Huh?*" Drake tilted his head.

"Ricky's ribs," Emma said. "Double plate, special barbecue sauce. Jug of cold beer." She threw an arm around Ben's waist. "My treat."

He hugged her in close and looked to Drake. "Play your cards right, you might just get an invite." His face became serious, as someone else came to his mind. "Cynthia, Mom, is she still…?"

Emma nodded. "Yeah, still there, still hopeful. Took every ounce of my strength and persuasion skills I had to keep her from coming along."

Ben laughed. "Yep, that'd be Mom."

They walked on in silence for another few minutes before Ben noticed that the swamp was drying and the ground was becoming harder beneath their feet. "This the right way?"

"I should be asking you, Tarzan. This has been *your* home for the last ten years," Drake said.

Ben stopped. "No, it hasn't. I stayed well away from here. For good reason."

"The snakes, *huh?*" Drake asked. "Yeah, pretty badass. We saw one in the temple."

"No, we saw a juvenile," Emma said. "The adults are three times as large."

"O-*oookay*." Drake's jaw clenched for a moment. "Nothing Ajax and Fergus can't handle."

Ben grunted. "I'm glad Fergus is there. Ajax is a little…impulsive."

"He can be. But he's matured…a little." Drake didn't sound all that convincing.

"Hope so; he was a damn hothead. Up here, that won't just get him killed, but everyone killed, and eaten alive." Ben sighed. "This is no

Garden of Eden." Ben gave his friend a half-smile. "Thank you for coming. But you're insane for doing it."

Drake winked. "Gotta tell you, buddy. We came for the money. I thought you were just a pile of bones somewhere in the Amazon Jungle." He looked around. "Never expected to find you, and sure as hell never really thought all this was going to be real."

"You and me both." Ben nodded sagely and walked on for a few minutes. He half-turned. "You're still invited for the ribs."

They continued to push through heavy fronds dripping with moisture, trying to move fast but in silence. After another moment, Ben thought he heard and felt something. He held up his hand.

"Quiet."

He turned back the way they'd come, staring into the darkness. He tilted his head, straining to listen, and then crouched to place a hand flat against the ground. This time, he closed his eyes, concentrating.

After a few minutes, he opened his eyes. "*Goddammit.*" He stood. "That big bastard is following us."

"The *Giganotosaurus* again?" Andy asked. "*Shit.*"

"Good and bad news," Ben said. "The good news is that the smaller hunters will head for the hills with a big theropod in the vicinity. The bad news is, there's a big theropod in the vicinity. This is usually the time I run and hide—into a cave, or to a treetop."

"How far back is it, you think?" Drake asked.

"Half a mile, less," Ben said and shrugged.

"We can make it. I'm sure the temple is less than that. If there's no smaller carnivores, then we can double-time it," Drake replied.

Ben grabbed Emma's hand. "Good idea."

Drake pulled his longest blade and turned to the wall of green. "Let's push it." He hacked at a vine and then began to jog, thrashing away in front of him. Ben and Emma followed, with Andy lagging a little behind.

*****

The four of them crouched just behind the last line of hanging vines. Before them was the temple, still imposing and draped in shadows within shadows. At the eastern horizon, a tiny blush of red indicated that sunup wasn't far off.

Ben snorted softly. "Just like on the jungle floor all those years ago. Even the gargoyles out front; the monster snake in battle with the beast."

"Same culture," Emma said.

Drake rested on his haunches and had his binoculars up to his eyes. "All calm and quiet." He handed them to Ben.

Ben scanned the entrance. "I'd be happier if there was someone waiting for us."

"Think positive," Emma said. "They've already made it to the base of the plateau and are waiting for us down there."

Ben turned and grinned. "Yeah, I like it; that's what happened."

Behind them, Andy had his night vision goggles over his eyes, but was furiously scribbling something on a piece of notepaper with a pencil.

"See anything?" Ben asked him.

"*Huh*?" Andy looked up. "Oh." He turned to the temple and stared for a few seconds, his mouth slightly open. He slowly shook his head. "Nope, no one and nothing."

Ben looked up at the sky between the branches and saw something familiar that filled him with dread—the clouds were low and ominous, beginning to rotate like they were in the eye of a cyclone, even though the wind was still gentle. For now.

"Let's get this over with." Ben turned to the trio, and thought he saw Andy pull his hand back as if he had been about to touch Emma's leg. *Weird kid. Smart, but weird*, he thought.

"Ready?" he asked Emma first.

She nodded. "When you are."

Ben half-turned. "Guys?"

"Yo." Drake's eyes were gun barrels on the temple, and Andy nodded but still looked distracted.

Ben turned back. "Count of 3, 2, 1...*go*." He led them out of the cover of the jungle and across the clearing. He ran hard, but not fast enough as to leave Emma behind. He needn't have worried, as she kept pace with him easily and was probably fitter than he was now.

In another minute, he bounded up the huge stone steps and stopped just inside the heavy carved doorframe. Emma came in and flattened herself against the wall next to him. Drake came in on the other side.

Ben was breathing hard, waiting for his eyes to adjust. Drake and Emma flicked on flashlights.

"Where's the kid?" Ben noticed Andy hadn't arrived.

"What?" Emma immediately looked back out across the clearing to where they had come out of the jungle.

Ben followed her eyes. "Were there hunters there?" His stomach suddenly felt leaden.

There was no one and nothing in the clearing, and no man or beast still in the jungle they could see.

"Unlikely," Drake said.

"What the hell happened to him?" Emma asked. "I don't… I don't even remember him running with us."

"We go back," Drake said. He moved to the entrance and looked out over the clearing.

"Wait."

Ben had a mad thought. Impossible, but…

"Emma, check your pockets," he said softly.

She frowned and reached a hand into one, then the other. From her right pocket, she drew forth a folded piece of paper. She looked down at it as if it was the strangest thing she'd ever seen. She held it out and lifted her querying gaze to Ben.

"What does it say? Read it."

She quickly unfolded it, and Drake held his light over her shoulder. She began:

Emma, Drake, and Ben, thank you. Thank you for bringing me here. My life's love has been to immerse myself in the distant past. I used to just use my imagination to reconstruct the wonders of that time. But you have managed to take me there, for real.

But there's still so much I want to see—must see.

I want to see a sunrise over a prehistoric ocean. I want to see the colors, the habits, and the behaviors of creatures long gone. I want to see the creatures that never even made it into our fossil record.

I'm sorry. Please tell Helen I love her and will miss her.

But don't try and look for me. This is my decision. And I'm already gone.

Yours truly, Andrew Francis Martin."

"That goddamn idiot," Drake said. He bared his teeth and leaned around the doorframe again. "He can't be that far ahead of us."

"No," Emma said with heavy resignation in her voice. "Let him go."

"No one on my watch gets left behind," Drake insisted.

"Drake, he's not being left behind. He's made a decision to stay;

respect it," Ben said. He pointed up at the sky. "See that?"

Drake turned to where Ben indicated.

"That spinning cloud is just the start. Soon, the wind will rise, the cloud will drop, and then all hell breaks loose as this place goes back to where it belongs." Ben looked at his friend. "We need to be long gone by then."

Drake dropped his head for a moment. "Yeah, I get it." He took one last look out at the clearing. "That's the plan. So let's go see if any of our wayward clan is still here, or left us a sign." He checked his gun and then held his flashlight high, locating the room that held the steps down to the basement. "This way."

The trio entered the room, and Ben saw the hole in the floor. He sniffed. "Not good."

"Yeah, snakes. Seems there was a nest in the chute," Emma said.

"Well, as long as Ajax didn't bring the entire roof down on his head, I expect to find a lot of snake bodies."

"Here's hoping," Emma said, uncertainly.

Drake turned to her. "Don't worry, he and Fergus know their stuff and had enough firepower to do some serious damage." He lit a flare and tossed it down into the darkness. The red glow was anything but warm and welcoming as the soldier was first to descend.

Ben paused for a moment; the smell alone put him on edge. He also noticed that Drake went down the steps like he did—as far up against the wall as he could get. For all his confident words, he noticed the guy was on edge.

They inched down, toes alighting first, softly, followed by the rest of the foot. Add weight, and then onto the next step, doing the same over again. Just the sound of the flare fizzed below them.

Ben and Drake came into the room first with Emma at their heels. Ben went to push Emma back, but she swiped his arm away and held her gun in both hands.

Then he saw it.

Ben dry-swallowed down some bile. The place looked like an abattoir, and even though the pyrotechnic smell of the flare was strong, they could still detect the overpowering smell of the blood and viscera.

"What the fuck happened here?" Drake had his gun up. "Is it snake's blood?" he asked hopefully.

"No, look, there's torn cloth, boots, clothing strewn about." Ben pointed at a shred of camouflage material. "I think one of the guys bought it right there." He put an arm across his lower face as he saw the glistening thing. *"Jesus Christ."*

Ben stared down at the mess on the ground. It was about 10 feet long and was roughly compressed into a giant, wet-looking cigar shape. But in amongst the red of the meat and speckled fragment of bone, there was a boot on one end.

"I think that's Ajax," Drake said. The tough soldier's jaws clenched as though he was also fighting to keep down his sick down.

"Regurgitation," Emma said softly. "I remember Andy telling me that big snakes do it from time to time. If they've had their fill, even after crushing and swallowing something, they might decide to vomit it up and come back to it later."

Ben was nauseated but found it hard to drag his eyes away from that crushed boot. He didn't want to, but his gaze was now drawn to the other end of the thing, where the man's head should have been. In amongst the mess, he could just make out some hair, an elongated skull, and a single eye floating in the mess. The jaws were still there, but now torn wide in a perpetual scream of agony.

Now he knew how Drake had identified Ajax—there was a silver tooth floating in the gore. He grimaced. "Poor sap."

"Fuck, fuck, fuck," Drake spat the words through clenched teeth. "We've gotta get out of here. Get off this damn plateau." He edged up to the portal in the wall and darted his head around the carved stonework, and then pulled it back. When nothing jumped out at him, he looked back in and shone his flashlight deeper into the hole. He looked about to step inside.

"Don't!"

They all spun, three guns pointing to where the voice had come from.

About five feet up on the wall, there was a crack, no more than a foot high and six feet wide. Probably where some sort of earth movement had caused the heavy stone blocks to settle at an angle.

A slim hand emerged, followed by a dirt-covered woman—Helen. Drake rushed to her, helping to extract her from where she had wedged herself in tight. He carried her down to the floor of the room, and she clung tight to him.

"You're okay now." Drake tried to calm her, but Helen just shook her head, and wouldn't let him go. Drake tried again. "Can you tell us what happened?"

"Out, out," she hissed.

"Let's take her upstairs," Ben said, keeping his eyes on the hole in the wall.

Drake looked up and saw where he was looking. "Yeah, good idea." He helped the woman to her feet, putting an arm around her and literally dragging her up the steps. Emma quickly followed.

Ben spotted some things near the hole and ran for them. He snatched them up—one of the M4 rifles and a bloody ammunition belt that held stubby can-like rounds. He could feel by the weight of the gun that the magazine wasn't empty. There was also a slime-covered handgun. He took one last look at the dark portal, and then backed up the steps, keeping his eyes on the impenetrable blackness inside every step of the way.

Drake sat Helen down and gave her a sip from his canteen. She immediately lurched forward and vomited onto the ground. Emma rubbed her back and spoke softly to her and she sobbed once, wiped her mouth and nose, and sat back. Her eyes remained tightly closed.

"We can't stay here," she said. "We can't."

Drake put a hand on her shoulder. "Tell us wh—"

Helen grabbed his arm, her eyes round. "We've got to go."

"We're here, you're okay now." He kept his voice soft.

"You don't understand." Helen seemed to deflate and leaned forward onto her knees. "The *Titanoboa*; much bigger than I ever expected. And fast, so fast." She started to laugh, but her eyes began to redden again. "Couldn't kill it." She turned to Drake, shaking her head. "Nope, wouldn't die."

Helen's eyes took on a faraway look. "It trapped us; ambushed us." She slumped again.

Emma's eyes went to Ben momentarily, before she took the woman's hand. "From the pit?"

"Yes, no…" Helen grimaced. "The snake came, but not from the cave. We all thought it was in there, and Ajax tried to lure it out." Her eyes went wide. "But it came from behind us, trapped us. The bullets didn't seem to hurt it at all."

"Shit," Drake said under his breath and looked up at Ben.

"I had to hide. I couldn't do anything but hide." Helen shook her head. "I've been in there ever since. The snake ripped them to shreds, crushed them down to nothing and ate them all." Her face screwed up in horror. "Then the others came, the smaller ones, and she fed some of the bits to them."

Helen buried her face in her hands. "Camilla, Fergus, all of them, crushed, eaten." She took her hands away, her eyes wild. "We need to get out, run, *now*."

She went to get to her feet, but Emma grabbed her, and sat her down hard. "No; there isn't time." She looked at Ben, and then Drake, her teeth showing. "We stick to the plan." She shook Helen. "Look!" She pointed at Ben. "You know who this is?"

Helen shook her head, and then realization must have dawned on her. "You're Ben Cartwright?"

Ben nodded.

Emma's eyes drilled into Helen, and she still gripped her arm. "He survived here for ten years. We only need to do it for another few hours. But we need to escape. Nothing is going to stop that from happening. *Got it?*"

"We'll never make it." Helen looked panicked. "You didn't see what happened." She tried to pull out of Emma's grip. "Andy and I..." She stopped dead and looked around, as if realizing for the first time her brother wasn't with them.

"Where's Andy?" Her voice was small.

Emma finally let her go. "We think...he decided to stay here. No, we *know* he decided to stay. He left us and vanished when we were just outside."

"He left a note," Ben said. "He wanted you to know that he loved you, and not to worry about him."

"Oh God." Helen grabbed her head and squeezed her eyes shut. "That little fool. Ever since he was a kid, he'd do things like this."

"He's not a kid now. This is what he wanted," Ben said.

"Andy's a dreamer. He hasn't seen what I've seen," Helen quaked out.

"Too late; he's gone. Nothing we can do now." Emma sat back on her haunches. "So, now we need to save ourselves."

"We stick to the plan," Ben said softly.

"Only one we got. And the clock is ticking," Drake added. "Weapons check. Whatta we got?"

Ben checked the rifle he found; he wasn't familiar with the new model but knew he could operate it. He pulled out the magazine, checked it, and then noticed the undercarriage wasn't holding the grenade launcher. "Magazine is half-full, grenade launcher is gone. So I have a belt with three grenade cartridges and nothing to fire them with. Also a handgun that has five rounds remaining."

"Good," Drake said. "I've got two knives, M4 handgun with half a magazine, and a spare mag in my belt. I've also got two flares remaining."

Emma checked her handgun, popped out the magazine, and saw there were only two rounds left. From a pouch on her thigh, she drew forth a full magazine and snapped it in, and then snapped the slide forward and back. "Full magazine, plus another full mag in my pocket, and two rounds in another. I've got the bush knife and three flares." Her lips compressed. "Not much, but it'll do."

Drake raised an eyebrow. "It'll *have* to, and it *will* do."

Ben had extracted one of the copper-colored grenade rounds. He held it up—it was like a stubby bullet with a red tip. He'd never seen one like it before. "Are these DOI?"

Drake looked at him and grinned. "M203 cartridges can be DOI— detonate on impact—or air burst, incendiary, and even water detonation. We've come a long way in a few years, buddy."

Ben turned the fat cartridge in his hand. It still had streaks of blood coating it, and it stained his palm red. "What sort of velocity for DOI?"

"Baseball pitch. Impact detonation, on paper, means if you can just throw 'em hard enough, they'll detonate. But you've got to have a good arm and a hard surface to strike."

"Got it," Ben said, resheathing the plug.

Helen turned to him. "Ben Cartwright?"

"Yep."

"If you survived here by yourself, do you think, *um*, that maybe there's a chance that Andy can too?" Her eyebrows were high, and there was real fear in her eyes.

Ben got down on one knee close to her. "Sure he can. He's a smart guy; smarter than I am." He smiled crookedly and patted her hand. But he didn't believe it for a second.

She nodded back, her eyes still wide. "And then I can come back for him, like Emma did for you." Her eyes were pleading now.

Behind him, he heard Emma exhale. "Anything's possible." Ben patted the woman's hand. "Helen, I need to ask you something. It's important."

She looked up. "Of course; what is it?"

"We're going to have to move quickly, climb, maybe fight; can you do that?" He waited.

"Fight?" Her brows drew together in confusion.

"Yes, fight to live." Ben kept his eyes on hers.

"I don't want to go back down there." She looked away. "But I'll do what needs to be done."

"That's all we can ask. Thank you." Ben squeezed her hand and then stood. He walked to the doorway and looked out into the jungle. He had to squint now as the wind blew debris in at him. He momentarily recoiled as a long thread of lightning traveled horizontally, branching up and down like a blinding river of light.

"Not much time now." He sucked in a breath right to the bottom of his lungs. "This is where the shit gets real." He looked along the jungle wall and saw what he needed just in through a stand of trees. "We need to make use of every advantage we have. And every tool and weapon we have. We're going to war, and the odds are not in our favor."

Drake looked back to the room with the steps leading to the portal. "Might be more we can salvage down there."

"Yeah, you do that," Ben said over his shoulder. "I'm going to grab a few things. Be back in ten minutes. Em, can I borrow your knife?"

"No." She scowled. "But you can borrow me and I come with a knife. You're not going anywhere by yourself right now."

Ben sighed. "Don't have time to argue." He pointed. "See that stand of trees, the larger ones with the collars of thin leaves around their base? That's where we're going."

"No problem; ready when you are," she said.

Ben turned to nod at Drake. "Ten minutes. Be ready." He turned, took one last look up and down along the tree line, and then sprinted from the temple doorway. Emma was right beside him.

*****

Emma beat Ben to the tree line, and immediately went down on one knee, gun up in a two-handed hold. She scanned the trees, but there didn't seem to be anything moving. *It was damn hard to tell now*, she thought, as the branches whipped about and the low moan of rushing wind dominated everything.

Ben crouched beside her, also scanning the brush. She looked back at the temple; the dark mouth of the doorway was now empty as she assumed Drake and Helen were down in the basement room retrieving anything of use they could salvage from the carnage.

Good on Helen, Emma thought; couldn't have been easy going back down after what she had seen take place.

She winced as thunder cracked, and looked up to see the boiling clouds rotating like froth in a bath about to go down the plug. They were getting down to the last hours or maybe even hour now—seconds counted.

"What do we need?" she yelled.

Ben held out his hand. "We need to cut some straight branches, some vines, and collect some of that resin." He pointed.

She handed him the long knife. "I'll get the vines." She withdrew her smaller blade.

The pair worked fast. Ben hacked down five-foot trees and stripped them of their branches and leaves. Emma extracted elastic vines from around the tree trunks, and quickly scooped up some of the dark sticky resin onto broad, flat leaves.

Ben then shaped the ends of his rods, cutting a groove a few inches from the top, and then making a small notch in the top like a saddle. Emma brought him her pieces.

"I think I know where you're going; and I like it."

He grinned as he worked. "Every bit helps." He took one of the grenade cartridges and sat it in the saddle at the top, rounded head as the spear tip. Ben then lashed and tied them with the vines, and finally liberally coated them with the sticky and fast-drying resin.

He examined it and handed it to Emma. "One." He worked quickly; creating two more, and then wiped off his hands and turned to her. "Seems fitting that in this place we're back to resorting to spears." Ben got to his feet.

"One more thing." Emma came up beside him. Her eyes were luminous, and he couldn't help bending toward her. She smiled and pushed her face back at his, their lips meeting, hard. She broke the kiss.

"For luck."

"I've loved you…" He grinned down at her. "…for 100 million years."

She laughed and the pair turned, about to leave the jungle edge, but Ben threw an arm out in front of her.

"Don't move."

From the other side of the clearing, the monstrous snake slid from the jungle like a waterfall of dark brown and green scales. It was on its belly, but the arm-thick tongue continued to dart out, tasting the air. The tongue's movements became more frantic and then the snake reared up, raising its head around 20 feet from the ground.

Emma couldn't help her intake of her breath—to her, the nightmare was back. Out in the open, its size was colossal, and even though she had witnessed a full-grown creature before, her modern mind still had trouble processing it as being real.

They both eased back behind the trees and tried to stay motionless. The red, glass-like eyes of the *Titanoboa* were impossible to read, but the tongue began flickering again, and the head began to turn as it looked along the line of foliage.

"Drake and Helen will be sitting ducks," Emma whispered.

"So are we," Ben responded.

"We can run for it," she replied.

"To where? And for how long?" Ben answered. He hefted one of the spears. "No, we've got to discourage it from entering—we *need* that temple."

"Yeah, we do." Emma swallowed. Suddenly, the spears and her handgun seemed a joke when contemplating a war on this thing. She wanted to run and hide, but Ben was right. Running and hiding might mean life for now, but it would also mean missing their window of opportunity. Did she want to try and live in this place for 10 years? Or condemn Ben for another decade?

"Goddamnit," she whispered.

"No, this is a good thing." Ben pulled her along behind the tree line. "We wanted to flush it out. Now we don't have to." Ben's jaw worked for a moment, as he seemed to come to a decision. "Cover me."

"*What?*" Emma grabbed at him, but he had already moved further along behind the line of trees, getting closer to the snake.

Even though Ben crept along and tried to stay behind cover, the snake spotted him almost immediately. Its five-foot-wide diamond-shaped head swung around to watch him. The creature's body was around four feet wide at the neck, but then broadened to be about seven wide at its girth. It was a monstrous animal and emanated power and lethality. Ben would have made a perfect bite-sized snack for the creature.

"Oh no." Her mouth dropped open as Ben broke cover and sprinted at the monster, yelling and holding up one of his spears. The snake must have been taken by surprise by a prey animal charging it, and stopped its advance, rearing up even higher in a defensive display.

When Ben was just 50 feet away, he whipped his arm forward and propelled the spear like a javelin.

It flew, wobbling, and as a first effort, it wasn't bad. But it was obvious that Ben needed practice as the swirling wind caught the missile and nudged it just enough to make it land several feet wide.

"*Shit!*" Ben yelled.

It got worse, as it struck a patch of thicker grass and didn't even detonate. Emma grimaced, her teeth clamped together so hard they hurt.

Ben fumbled with another of his spears, but it was obvious that the odds had moved even more out of his favor.

"Fuck it." Emma gripped her gun tight and stepped from the line of trees, knowing they were now on a suicide mission.

But instead of the snake bearing down on them, it swung away as an earth-shaking roar came from the other end of the clearing.

The thundering, predatorial bellow of the carnivore was a challenge, a warning, and designed to freeze its prey to the spot—it worked, as Emma cringed to be rooted to the ground from the noise alone.

She watched in awe as the massive theropod emerged from the jungle. *Giganotosaurus*, she breathed. The thing had tracked them from when she was in the crevasse. It seemed the monster decided it still had unfinished business with them. One problem: to get to Ben and Emma, it might have to fight for them.

The effect on the snake was instantaneous—Ben was forgotten, and the colossal snake reared up, rising high from the ground. Its head shivered slightly and the tongue flicked out, faster and faster, in clear agitation. Amazingly, its throat flared red with aggression.

Ben backed up, trying to keep watch on both monsters, but he was insignificant and nothing more than food to the victor, and right now, the two formidable beasts, both territorial, undoubtedly knew their meeting could end in only one way.

He joined Emma back in the tree line, and both could only watch with mouths gaping.

Though the snake was colossal in size, the *Giganotosaurus* lived up to its name—it was the biggest carnivore on this primitive continent, and this one was 40 feet long and stood 18 high at the shoulder. Though the snake was longer, the saurian massively outweighed it by many tons.

The *Giganotosaurus* roared, and its massive box-like head split open, showing the rows of razor-sharp, backward-curving teeth, each about 10 inches in length. It started to move, keeping its eyes on the snake and trying to circle it.

With small twitchy movements, the snake kept itself facing toward the threat. The dinosaur edged sideways, bellowing and snapping massive and powerful jaws at the *Titanoboa*. It looked like a monstrous guard dog threatening an intruder.

"No, no, no, not that way," Emma said.

The dinosaur was moving the snake, and they could see that the *Titanoboa* was going to end up between them and the temple. If the snake decided to cut and run, it'd be back inside with Drake and Helen before they could blink. That'd leave them alone with one of the most fearsome creatures of the Late Cretaceous Period, and Emma knew how that would go.

There came a long hiss from the snake, and it tried to rear up even higher, perhaps to make itself seem even bigger. It didn't work; the dinosaur charged.

The ground shook beneath their feet as the three-toed monster closed the gap between them in seconds. Ben and Emma were transfixed, watching the two land leviathans come together.

The *Titanoboa* snake was reputed to have fed on dinosaurs, and it was easily big enough. But the *Giganotosaurus* was a species of theropod that ruled its domain for a good reason and amazingly, for something of such a titanic size, was even faster than the snake probably suspected.

The snake went to strike the beast on its flanks, but the dinosaur lowered its head like a bull. The front of the creature's skull was a massive plate of many-inches-thick bone, and even though the snake's teeth caught and dug in, they inflicted little real damage.

In turn, the *Giganotosaurus* angled its head and opened its massive jaws wide and clamped them down on the snake's upper body. The machine-like head brought a bite pressure of 1,000 pounds per square inch to bear on the giant pipe of scale and muscle.

The *Giganotosaurus* clamped down with an audible crunch, and the snake went mad. It became a monstrous worm in a bird's beak. The body and tail of the snake whipped and thumped down, raising dust and making the ground shake.

"Now's our cue," Ben said, snapping Emma out of her trance and grabbing her hand. They sprinted across the clearing and were at the temple doorway in seconds. But just as they reached the steps, they were both thrown backward as a second colossal snake flowed from the doorway.

This snake was even bigger than the one locked in its death roll with the dinosaur. Perhaps it had been called by the first or had heard the commotion via vibrations in the ground, but it ignored the humans and poured forth toward the fighting pair.

Ben and Emma leaped aside but got to their feet quickly when it became clear the snake was going to pass them by. They watched it go and still couldn't tear their eyes away as the second snake sped into the fighting pair.

It didn't stop or even deviate, but simply accelerated, opened its mouth, and shot its head and neck forward to thump into the flanks of the *Giganotosaurus* and then clamp its jaws down hard. Immediately, the snake's massive body was brought into action, throwing itself forward and wrapping itself around the great beast's torso.

The *Giganotosaurus* must have known the dynamics of the battle had shifted as it dropped the first snake, which fell limp to the ground, and tried to bite at the muscular coils that were now wrapping around it.

The two colossal legs of the dinosaur planted and it raised itself to its full height as the body of the snake engulfed it—loop after loop, until the massive theropod, still upright, was bound in place and could only scream its primal rage.

"Look." Ben nudged Emma and pointed to the gargoyle images of the carved intertwined deities at the temple's entrance.

She nodded. "Yeah, this battle has played out before."

"Come on, quick." They bounded up the steps and sprinted inside.

"*Drake, Helen*," Ben yelled into the cavernous space so his voice could be heard over the titanic struggle going on outside.

"Yo," came an answer from the furthest room. Drake's light appeared and then he and Helen followed it.

"Goddamn monster burst outta that portal. Went past us like we didn't exist." Drake looked pale but managed a grin regardless. Helen just looked ill.

Ben pointed to the room with the steps to the basement. "Now's our chance. Those bastards have bigger fish to fry than us."

Ben led them down the steps and slowed as he approached the ink-black hole in the wall. He leaned in and shook his head. "Still stinks in here. A nest for sure."

"Yeah, and even the young ones are bad news." Drake lit a flare and tossed it as far in as he could manage.

The red glowing stick bounced a few times and came to rest about 60 feet in. The carved portal opened out into a cavern. The smoke of the flare blew toward them.

"A breeze," Emma said. "Warm air rises, so this is the best news we've had in days."

"Years." Ben grinned at her, but then turned back and tilted his head, listening.

Emma watched him for a moment. "You hear something in there?" she whispered.

"No, and that's the problem. It's gone quiet, but I mean from outside, and that tells me the fight is over." He moved his remaining explosive spears from one hand to the other. "There's no choice now; we've got to stay ahead of the snakes, and stay ahead of the gateway closing."

Ben stepped inside.

CHAPTER 41

Ben led them in, walking carefully, holding the rifle up. Emma was at his left shoulder, gun ready but pointed down for now. Her eyes were wide and she was as alert as a hawk.

On Ben's other side, Drake also had his gun ready, but also had Helen clinging on tight to his arm. She looked on the verge of panic— *not good*, Ben thought. If things went bad, they needed to remain cool and clear-headed, and able to move quickly. Ben knew from his mission firefights that it was indecision, hesitation, and panic that were always the first killers.

He had a spare gun and would have liked Helen armed, but given her state, he bet that when the chips were down, she'd more than likely drop it, or shoot one of them by accident.

Ben held up a hand. The cavern had opened out and then forked. There were several passages before them, and the gentle slope of the ground they'd been traveling on meant they were probably already quite a way below the surface. They'd left the flare far behind and were at the edge of its faint red glow, but their next discovery told Ben they were still well within the danger zone.

"Coprolite," Helen observed as they passed the balls of chalk-like packages.

"Their shit," Emma added. "And no, not fossilized."

Some of the crap balls were the size of footballs, and some the size of large watermelons. In amongst the droppings, there were the remains of crushed bones. Ben didn't want to think that the remains of Fergus or the others would soon end up deposited here. He shuddered; for that matter, he didn't want to end up that way either.

The rocks inside the cave were smoothed, as if they had been polished by something heavy sliding over them over and over. And he knew what.

"Is this the nest?" he asked.

Helen peered around Drake. "No; there'd be clutches of eggs scattered around. This must just be an antechamber."

"Damn; I have no idea which way," Ben whispered as he flicked his light into each of the passages in front of them. "Emma, this is your field. Which way do we go?"

Emma turned slightly, spat on her hand, wiped it on her pants, and then held it up in front of her face. She moved it around and then pointed.

"The entrance on the left; that's where the breeze is coming from."

"Good enough for me," Ben said.

"Hey, look." Drake had his flashlight shining up against the flat wall. It was heavily carved with glyphs and drawings. "Je-*zuz*." He shook his head.

Ben added his light. "They were as bad as the snakes." The images showed men, women, and children all roped together by the neck, dozens and dozens of them, and all being led out past the gargoyle statues of the carved snake and beast.

The next image showed them standing before the monstrous snake. And the last image was of the snake beginning to consume them, as the tied-up victims stood calmly as though simply waiting for a bus ride.

"Bastards," Emma spat. "I used to think they killed their people first and then fed the parts to the *Titanoboa*. That was bad enough. But it's worse; they fed the snakes with their own people goddamn alive."

"I think they got what they deserved," Ben said. "Looks to me like the snakes got tired of waiting for their dinner to be brought to them and decided on a little self-service."

"Karma is a bitch," Drake said, chuckling. "And now the snakes run the place."

"Let's keep going." Emma glanced over her shoulder.

"How much time have we got?" Ben turned to see her still looking over her shoulder the way they'd come. "Emma?"

"Huh?" She turned to him. "Sorry?"

"You okay?" He followed her gaze, but there was nothing to see and the cave now extended back well beyond their light beams. "Time left, how much have we got?"

She didn't even need to check her watch. "Based on the last apparition of Primordia, I estimate we've got 1 hour and 20 minutes. We must be below whatever line it is, or we all stay."

"Okay. Give us a countdown every ten minutes to keep us focused and, you know, motivated." Ben half-smiled at her.

"Yeah, *motivated*." She grinned back.

He led them on through the passages that were still large enough to run a truck through. Ben had hoped they'd narrow, but guessed it wouldn't matter, as the snakes were able to fit in fairly small spaces. He hoped they could go some places where the snakes couldn't, but anything real tight, there was a chance they'd get stuck. *He'd risk it, they all would,* if it gave them even the slimmest chance to get the hell out of this place.

Ben swept his light from one side of the cavern to the other, spotting an alcove in the left rock wall that seemed incongruous. It narrowed to no more than a few feet wide, but inside, there were stones—cut stones—stacked up, almost sealing it off.

Around the outside, there were gouges in the rock walls, as though something had tried to force its way in. Ben leaped up and shone his light in between two of the stacked rocks.

"Well, I'll be damned." He stood back. "Looks like I wasn't the only sap to get trapped up here once."

The others took turns crowding around and looking inside the walled-off alcove. Ben knew what they were seeing—a skeleton, small, and brown with age. There were the remains of feathers and colored stones that were dappling the ribs and must have been some sort of necklace jewelry.

Whoever it had been, man or woman, they had sealed themselves in. And as the snakes had obviously been trying to get in, they had never been able to get out.

"They were trapped," Ben said. "So they just sat back and waited to die."

"Jesus—trapped in Hell." Drake bared his teeth. "That doesn't exactly fill me with confidence."

"Yeah, it's Hell. But you know what they say, *when you're going through hell…?*" Ben turned and grinned.

"*You keep going,*" Ben, Drake, and Emma both said at once.

Helen had her arms wrapped around herself and stayed closed to Drake full time now. "Appropriate, this being Hell, I mean." She gave them a broken smile. "Some ancient Amerindian races believed that down, being the underworld, was Heaven. And the sky was where the devil lived. That's why they used to carry their dead deep into caves."

Drake turned his back on the tunnel to face her. "Then we better find our way back to Heaven."

The snake struck then, grabbing Drake by the thigh. The soldier yelled, more in surprise than pain, and was thrown backward by the force of the attack. Helen screamed and Drake pummelled down on the reptile's head as it immediately began to throw coils as thick as the man's waist around him.

Ben remained calm, turned, and fired controlled bursts from his rifle. The gunfire was near deafening in the confined space, and the bullets zippered along the snake's flanks.

Emma held her gun in a two-handed grip and also fired, taking care to avoid the downed man. Helen backed up against the wall and held her hands over her ears.

Drake managed to pull his knife, and using the entire upper half of his body, swung the blade into the eye socket of the creature, sinking the steel deep.

It opened its mouth and hissed with pain and fury. Drake then twisted the blade, and it was like the creature was receiving an electric shock, as the snake went mad, thrashing around and jerking Drake up and down. Eventually, its head lay still, while its tail seemed to be trying to coil itself into knots.

Ben was first to his friend and dug his fingers into the mouth and pried the jaws open. It took a while to unhook him, as the backward-curving teeth were sunk like fishhooks into his flesh.

"Fuck it," Drake yelled, as Emma wrapped her belt around his thigh.

"You were lucky," she said.

"Yeah, for some reason, I don't feel it." He grimaced as she tightened the tourniquet.

"She's right," Ben said. "It was a small one. If it was an adult, next time you made an appearance, it'd be like that." He pointed to a huge ball of snake shit in the corner. He helped pull the man to his feet.

Drake hopped for a moment and then put his foot down gingerly. He shook his head. "I can move, but if it comes to running…" He just shook his head. "Ain't gonna win any medals this week."

Ben handed him the rifle, and Drake used it like a walking stick.

"Yeah? Well, I'm betting if that big mother makes an appearance, you'll win medals." He slapped Drake on the shoulder. "Let's move out."

CHAPTER 42

Rib bones the size of a full-grown man's torso on the theropod began to compress. The *Giganotosaurus'* massive jaws were of no use if it couldn't get anything between them, and the *Titanoboa* knew to keep away from them, using the coils of its colossal body to bring a titanic pressure onto the huge predator's chest.

It squeezed some more, and the eyes of the theropod bulged and its mouth sprung open. A few large gasps emanated from its throat as it tried to suck in air. Another squeeze, and then like cannon fire, the ribs broke, one after the other. Finally, the massive heart exploded under the pressure.

The monstrous snake lowered its head close to the open mouth of the *Giganotosaurus*, and its tongue flickered out. It tasted the saliva, the blood, and felt for any trace of breath or a heartbeat—there was none.

The giant theropod predator was too large for the *Titanoboa* to eat, but hunger always burned within it. The snake could continue to crush the beast down, turning it to mush, but even then, it would be a challenge.

At that moment, the booming sounds emanated from the stone building. The snake released the gigantic corpse and turned to the temple, and its nest. Like a molten river of glistening scales and muscle, it flowed toward the doorway.

CHAPTER 43

"This way." Emma followed the faint movement of air. Her hands ached from gripping the gun and flashlight. Added to that, her nerves were piano-wire tight. She didn't doubt for a second that there were more snakes in the caves, and only prayed that they ran out of snakes before their bullets did.

Ben had dropped back to cover their rear now. Though Drake would still be a formidable fighter, his ability to move quickly was compromised. She turned and looked briefly at Helen, who looked pale and scared half out of her wits. *As long as she kept up, then that'd do*, she thought.

Emma wiped an arm up over her face that streamed with perspiration. Thank God she could feel the soft kiss of a breeze on her cheeks. It had to be coming from below—it had to be another entrance—*please* be another entrance.

She dared to check her watch and winced. Time was moving too fast on them. "We got forty minutes to go," she said over her shoulder.

"Got it," Ben said from back in the darkness.

They'd come too far to turn back now, she knew. There was no backtracking and trying another route. It was all in or bust.

After another few minutes, the cavern began to get smaller and the gentle breeze started to turn into wind. As of yet, there was nothing but the smell of dry dirt, ancient dust, and just a hint of the musky scent of the monster reptiles.

As a caver, what she was desperate to find was a chute that dropped them down into the heart of the flat-topped mountain. One that was climbable, yet steep enough to get them below the distortion line quickly.

She held a hand up and shone her light at her palm. There seemed to be a mist or fog filling the cavern, and it rushed past her on the breeze.

"It's starting to happen," she whispered.

But then the mist slowed, and then stopped, just hanging listless in the air. *Oh no*, she thought. Emma turned slowly. The wind had stopped dead now, and the mist hung heavily around them.

There was only one reason for it—a blockage. She turned and met Ben's eyes. "Something's coming."

CHAPTER 44

"From in front or behind?" Ben spun to look over his shoulder, and then back to Emma. "Shit." Where they were, there were few vantage points, no places of concealment, or even opportunities to mount a real defense.

It didn't matter; he'd seen what the monsters could do, and trying to fight one in an enclosed area was not a good tactical move. He had to assume it was one of the creatures coming up from behind them. And a cave blockage meant it was a big one.

"We stay ahead of it." Ben spun to Drake, and his voice became authoritative. "*Sergeant.*"

Drake's head snapped around. "Sir."

"We are going to double-time it, and you *will* keep up." Ben glared at his friend.

"Damn right I will, Captain." He put more weight on his leg and grimaced.

Helen grabbed his arm tighter. "I've got him."

"Go." Ben began to jog, taking the lead with Emma who was right on his shoulder. A few more paces back, he could hear the quick clacking sound the gun muzzle made as Drake jammed the barrel into the cave floor.

Ben spotted the narrowing of the cave and went through a natural archway. He immediately slowed as they found themselves in a huge cathedral-like cavern.

He began to walk. "Ah, shit." He lifted his gun. Emma did the same. The huge cave was filled with piles of eggs, eggshells, and twisting snakes. Most were no more than 20 feet in length, but some were larger.

"*Look*; at the far end of the cave." Emma pointed.

On the other side of the huge cavern, there was what looked like a well, with hand-carved stone blocks built around a hole in the floor. Around its edge were eight-feet-tall stone idols of natives in headdresses, huge, two-legged beasts roaring to the sky, and rearing snakes with the green gem eyes.

"This must be it. This is how the natives were climbing up here in the wettest season," Emma said. "We just need to get through."

"Well, no time for diplomacy." He turned to Drake. "Shock and awe."

"My thoughts exactly." Drake grinned with zero humor.

Ben turned back. "Then let's make some space." He pointed his gun at the largest snake and fired twice in quick succession. The bullets created twin holes right between the 30-foot snake's eyes, and it shuddered and fell to the cave floor.

Drake balanced on one leg and started firing the rifle, picking his targets and never missing. Emma followed, drilling holes in anything that moved.

The room quickly filled with a mist of blood, smell of cordite, and the sound of a furious hissing that grew so loud that it almost hurt the ears. But in just seconds more, most of the remaining snakes had vanished like smoke.

"Cease fire," Ben yelled, but he had no choice. "I'm out anyway."

"Me too," Drake said.

Emma jammed in her last magazine and went to point her gun at a rapidly retreating, but wounded snake.

"No!" Ben yelled again. "Save it. It's all we have left."

Emma reholstered her weapon and looked quickly at her watch. "*Shit*; hurry."

They ran to the edge of the well-like pit and looked down. Emma grabbed her last flare, punched it against her thigh, and dropped it.

It floated for a moment on a wind rushing up into their faces, and then fell slowly. It kept on spinning and falling into a pit that seemed bottomless.

"Look." She pointed. On the outside of the 20-foot-wide hole, there were steps carved into the stone in a corkscrew design.

Ben stared down and waved a hand in front of his face. The fog was thickening, and he looked to Emma. "Time to portal close?"

She quickly checked her watch and grimaced. "We've got twelve minutes, and we need to be down…" She shook her head. "…I have no idea how far."

"Then no time to waste—and deeper has got to be better. So…" Ben was first over the side. Stuck in his belt were a few of his spears tipped with the grenade slugs.

Drake had discarded the empty gun and hobbled as best he could. He moved Helen in front of him but grabbed her arm and looked deep into her eyes.

"Don't look back. Just keep your eyes on Ben the whole time, okay?"

She nodded but looked like she didn't trust herself to speak. Ben looked into the pit, and what looked like miles down deep, there was a pinprick of red light. With his back to the wall, he began to navigate a set of steps that were narrow, crumbling, and in some places coated in moss.

He moved as fast as risk would allow—too slow, and they were all staying—too fast, and he'd slip and tumble into the void.

Concentration, persistence, patience, his mind whispered to him as he descended. His legs wanted to run, and he fought with them every step of the way. *Concentration, persistence, patience,* he told himself over and over.

*****

The snake burst into the nesting chamber and reared up. The bodies of the young were everywhere, and even some of the eggs were riddled with holes and leaking their precious life fluid.

Its tongue flicked out, sensing the fresh blood, and also tasting the chemical traces of the small beings.

The massive 70-foot creature had been challenged many times in its long life, and it prevailed every time. In its primitive reptile brain, it was concerned with territory, mating, eating, and survival.

But surveying the destruction of its brood created another sensation not felt before in its entire life—*hate*.

It surged toward the hole in the cavern floor and without stopping went over the surrounding stones.

In the darkness of the pit, it could see the creature's flaring warmth—they weren't far ahead of it. The *Titanoboa* increased its speed as it flowed like water around the outside of the shaft.

*****

"Five minutes!" Emma yelled.

She heard Ben curse and try to speed up. He succeeded in slipping on one of the steps, and cursing even more.

The wind rushed up past them as it was sucked up inside the tunnel. The mist was so thick now that they could only just make each other out by their shapes and the glow of their flashlights.

"How far down—do you think—?" Ben continued to edge along. "—we need to get?"

Emma followed closely, her fingertips almost touching his, but he still became indistinct in the foggy darkness. She had to squint from the flying debris smashing into her. Behind her, Helen and Drake were just shadows.

"I remember, that first time, when I came out of the mist layer, everything just seemed to…settle down." She wracked her mind, but the detail wasn't there. "But I can't remember how far I had to climb." She grimaced. "It took a while. I think."

"We must hurry." Ben turned and yelled up the shaft. "Drake, get a move on."

Ben turned back and kept going, and as his foot alighted on one of the steps, it simply crumbled underneath him.

Ben's arms pinwheeled for a moment, and then he fell.

"*Ben!*"

Emma went to grab for him, but nearly overbalanced herself. Ben spun in the air and threw out both arms. His fingertips caught the edge of the next step down and he swung hard but managed to cling there.

Drake and Helen bunched up behind her, but their path was so narrow, no one was getting past anyone else. Emma carefully straightened and went to step over Ben's fingers to try and get below him.

Immediately, the rushing wind stopped dead in the shaft.

She froze. "Oh no." Emma lifted her gun, pointing it upward. "Everyone…get down."

"Down where?" Drake said.

The huge snake came dropping down at them like a missile of scales and teeth. Emma immediately fired several rapid shots into a head that seemed to fill the entire shaft.

Drake could do little other than throw an arm over the shrieking Helen and cover her with his own body.

Ben screamed his frustration and tried to lever himself up. The monstrous snake seemed to coil around the outside of the shaft, its muscular body laying on the winding steps, and pressing outwards to hold itself in place. With the snake now not fully blocking the shaft, the gale-force wind started to howl upward again.

Ben released one hand to reach down for his spears, knowing he couldn't possibly get the leverage to throw them, but thinking he might be able to pass them up to Emma or Drake.

As he fumbled them out, the snake lunged, and Emma fired her remaining rounds into its open mouth. The snake pulled to the side just over Drake and Helen, smashing into the side of the shaft to avoid the stinging pellets.

"I'm out!" Emma yelled and looked down at her watch, and Ben could tell by her face, their time was up. Around them, the entire shaft shuddered, and chunks of the steps, dust, and debris rained down.

Ben held out the spears. "Take these…"

A baseball-sized chunk of rock flew down from above and struck his wrist, smashing the spears from his hand, and they tumbled away into the void.

"*Shit!*" he yelled. He looked briefly over his shoulder, but they were already gone. He'd lost their last weapon, but more importantly, he wondered would they…

The detonation was like a thunderclap. The shaft lit momentarily as an orange flower bloomed several hundred feet below them. The snake pulled back on itself a few dozen feet, as the hurricane winds first brought the heat of the blast, to be quickly followed by the sound of collapsing stone.

And then there was just dead air.

Ben stared downwards, knowing what that meant. He turned away to look up at Emma, and their eyes met.

She mouthed the fateful words he already knew.

"Time's up."

He felt like just letting go and letting himself drop to the bottom of the collapsed shaft. *They were all doomed now anyway*, he thought.

Ben looked past Emma and saw the snake still hanging above them, glassine, soulless eyes on them again. It seemed confident now that the bloom of the explosion didn't mean any harm to it, and then it burst into action.

The *Titanoboa* came down on them and its coils against the blocks sounded like a miller's stone crushing the rock to dust. Drake turned toward it, and then stood, defiant and waiting. But as the monstrous reptile opened its enormous mouth, displaying rows of backward-curving, tusk-like teeth, the air around it became indistinct.

It just seemed to become frozen, like an old movie on a projector where the film wheel has stopped.

"What?" Ben's mouth hung open.

And then…it simply vanished.

Everyone just stared, mouth's gaping, and no one able to speak for several moments.

"What. Just. Happened?" Ben asked softly.

"It's gone," Emma said with a chuckle. "The snake, the world, Primordia, it *must* be all gone."

"Primordia has left us and taken that goddamn snake with it," Drake whooped. "*Yes!*"

"Little help here." Ben still dangled on the step, his fingertips now bloodless from the strain.

Emma finally was able to step over him and help him get an arm up over the remaining steps. Ben climbed back up and sat with his back against the wall. He looked up at her. "We can't go down."

"So we go up." She grinned and rubbed his shoulder.

Ben nodded. "We go up. And we pray."

CHAPTER 45

They scaled upward, taking them hours this time. At first, the massive body of the snake had crushed the stone steps, but further up, they simply ceased to exist. The carved steps had been totally eroded back into the wall.

Emma's rock climbing skills allowed her to lead the way, and when they finally reached the top, she found there was no well-like structure built around the rim, but instead a roof of solid stone over the top of them. There was a slim crack of light showing, and together, they battered, beat, and bludgeoned the hole wide enough for Emma to be able to slide through.

She stayed down on her belly for a few more seconds, hugging the stone, and trying to shake off the fatigue and disorientation. They weren't in a cave anymore, and she felt slightly nauseous as she got slowly to her feet.

"Wow." She took a few halting steps, looking one way then the other, before quickly coming back to pick up a rock and bash the hole wide enough so Ben, Drake, and Helen could slide out.

They stood shoulder-to-shoulder, not moving, but simply adjusting, as they let their eyes move over the landscape.

Drake limped forward a few paces. "Ho-*oooly* shit." He turned. "Did this just happen?"

Ben nodded slowly but reached up to wipe streaming eyes. "Yeah, yeah it did." He smiled through his tears. "And now it's over." He threw his head back and whooped.

The tepui was different—very different. There was no monstrous snake, no gargantuan dinosaurs, or flesh-eating bugs. There was no primordial jungle, no lake, no temple, no nothing. It was like they had been transported to another planet.

Instead, there was just a weather-beaten, heavily cracked surface of a flat-topped mountain. Instead, there *were* a few stunted trees, wind-ravaged spindly grasses, ponds of water, and a clear blue sky above them.

"Gone, all gone." Emma turned, arms out. Her face broke into a broad smile and she rushed to Ben to wrap both arms around him. "*We made it.*"

"We made it. WE MADE IT!" Ben lifted Emma off her feet and spun her around. "We're back."

"Thank God," Helen said and tilted her face to the sun. "Home."

Drake hobbled back to them. "We're not home just yet." He pointed. "We're still right in the middle of the Amazon jungle."

Emma looked out at the endless landscape—the tepui mountain was a floating island in a sea of impenetrable green for as far as the eye could see in every direction.

"Not this time," Emma said. "Cynthia knows where we are." She looked at Ben. "And you just try and keep this guy's mom from seeing her little lost boy."

Ben laughed out loud. "Today is a *good* day." He put his arm around her and looked up into the sky. High up and toward the west, there was a faint streak, like an artist had daubed a tiny dash of white.

"Primordia is going again."

"Good riddance," Emma said.

"It'll be back again," Ben said. "In ten years."

"Yeah, well, when it is…" Drake grinned. "Please don't call me." His face became serious, and he fumbled in his pocket for his canteen. He shook it, eliciting the sound of a few drops sloshing around inside. He then uncapped it and held it up.

"To our friends not with us—to Brocke, Ajax, Fergus, Camilla, Juan, and Andy. We thank you and will miss you." He sipped and passed it to Emma, and then Ben.

"*Um*." Emma winced and turned to see Helen walking away, looking down at the bleak rock.

"No, we didn't lose him," Ben said. "He chose his path. I just hope he finds what he's looking for." Ben looked out toward the east. He knew just over the mountains there lay a sparkling blue ocean. On its shore today were the bustling metropolises of Georgetown, Paramaribo, and hundreds of smaller villages like Mahaica and Suddie and countless more. But it wasn't always like that.

"Yeah, I just hope he finds what he's looking for." He turned away. "And lives long enough to enjoy it."

227

CHAPTER 46

End of Comet Apparition

Primordia was gone from the third planet, and already on its way to the middle star where it would be grabbed by its gravitational forces and then flung back to begin its decade-long elliptical voyage around our solar system all over again.

The monsoon-like rains dried, and the clouds parted, then cleared. The magnetic distortion on the eastern jungles of Venezuela had ceased, doorways closed, and pathways were erased. On the surface of the tabletop mountain, silence and stillness settled over the sparse grasses and fissured landscape.

A few tiny skink lizards, insects, some hardy birds, and a handful of human beings were all that remained on the huge plateau. The wettest season was at an end, and once again, there would be 10 years of calm over a single jungle mountaintop in the depths of the Venezuelan Amazon jungle.

CHAPTER 47

Venezuelan National Institute of Meteorological Services

Nicolás frowned, fiddled with the resolution, and frowned even deeper. He leaned back.

"I think I can see something in there."

"Huh?" Mateo turned. "In where?"

"The Amazon, *ah*, over that tepui. The clouds have dissipated, and the localized effects are now gone. That wettest season of yours seems over." He licked his lips and rolled his chair in closer to his desk. "So I've been playing around with the saved data from the last twenty-four hours. And I can tell you there is, I mean *was*, something weird inside there."

Mateo folded his arms and waited. "Weird, *hmm*?"

"It looked like a balloon, and it traveled into the eye of that storm, and then vanished." Nicolás shrugged.

"Balloon, huh?" Mateo looked at him from under lowered brows. "Are you sure it wasn't a lady with an umbrella?" He chuckled.

Nicolás didn't get it. "No, a balloon. But it's a little hard to make out as the image is heavily distorted. Plus, there looked to be a lot of other debris flying around."

"Yeah, that happens in storms." Mateo sighed and rolled his chair closer to where the young meteorologist had set himself up. His bank of screens were all analyzing the data, but the largest held an image of the swirling purple clouds that had hung over the tepui for over 24 hours.

Mateo squinted. "Could be." He bobbed his head, and let the image roll forward and rewound it, and rolled it forward several more times. The entire grab was only three seconds, and blurred, but there was definitely something there. He thumbed to another server.

"Use the Paradox software to try and clean it up."

"Oh yeah, yeah. Good idea." The young man jumped from his chair and brought the smaller server online. The Paradox software program used a heuristic analysis application to apply a best-guess logic to images that were indistinct. It could never be relied on as 100% accurate, but it did give the user a high-probability suggestion based on what it saw, and what it could be.

"Working now," Nicolás said and craned forward, watching the screen closely. The image cleared, then cleared some more, as a bar along the bottom of the screen filled up to ping when at 100% complete.

"Run it," Mateo said.

Nicolás rewound and then ran the portion of video they were interested in. Their mouths hung open—a large orange balloon, with what could be several people jammed into the basket, dropped toward a funnel-shaped vortex in the center of the cloud mass. But what happened next had both men feeling lightheaded.

Things, big bird-like *things*, came out of the cloud and attacked the balloon. Then it was gone.

Nicolás ran and reran the film several more times, and for the last, he froze the image of one of the giant bat-like creatures on the screen. Both men just sat in silence, staring at it. Nicolás finally cleared his throat and turned to his senior colleague.

"What do we do now?"

Mateo blew air through pressed lips and shook his head slowly. "Normally, I would say, make a note, sign it, and then leave it for ten more years' time. But instead, today I say, we didn't see a thing."

"But…?" Nicolás swung around.

Mateo held up a hand. "Don't worry, we'll check again." Mateo rolled back to his desk. "In ten years' time."

EPILOGUE

South American East Coast, Late Cretaceous Period, 100 Million Years Ago

The ocean seemed endless, and under a clear azure sky, the water was a blue blanket sprinkled with glittering diamonds as the sunlight caught tiny ripples on its surface.

On the cliff top, Andy turned his head slowly, scanning the horizon. There were no dots of ships, large or small, and wouldn't be for another 100 million years. There was also no high-tide line on the beach crowded with rubbish, no islands of floating plastic, no slicks of oil, and no brown haze on the horizon creating unnaturally colored sunsets.

The young paleontologist inhaled the fresh sweet sea air, and his face split in a broad grin. He was in heaven and he only wished his sister could see what he was seeing.

He sat and wrapped his arms around his legs and watched as long necks of plesiosaurs rose from the sea surface, and then dived down, returning with flapping fish in sharp-toothed mouths.

In the time he'd been here, he'd seen ocean giants, like the mosasaur, tylosaur, and even once a monstrous kronosaur that was like a flipper-finned blue whale, attacking pods of plesiosaurs like those in the ocean now. He had watched, mesmerized, as gliding pterosaurs lifted fish from the sea surface, and also packs of theropods scouring the tide line for the carcasses of dead sea beasts washed up to scavenge upon.

Every day brought something weird, wild, or fantastic. He knew, to a man like Ben Cartwright, these things would have been perceived as a threat, *and they were*. But to him, they were his life's work brought to life. Even if he only had one more day to live, he could die happy.

Down on the rocks below, there were the raw bones of a boat he had begun to construct. It would take him more months to build, using old construction methods of wooden pegs instead of nails, rope from vines, plant resins as sealants, and a beaten-out dinosaur hide as a sail.

But he knew he could do it. He figured the great land bridges between the continents would still be accessible, and the waters shallow all the way up the east coast.

Andy wanted to sail up along that shoreline and see what America was like. He felt a thrill of excitement run through him that made his scalp tingle.

"I have no bucket list left," he said to the breeze. It had taken him three long months to reach the coast, using his knowledge of the great beasts, following the tips Ben had dropped, and traveling mostly by night. He even copied Ben by burying himself in mud when he needed to. But when he arrived, he knew he had found his heaven.

The young paleontologist turned in the direction of the plateau and contemplated the future, that was strangely, now his past. The paradox of the time displacement made him wonder whether the portal opened at the same time, every time, or did it move around, by years or even days.

He smiled; for all he knew, he and Ben were here at the same time. It hurt his head thinking about it, and he wished his sister were here so he could ask her about it.

But then again, he was glad she wasn't here. He just hoped she wasn't missing him *too* much. Andy sighed and turned back to the prehistoric ocean.

"Don't come looking for me anyone; I'm already home."

THE END

AUTHORS NOTES & THE CUTTING ROOM FLOOR

Many readers ask me about the background of my novels—is the science real or fiction? Where do I get the situations, equipment, characters or their expertise from, and just how much of any element has a basis in fact?

In the case of the hidden plateau in the Amazon jungle, the novel, The Lost World, was my blueprint. However, all of the creatures I talk about in my story actually existed—see my notes below on some of the new creatures featured in this book.

As for the sightings of these monsters from our primordial past existing today, well, there are myths and legends of just that occurring all over the world. But none has so much credence as the ones emanating from our deep oceans or deep jungles—like the Amazon.

GIANT PREHISTORIC OCTOPUS

In his lagoon, Ben was attacked by an oversized octopus. It was exciting, but was that likely? Well, the problem with soft-bodied creatures from our past was that they don't fossilize very well, but they could well have existed.

There are massive cephalopods still living today. The giant Pacific octopus is a powerful creature and the largest specimen found (to date) was 30 feet across and weighed over 600 pounds. There is also the colossal squid living in the sunless depths that can attain a length of 46 feet and weigh in at nearly 1,700 pounds. Big, but were there even bigger cephalopods in our prehistoric past? Maybe. Probably.

In a presentation made at a meeting of the Geological Society of America, evidence was presented for a monstrous-sized creature that may have even been the basis for the legendary Kraken. It was a theory derived from some strange 'scoring' scars found on the bones of nine 45-foot ichthyosaurs from the Triassic Period.

How these huge ichthyosaurs died had always been a mystery. In the 1950s, it was hypothesized that the ichthyosaurs had fallen victim to a toxic plankton bloom as water temperatures changed. But recent work on the rocks surrounding the fossils seem to suggest that many of the creatures died in deep water...very deep water. Strange, because these prehistoric fish inhabited shallower water.

However, when the fossil evidence was examined, and the vertebrae of some ichthyosaurs were organized, there was revealed some tell-tale patterning—scars on the bones that resembled gigantic sucker marks like those from a giant cephalopod's tentacle.

A new theory was presented that suggested the ichthyosaurs had been snared by a massive cephalopod and then dragged back to its underwater lair.

These creatures would have been smart and aggressive, and would have lured their prey with many self-learned baiting tricks—not unlike my octopus that tried to lure Ben into deeper water with gifts of seashells!

THE GIANT BOBBIT WORM

In another scene from my story, I had Juan attacked by giant worms burrowing up from the soil to feast on his flesh. Sand worms (blood worms) on our shoreline do this to fish and animal carcasses today—I've seen them!

The present-day bloodworms are long, but usually no thicker than pasta ribbons. However, they weren't always so small. Jaw fossils recently found in the Devonian sedimentary layers in Canada show that giant carnivorous worms did once exist on Earth.

Websteroprion armstrongi is a new species of giant bristle worm described based on partial jaw fossils. Despite being soft-bodied, and therefore rarely fossilizing well, bristle worms have a decent record due to their numbers. They have been around since the earliest of evolutionary ages (Paleozoic, 541–251 million years ago).

Only the hard pincer-like jaws of the bristle worm remained to be fossilized, but the jaws themselves measured just under half an inch (12–15mm), and though this doesn't sound all that awe-inspiring, in the subterranean world of worms, these guys were giants, considering that most fossil polychaete jaws only come to about 0.1–0.2mm.

By using this ancient jaw size and doing an extrapolation, specialists estimate that *Websteroprion armstrongi* could have been seven feet in length and nearly as thick as a soda can. In addition, the jaw fragments indicate that the animal was an adult but not fully grown, so the worms could have attained even greater sizes.

Gigantism was a trait common in prehistoric reptiles, dinosaurs, and, later, the mammals. It also manifested in mollusks, crustaceans, and cephalopods. Now we also know that even the creatures burrowing beneath the ancient soil were giants and presented danger to the unwary.

PULMONOSCORPIUS – THE MONSTER SCORPION

The largest scorpion living today is the *Heterometrus swammerdami*, coming in nose to tail at an impressive nine inches. But during the Carboniferous Period—some call the *age of insects*—there was a monster that was an armor-plated hunter that seemed straight out of science-fiction.

The *Pulmonoscorpius* was over three feet in length, armed with powerful and sharp claws, and also had a venomous sting. We can't determine from fossil records just how powerfully toxic the venom was, but considering the scorpion's size, the amount it could inject would be certainly overwhelming. Also, in all scorpions living today (1,750 species), their venom is a mixture of compounds that are neurotoxins, enzyme inhibitors, or corrosive chemicals designed to stun and then speed up the liquefaction of flesh.

The giant *Pulmonoscorpius* scorpion was a predator and roamed the swampy forests of the Carboniferous. Its prey would have been anything it could catch, but more than likely, the giant scorpion lived on giant bugs like cockroaches the size of dogs, *Meganeura* dragonflies as big as a model airplane, and even the huge *Arthropleura* centipede that was nine feet in length.

PTEROSAURS – RULERS OF THE PREHISTORIC SKIES

The skies in a prehistoric world didn't stay empty for long. Flying creatures evolved called pterosaurs that were prehistoric archosaurian reptiles closely related to dinosaurs, but *not* dinosaurs. They flit from tree to tree, skimmed lakes, or soared majestically on updrafts.

Many of the pterosaur species were small, but the largest of their kind had wingspans of more than 43 feet and weighed in at around 600 pounds. To give an idea of size comparison, the modern bird with the largest wingspan today is the wandering albatross, which has a tip-to-tip wingspan spread of 11 feet (and in fact, the average-sized single-propeller plane wingspan averages about 36 feet).

It has often been debated about why they grew so large. Factors such as the warmer climate of the Mesozoic Era, or maybe higher levels of oxygen in the atmosphere, have been suggested. But the fact is, they had millions of years to command an environmental niche, and with no competitors, they simply became dominant, and only needed to compete with each other, so only flying distance, size, and strength mattered.

The pterosaurs filled many types of environments, ranging from ocean, to swamp, and to forest. And they were global. The smallest known pterosaur was *Nemicolopterus* with a wingspan of only 10 inches. Below is a top-three list of the largest pterosaurs known.

1. *Arambourgiania philadelphiae*—23 to 43 feet (7–13 m)
2. *Hatzegopteryx thambema*—33 to 36 feet (10–11 m)
3. *Quetzalcoatlus northropi*—33 to 36 feet (10–11 m)

GIGANOTOSAURUS – THE GIANT SOUTHERN LIZARD

The *Giganotosaurus* was a genus of massive shark-toothed dinosaurs that lived on the South American continent during the Late Cretaceous Period (100–97 million years ago).

The powerful theropod was up to 45 feet long, 12 feet in height, and weighed in at around 13 tons. It walked on two large and powerful hind legs, had a small brain, and enormously powerful jaws, with 10-inch, backward-curving serrated teeth in a six-foot-long skull. Like most of the giant carnivore theropods, its forelimbs were much smaller, ending in three-fingered, clawed hands.

Giganotosaurus was also thought to have been fast and agile, thanks to its thin, pointed tail, which may have provided balance and the ability to make quick turns while running. Another advantage the huge dinosaur possessed was that it was thought to have been homoeothermic (warm-blooded), with a metabolism between that of a mammal and a reptile, which would have enabled rapid growth.

And though the huge beast was powerful, it was also fast with a maximum running speed of 31 miles per hour. It would have been capable of closing its jaws quickly, capturing, and bringing down prey by delivering cutting or crushing bites.

The *Giganotosaurus* was an undisputed alpha-apex predator of its habitat, and would more than likely have fed on the plant-eating sauropods, as well as other carnivorous theropod dinosaurs.

MACHIMOSAURUS REX

In PRIMORDIA II, Ben's time at the coast is ruined by the appearance of a giant sea-going crocodile. Though the sea-going variety never attained the size of some of the freshwater estuary types, they were still monstrously huge, powerful, and would have made a formidable predator.

The world's biggest ocean-dwelling crocodile was twice the size of any crocodile living today. It was named *Machimosaurus rex* and would have weighed in at least 6,600 pounds and been up to 34 feet in length.

Crocodiles aren't much fun for evolutionists as they remained nearly unchanged for hundreds of millions of years. For the *Machimosaurus rex*, it would have looked like a modern-day crocodile except for a slightly narrower snout, which was better designed for speed when going after prey in the open ocean.

The skull of this crocodile alone would have been nearly seven feet in length, and the ocean lagoons where it lived would have been filled with sharks, huge fish, and turtles—all favorite prey of the prehistoric sea hunter.

Many of the giant crocodiles died out during the mass extinction event that is believed to have happened between the Jurassic and Cretaceous Period about 150 million years ago. However, the *Machimosaurus* lived for tens of millions of years beyond this cataclysmic event, suggesting the mass extinction was not as widespread as some paleontologists first thought.

The *Machimosaurus rex* was an enormous beast, but he was still dwarfed by even bigger crocodiles that lived on land. Species, such as the world's largest freshwater crocodile, the *Sarcosuchus imperator*, lived around 110 million years ago, grew to 42 feet, and would have tipped the scales at an astonishing 17,500 pounds (8,000kg), nearly triple the weight of the *Machimosaurus*.

I admit, I'm a little like Andy Martin in my story, where I would love to see these mighty creatures, if only for a moment. But the cryptozoologist's spirit in me is encouraged whenever I read about some fantastic creature being discovered to have lived through its supposed extinction event. It is yet more evidence that points to some of the massive creatures of our prehistory confounding those who tell us they no longer exist.

One day, in a jungle, on a mountaintop, frozen land, or in the depths of a deep, dark ocean, we'll meet one. Until that day, I'll just have to go there and see them in my stories.

CHECK OUT OTHER GREAT DINOSAUR THRILLERS

JURASSIC ISLAND
by Viktor Zarkov

Guided by satellite photos and modern technology a ragtag group of survivalists and scientists travel to an uncharted island in the remote South Indian Ocean. Things go to hell in a hurry once the team reaches the island and the massive megalodon that attacked their boats is only the beginning of their desperate fight for survival.

Nothing could have prepared billionaire explorer Joseph Thornton and washed up archaeologist Christopher "Colt" McKinnon for the terrifying prehistoric creatures that wait for them on JURASSIC ISLAND!

K-REX
by L.Z. Hunter

Deep within the Congo jungle, Circuitz Mining employs mercenaries as security for its Coltan mining site. Armed with assault rifles and decades of experience, nothing should go wrong. However, the dangers within the jungle stretch beyond venomous snakes and poisonous spiders. There is more to fear than guerrillas and vicious animals. Undetected, something lurks under the expansive treetop canopy . . .

Something ancient.

Something dangerous.

Kasai Rex!

CHECK OUT OTHER GREAT DINOSAUR THRILLERS

WRITTEN IN STONE
by David Rhodes

Charles Dawson is trapped 100 million years in the past. Trying to survive from day to day in a world of dinosaurs he devises a plan to change his fate. As he begins to write messages in the soft mud of a nearby stream, he can only hope they will be found by someone who can stop his time travel. Professor Ron Fontana and Professor Ray Taggit, scientists with opposing views, each discover the fossilized messages. While attempting to save Charles, Professor Fontana, his daughter Lauren and their friend Danny are forced to join Taggit and his group of mercenaries. Taggit does not intend to rescue Charles Dawson, but to force Dawson to travel back in time to gather samples for Taggit's fame and fortune. As the two groups jump through time they find they must work together to make it back alive as this fast-paced thriller climaxes at the very moment the age of dinosaurs is ending.

HARD TIME
by Alex Laybourne

Rookie officer Peter Malone and his heavily armed team are sent on a deadly mission to extract a dangerous criminal from a classified prison world. A Kruger Correctional facility where only the hardest, most vicious criminals are sent to fend for themselves, never to return.

But when the team come face to face with ancient beasts from a lost world, their mission is changed. The new objective: Survive.

CHECK OUT OTHER GREAT DINOSAUR THRILLERS

SPINOSAURUS
by Hugo Navikov

Brett Russell is a hunter of the rarest game. His targets are cryptids, animals denied by science. But they are well known by those living on the edges of civilization, where monsters attack and devour their animals and children and lay ruin to their shantytowns.

When a shadowy organization sends Brett to the Congo in search of the legendary dinosaur cryptid Kasai Rex, he will face much more than a terrifying monster from the past. Spinosaurus is a dinosaur thriller packed with intrigue, action and giant prehistoric predators.

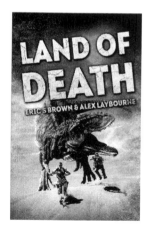

LAND OF DEATH
by Eric S Brown & Alex Laybourne

A group of American soldiers, fleeing an organized attack on their base camp in the Middle East, encounter a storm unlike anything they've seen before. When the storm subsides, they wake up to find themselves no longer in the desert and perhaps not even on Earth. The jungle they've been deposited in is a place ruled by prehistoric creatures long extinct. Each day is a struggle to survive as their ammo begins to run low and virtually everything they encounter, in this land they've been hurled into, is a deadly threat.

Printed by Amazon Italia Logistica S.r.l.
Torrazza Piemonte (TO), Italy

11896053R00144